The Normal State of Mind

Susmita Bhattacharya is a Mumbai-born writer. She has a Masters degree in Creative Writing from Cardiff University and her short stories have been published in the UK and internationally. Her work has been featured by the BBC and received a nomination for the Pushcart (literary) Prize. She lives in Plymouth with her daughters and husband. This is her first novel.

http://susmita-bhattacharya.blogspot.co.uk

@Susmitatweets

The Normal State of Mind

Susmita Bhattacharya

PARTHIAN

Parthian, Cardigan SA43 1ED
www.parthianbooks.com
First published in 2015
© Susmita Bhattacharya 2015
ISBN 978-1-909844-62-9
Editor: Susie Wild
Cover design by www.theundercard.co.uk
Front cover image: Shipra Bhattacharya
Typeset by Elaine Sharples
Printed and bound by Edwards Brothers Malloy
Published with the financial support of the Welsh Books Council
British Library Cataloguing in Publication Data
A cataloguing record for this book is available from the British Library.

For Ma and Bapi

PART ONE

1990

1

Dipali

Cinnamon and mint. Those were the first tastes she got when he kissed her. Dipali shut her eyes, concentrating on the waves riding down her stomach. She inhaled his scent, sweat and aftershave mixed with Pears soap. He embraced her and then hesitated. They looked at each other, unsure of the next move.

She leaned away from him, crushing the jasmine and marigold garlands that hung from the bedposts. The floral fragrance filled the bridal suite, her mother's room, obscuring their sweat and nervousness for a moment.

Sunil cleared his throat, his Adam's apple bobbing as he smiled at her. She held his hand lightly to reassure him. She felt a bit— silly, but what else could she do? Why wasn't he just pouncing on her or something? She'd readily comply— if only he *did* something.

It was her wedding night, and she was with her husband, Sunil, but he was a stranger three months ago. An advert in the matrimonial column, circled in red by her elder brother. A good catch, her brother Ashish had said, from a respectable family and with a promising career. And now, he was her life partner, with whom she would have children and grow old. She had to love him, and she prayed that he'd be easy to love.

Dipali bit her lip and lowered her gaze. Was it really mandatory to have sex on the wedding night? All those years of dreaming about it, waiting for it and now she was backing away?

'What's the matter?' Sunil asked, tightening his grasp on her hand.

Being a Bombay girl meant most of her metaphors and symbolism were inspired by the film industry. Scenes from Hindi films flashed in her mind. Drunken bridegroom chewing paan swaggers into bedroom and forces himself on stricken bride. Romantic couple giggle and jump under the covers. Cut to flowers that sway suggestively on a mountainside, with a full orchestra playing to a climax in the background. Husband sings a soulful ballad while bride thinks of ex-lover and sobs.

'I'm sorry, but it's all very new. I'm not sure what we're supposed to do now. They should have classes for these situations. Typing class, dance class don't help. 'What to do on wedding night' class would certainly help. For arranged marriages. I'm making a mess of things, na? I'm talking too much.' Dipali stopped for breath. She thought back on her sister-in-law Shikha's advice, which didn't seem appropriate in this situation. After all, she had known her husband for years before they married.

'No, you're not talking too much. Hey, look. I'm not sure what we should do either. Maybe I should have enrolled in a class for bridegrooms too. All this feels wrong.' Sunil edged away from her. His silk kurta caught on the edge of the bedpost and ripped.

'I hate these clothes. Why do I have to wear them?' He

4

tugged at the torn cloth and Dipali put her hand forward to stop him from ripping it even further.

'Because you are the bor, the bridegroom! Don't worry, the dhobi will mend it.'

Sunil's eyes flicked on her again. 'So what now?' he asked.

'Well, I don't mind being kissed...'

'I don't want to force you...'

They spoke simultaneously and laughed.

'I was thinking of the wedding scenes from Hindi films,' Dipali said, arranging her sari around her in a way that she resembled a flower with its petals unfurling. Just like in those films where the bride sat on the bed, shy and cowering under the bridegroom's stare.

'How appropriate. Look, I'm even dressed like a typical one. All I need is a whiskey bottle and paan.'

They laughed again, and Dipali was pleased to have him as a husband. He seemed so different from the photograph that had accompanied the letter from his father to her brother, stating all the details one needed to know to find the suitor acceptable. In the photograph he had looked so uncomfortable, squinting at the camera. Like he knew why he was being made to pose, in a suit and tie, among the hibiscus flowers in the middle of the day. He must have had an argument with the photographer, in all probability his mother, just before she clicked. When she met him though, she noticed the way his eyes crinkled when he smiled, or chuckled as when they were made to play games at the wedding. When she had been brought before him, her eyes covered with paan leaves, she had been too nervous to look at him. But when she did, he had winked at her. Discreetly. And that had comforted her, like they both were in this together. The world took a back seat – all those teasing relatives, the heat, the music –

everything disappeared. It was just the two of them, facing each other, making promises to love for life.

Her college friend had once told her that a man's flat wrists, the white shirt sleeves rolled up, an expensive watch glinting, was the ultimate sex appeal. She hadn't understood it then, nor cared. But noticing now, his wrists did look very attractive, especially the long fingers that seemed so afraid to touch her.

'When you kissed me, I thought of Rhett Butler in *Gone with the Wind*. I mean, I read somewhere that Vivien Leigh complained of Clark Gable smelling of garlic, and she hated being kissed by him. I was wondering what you would smell like. I mean, you smell very nice. Sorry, I always babble when I'm nervous. Shit—'

Dipali bit her tongue and stared at Sunil. Swearing as a bride dressed in gold and silk did not seem right. 'Sorry. I'm just not myself at the moment.'

'Relax,' Sunil threw his head on the pillow. He pulled her down beside him and drew the covers over them. 'We'll just chill tonight. Let's compare notes on which film inspired you to say yes to me, shall we?'

Dipali watched him as he slept. In a year's time, I'll call that snoring, she thought. They had talked into the night. He had stroked her arm and played with her fingers. And then he had yawned, and suggested they get some rest. They hadn't slept for nearly two nights. The first night, they had been married. But as was the custom, the bride and groom were kept separate from each other for one more night, when family and friends partied through till morning, laughing and joking and singing. Who had planned such thoughtless traditions? After two sleepless nights, the couple were pushed into a room full of nauseating flowers to consummate their marriage. What a daft idea. Was her own wedding night going to end up this way? Husband fast asleep and she nodding off as well? She willed him to wake up and make love to her. She was sure Shikha and the rest would ask her in the morning, and she'd still be an ignorant fool. But he slept on.

Her shoulders ached from the weight of her sari, and the gold jewellery clanked and chinked with every move she made. Slowly she got out of bed, unwrapped her body from the Benarasi silk, and then placed her necklaces and bracelets in her mother's dressing table drawer. One of this week's many rituals, the gaye holud, when her friends and cousins had applied turmeric paste on her arms and face as a cleansing ritual, had left a pale yellow glow on her skin.

'You'll shine like a lantern on your wedding night, didi,' one of her cousins had teased. There were peals of laughter when she turned red. She checked her face and arms to see if they were still yellow, but the make-up had added another thick layer to her skin.

Dipali stepped into the shower and washed her stiff hair, letting the water strip the chemicals and artificialness from it. When she finished, she was herself once more. Her face was clean and bare. Her black hair fell about her shoulders in tangles. She stuck her chin up and peered at her sleeping husband. No, she was not going to lag behind on the marital front. This was their wedding night, not appropriate for sleeping. She slipped into bed, still damp from the shower. She touched his cheek and felt him move. She stroked his hair, and he awoke. He turned and her mouth was on his. He responded eagerly. She slid under the covers, and waited for him to make the next move.

7

2

Moushumi

Heart racing, Moushumi sped up to the terrace, and then waited, like she did most days, hidden behind the potted allamanda shrubs. She felt stupid, child-like. As though afraid of being caught with a mouth full of sweets. But this was much worse. She closed her eyes in shame as she thought of the consequences if she ever was caught. The door to the terrace of the house opposite opened. She heard the metal bucket being dragged to the tap and the gush of water. She listened to the tinkle of anklets and the low voice singing. The maidservant appeared, carrying the bucket into a little corner where a thin corrugated metal sheet served as a partition. However, from Moushumi's point of view, she could see inside, just about.

A single star struggled to shine through the smog that embraced Calcutta on summer evenings. The terrace floor was still warm from the day's burning heat and she savoured the sudden cool breeze that ruffled her hair. She stayed close to the ground, watching.

The girl stripped and hung her clothes on the metal wall.

She was thin and dark, with small breasts that pointed jauntily upwards. She splashed water on her body and over her head; little rivulets ran down her face. She soaped herself, her hands gliding over her smooth limbs.

Moushumi held her breath. Her skin dimpled in spite of the tepid air. Fuzzy warmth spread from her toes up. She leaned against the wall and let the confusion of feelings flood over her. Why was pleasure always racked with guilt?

'Bina, Bina,' a voice called from below.

The maidservant emptied the bucket over her head. She hurriedly dried herself, tied on a fresh sari and ran down, returning the call. Moushumi sighed. The hot wet excitement of a moment ago dulled. Instead she slunk back to her house. The view from the terrace would return to her later that night, when she would agonise on why she was not of the normal kind.

ॐ

Moushumi wandered around the art gallery, studying the paintings. They were large canvasses. Bold splashes of colour – reds, maroons, oranges – streaked across the white surface, thick blue or black oil paint dripped through razor blade rips as if coagulated blood. She shuddered.

There were reporters taking pictures or talking into their Dictaphones. People spoke in one or two pitches above their normal tones and mostly included words or phrases like 'babe', 'love' and 'call me soon, darling'. They seemed more interested in appearing in media society columns than appreciating the paintings.

The artist was like her art: bold, colourful and loud. She tossed her knee-length hair while she laughed and chatted with the people who huddled around her. Her eyes were blackened with kohl and her lips a slash of red on diamond-adorned skin. In her floor-skimming orange robe, she looked like a psychedelic priestess straight out of the jatras.

'Don't stare so hard. You'll be blinded by the glare!'

Moushumi turned around, embarrassed. It was a woman, smiling mischievously at her.

'She's more interesting to look at than her paintings,' Moushumi said. They both turned to look at the artist and chuckled.

The woman, Jasmine, introduced herself and held out her hand. She wore diamond rings too, but more tasteful than the artist's.

'Enjoying yourself?'

'No. I'm afraid not. I don't think I can appreciate modern art. I mean, honestly, I think this is a waste of space.' Moushumi looked around the gallery, shaking her head. 'It doesn't do anything for me.'

'You are very blunt, I must say! I like that. And I agree with you. But Meera Sen spells money, a lot of money. So you have to appreciate her. She's Calcutta's hottest artist now.'

'Well, if you consider art as a business. But I don't. I'd rather stick to my old-fashioned ideas of Jamini Roy and Monet. Or Raja Ravi Varma.'

'Come on, let's sit somewhere and chat. I'd like to talk about the masters too. They will never become old-fashioned.' Jasmine led her to the corner of the gallery, where cushions and beanbags were strewn across the floor. 'Drink?'

'Yes— I'll have whatever you're having, thanks.'

'Fine,' Jasmine motioned her to sit down. 'I'll be back.' Jasmine's retreating figure looked elegant in her white chiffon churidar kurta, small, but with a confident walk, her heels clicking purposefully. She returned with two flutes of champagne.

Moushumi watched as Jasmine closed her eyes as she sipped her drink. She looked away hurriedly when she realised she had been staring and sipped her own drink. It had a sour aftertaste and she tried to rearrange her facial expression quickly.

'First time?' Jasmine asked.

Moushumi nodded.

'It takes experience to appreciate the finer things in life,' Jasmine laughed. 'That's why you have to pay through your nose for something you don't like. And when you pay that kind of cash, *voila*, it all looks good.'

'Yes, that makes sense.'

'Tell me, what do you do, Moushumi?' Jasmine asked, touching Moushumi's arm lightly.

'I teach English at St Francine's in Tollygunge. What do you do?'

'I dabble in art. I buy pieces from upcoming artists and then sell them later when they have made a name. Investment.'

A man stopped by them and placed his hand on Jasmine's shoulder. She turned and kissed the air around his face. People had become more animated now that they were a few more drinks down. The volume of chatter and laughter had gone up several notches.

'Are you going to sell any of Meera's work?' Moushumi asked when the man sauntered away.

'Yes, in fact I just have. To him,' Jasmine said. 'I know it's not what you appreciate, but she is very sellable. She is quite sought after in the Gulf market. So it doesn't matter if I like it or not, my clients do.'

'I see. You must have a very keen eye to figure out which

painting will make it and which will not.' Moushumi looked across the room towards Meera. 'The artist has to adopt a certain look to go with her art, doesn't she?'

Jasmine laughed. 'You are wicked! But yes, it is true. The artist must reflect her art. People have different personas in different environments.'

She raised her glass to Moushumi and smiled, locking arms with Moushumi and walking back into the crowd.

ॐ

Jasmine's house was in Alipore, the posh end of town. The street was red-carpeted with the petals of the Gulmohar trees, giving a sense of ceremony just walking down it. The cars which were lined up on both sides were mostly Mercedes or Mitsubishi Lancers. Stiffly starched chauffeurs leaned against some of the vehicles, reading a newspaper or listening to the cricket commentary on the radio. Moushumi walked past them self-consciously. She hoped the stench of the sweat and grime of the Metro didn't emanate from her clothes.

She found Jasmine's apartment block and entered. A Nepali security guard made her write her name and who she was visiting in an officious-looking register. As she crossed the marble floor of the lobby, Moushumi could not imagine how such a space existed in a crowded and polluted city like Calcutta.

Jasmine welcomed her with a hug and a kiss and sat Moushumi down by the large windows that overlooked the tops of the Gulmohar trees. It was as if they were both floating on red and yellow undulating waves. In the distance, the Victoria Memorial peeked over the trees.

They talked about various subjects. Moushumi found it disconcerting to have servants walk around, waiting on them yet being treated as invisible. Her own mother had a woman come to clean the floors and wash the dishes. She was a loud woman who gossiped about the neighbours and complained about the workload. She had a personality of her own, unlike these uniformed ghosts.

There were several photographs displayed on the piano. Moushumi gasped when she looked closer. 'You are Nandkumar Ghoshal's wife?'

Jasmine smiled, but said nothing.

'Goodness, I'm in Nandkumar Ghoshal's house, having dinner with his wife? Why didn't you tell me before?'

'Why? Does it matter?'

'Of course it matters,' Moushumi said. 'Calcutta's top builder. He's in the news every day, with the seven-star hotel he's going to build. Bring Calcutta into the twenty-first century, like he says. Why would his wife want to have dinner with me?'

'Maybe because she sees something in you,' Jasmine said. 'I've always been Mr Ghoshal's wife. Or Kamini Vakil's daughter. I want to have my own identity. My own space, my own friends.'

Moushumi sat down heavily. 'Kamini Vakil? The artist?'

'Yes. Don't look at me as though I'm an alien. I'm a woman. A needy woman.' She stepped over to Moushumi's chair and kissed her lightly on the lips. Moushumi sprang forward, looking for the servants. They seemed to have disappeared. She trembled. Jasmine held her arm gently and pushed her back in the chair.

Moushumi tried to stop her. 'What are you doing? I— I don't think this is appropriate.' A thrill ran down her body, but at the same time she objected to it. How could this woman assume she wanted this? How did she know?

'Why, am I wrong in doing this? Does it feel wrong?'

Jasmine continued to stand close, and Moushumi breathed in her perfume. She thought of her fantasies, mostly involving the poor maid from next door. And here was a beautiful woman, actually kissing her and telling her it was okay. But she was frightened, too stunned to react. The sensations racing through her body were similar to the time she had gorged on jamuns one hot summer day at her grandmother's house. She and her sister had snuck behind the house with a stash of maybe fifty or more they had plucked from the trees, and they had eaten them, smearing the purple inkiness all over their faces, clothes and hands. The juice dribbled from their chins onto their toes. The sweetness, elevated to a degree that couldn't be described once the jamun had mixed with the saliva, was heady and intoxicating. Yet they were sickly sweet. Their stomachs revolted against the feasting and they eventually threw up masses of purple-coloured puke. She remembered that cloying taste clinging to the top of her palate for days. The ache in her belly. Their mother's yelling. The confusion of pleasure and pain. Yet her mouth salivated at the very thought of jamuns. That was exactly it. Jasmine's kisses were like those jamuns. They were hard to resist even after knowing the consequences of over-indulging.

'I'm not sure,' Moushumi stammered. 'You're married. How can you do this? Why should I be interested?'

Jasmine returned to her seat. She examined her nails for a while, ignoring Moushumi who was shifting from one foot to another.

'...I think you *are* interested,' she said finally 'It's the way you looked at me the other night. I knew right away.'

'So what?' Moushumi challenged her. 'I just had a friendly chat with you. I didn't behave immorally.'

Jasmine threw her head back and laughed. 'Immorally? What a choice of word. Being attracted to a woman is immoral? First time I've heard that.' She clapped her hands, and a butler in a white uniform appeared. 'Accompany my friend to the lift,' she instructed him. She then turned to Moushumi. 'You have my number. Call me if you have the guts. I will show you how to live.' She turned and walked out of the room.

Moushumi was unable to move until the butler cleared his throat and guided her out of the house.

3

Dipali

'So, Dips, you excited about going back to your mother's as a married woman?' asked Sunil. They had just returned from their honeymoon in Goa and now most of their evenings were booked by various relatives and friends inviting the young couple to their homes for a meal, as was tradition. Dipali had mixed feelings about visiting her childhood home as a wife. Her mother had not been happy there. Her father, her father—

She closed her eyes and the images flooded her mind. Her father's face close to hers, breathing hard and gritting his teeth. His grip inflicting bruises on her arm. All because her school dress was too short and she hadn't asked to have it lengthened. His words, skilfully delivered to break her spirit. Her hunger, when she was made to go without food for bringing disrespect to the family. At seven years of age, for wearing a school tunic that had ridden above her knees. One of many memories that had seared itself in her brain.

'You don't have to worry about those things anymore,' Sunil said. 'You are my wife now. You can do what you like.'

She looked at him. In the space of a month, he could already guess what was on her mind.

The sky was darkening with thunderclouds. The monsoon was on its way. Rush hour in Mumbai was not a pleasant time to travel, especially when the rains came. The air was still and suffocating. The sea had turned into a dull metallic sheet. The clouds hung low, just skimming the water where the sun created an unexpectedly fiery line between the sea and the clouds. Neon signs flashed out promises against the sky and the road was dotted with red taillights as the traffic crawled on.

A bullock cart stood in the middle of the road, the bulls chewing cud. The driver hit them with a stick, even though he could see there was no way they could inch forward. They swished their tails, as if they were flicking away flies.

'Ma is so happy for me. But I feel guilty, Sunil. I don't want to look happy with my husband in front of her. Will we remind her of what she has missed?' Dipali took a deep breath. Sunil pulled her towards him. The blare of horns deafened them for a second. They sat cocooned in the car; the cacophony seemed to come from another place, another time.

Dipali was miles away, in her father's house, feeling the sting of his sharp words. 'Baba stopped me from going to college for a month because I had bunked a lecture and gone to the cinema. He said I was of questionable character. It was only a movie. My brother went every week, and even got money from Baba for his entertainment. But he was a boy, na.'

She forced her tears back and focused on the blinking traffic light. An old beggar started singing tunelessly to Sunil, clanking his tin cup on the windshield. There was a deep hole where his right eye should have been. Dipali winced and looked at her husband. He reached into the glove compartment and took out an assortment of coins. He threw a few into the tin cup and wound his window up. They could see the beggar mouthing good wishes and blessings to them. Blessing us with a thousand offspring, I'm sure, thought Dipali, and cheered up.

'Welcome,' smiled Asha Devi, rotating a brass tray before Sunil. Shikha, Dipali's sister-in-law, came forward to put a red tilak on his forehead. Sunil stepped back, embarrassed.

'Welcome,' Shikha echoed. She stood on her tiptoes to reach his forehead. She wobbled a bit, her bulk threatening to tilt her right onto him. Sunil caught her arm to steady her, and she lowered her eyes and laughed. Dipali watched them. Typical of Shikha, she thought. Always the flirt. Ashish and Shikha were returning to Delhi, where Ashish worked, the next day. They had stayed back to welcome the new couple and host their first meal with the family.

'Come in, come in.' Ashish, Dipali's elder brother, marched towards them, his sandals slapping the ground. He embraced Sunil and led him inside. They were such a contrast, the two men. Ashish, big built and imposing, made Sunil look so wiry. So insignificant. Ashish's loud voice obliterated Sunil's soft articulate speech. But Dipali could see the admiring glances towards her husband. Both her mother and sister-in-law seemed smitten and she felt superior for the first time in her life.

Returning as Mrs Rai would not be so bad, Dipali assured herself. Perhaps she would at last admire and grow to love this beautiful house. Ram Vilas was one of the few bungalows left in the city, the others giving way to ugly apartment blocks needed to home the never-ending stream of people coming to Bombay. The mango tree heaved with ripe fruit and parrots noisily feasted on its branches. The rooms had been spruced for the occasion, tuberoses from the garden adorning vases. Her mother's signature alpana decorating the threshold. Dipali hugged her gratefully, knowing how hard it was for her to bend for long and design the intricate patterns with rice paste onto the stone floor.

'Sorry about the time,' Sunil said. 'We got stuck in traffic.'

'Nonsense, Sunil,' Ashish said. 'Let's eat right away. You must be hungry. Or would you like a drink first? Beer, or anything stronger?'

Everyone stopped to look at Sunil. Dipali held her breath. She had warned him before, she hoped he would remember.

'No, thank you,' he said. 'Just water is fine. Or Coca-Cola if you have it.' He looked reassuringly at her. Dipali smiled at the knowledge of the fully-stocked bar in their apartment. It felt good to be rebellious.

'As you know, we don't allow alcohol in this house anymore,' Ashish said. 'Dipali must have told you why. Glad you don't either, but didn't want to be rude by not offering. Anyway, why talk about the past. Here's to the future.' He lifted his glass and toasted the couple.

Dinner was a big affair. Asha Devi had brought out her silverware, which had been part of her wedding trousseau. It saw daylight only on special occasions, like Ashish's birthdays and his wedding. Now it was brought out in Dipali's honour. A traditional Bengali feast for a son-in-law consisted of thirty-two dishes and Asha Devi had nearly achieved that. There was kosha mangsho, soft pieces of mutton cooked with spices; Hilsa fish steamed in mustard sauce; deep-fried aubergines; Mung dal, the little golden lentils dry roasted to exude an earthy fragrance; gobindo bhog rice, which was specially acquired from Calcutta; tomato chutney; mishti doi, rasgullas;

and homemade payesh, all set out with various other chutneys and curries.

Ashish led Sunil to the chair at the head of the table. He sat down at the other end. The women hovered around with serving spoons in their hands.

'Er, what about you?' Sunil looked at the women breathing down on him.

'Oh, don't worry about us,' chimed in Shikha. 'We'll eat later.'

'Aren't we all eating together?'

'No, my son. We'll serve you first. Then we'll eat. Don't worry. Just start.' Asha Devi ladled some dal over Sunil's plate of rice.

'Please, I don't feel comfortable about this,' Sunil said. 'Let's all sit together and eat.'

'This is our family tradition. Ma and Dipali never ate a morsel until Baba and I had eaten, did you Ma? Even Shikha insists on serving me before she can start. Maybe because then she gets the horse's share,' Ashish laughed between munching on a poppadam. He eyed his wife's big body and pointed at her. 'Look at the advantages of serving the husband first. Doesn't Dipali do the same?'

Shikha moved away from the table while her husband continued to snigger. Asha Devi sighed and piled more rice on Sunil's plate to distract him.

Sunil shook his head. 'No, we always eat together, because that is *my* family tradition.'

Ashish munched on his aubergine fry and the oil made his lips glisten. His fingers mixed the aloo posto, potatoes cooked in poppy seed paste, in the rice and deftly made them into little balls. He scooped one into his mouth and then motioned Dipali to sit down.

'Sit with your husband and eat,' he said, between chewing and swallowing. 'You have to follow his rules now, not ours.'

'They're not my rules,' began Sunil, but Dipali poked him in the back. She sat down quietly and Shikha promptly began to serve her.

ॐ

'So how's our new dulhan?' grinned Mrs Nath as Dipali entered the staff-room at St Philomena's Convent school where she taught English. 'Tell us, did you enjoy your honeymoon? Bet you did.'

Mrs Lal, the Hindi teacher, joined them. 'Arrey, Dipali, welcome back.' She hugged her and Dipali nearly gagged at her strong perfume. 'All okay? Is your dulha to your satisfaction or not?'

Dipali forced a smile. 'Yes, he's... he's okay, I guess.'

'Dipali,' Mrs Lal said, peering close to her face. 'You're not wearing sindoor?'

Mrs Nath leaned over to have a look at Dipali's forehead as well.

'No, actually, my husband asked me not to. He doesn't like it,' Dipali said.

Her mother had accosted her about this earlier. But Sunil had been firm. He didn't want her to wear the vermillion powder in her hair as a married woman should. His mother never wore it, and he didn't expect her to either. Dipali was finding it hard to explain this to the elderly women around.

'Tch tch, don't do away with old customs so easily,' said Mrs Nath, touching her own red-coloured hair parting. 'It is a way of acknowledging your married state. It says you are proud of being married to your husband.'

'Even though he smokes in the toilet,' said Mrs Lal, glancing sideways at Mrs Nath.

'Pramila, I'm not joking. It's very important to respect your husband. Say, in this country, what good is a woman without her husband? He is your identity, like it or not.' She glared at Dipali. 'All this modern thinking is alright. But it's alright only when you are married. When the husband is gone, no matter how much he irritated you in this life, you are reduced to nothing.'

'Mrs Nath,' Mrs Lal raised her voice. 'What are you saying to this poor girl? She's only just married. Let her enjoy her life. If her husband says no, then it's okay. As long as in your heart, you don't agree with him.'

The sensible Mrs Dubash walked in and Dipali sighed with relief. No airs and graces. No double meanings or hints and nudges from her. She never pried into other people's affairs either.

'Dipali, welcome back,' Mrs Dubash said, wiping the sweat off her face with her sari pallu. 'Ready to get back to work or still in honeymoon state-of-mind?'

'Back to work now.'

'Arrey, what an answer,' Mrs Nath poked Dipali on her shoulder. 'Happy to be away from your new husband? When I got married I didn't let my Mister go back to work for a month. I just clung to him and cried. I didn't want to be left behind with my mother-in-law.'

'And now you can't wait to push him out of the house every time he returns,' Mrs Lal laughed.

'I can't stand his smoking, Pramila,' Mrs Nath complained. 'I cannot take that smell anymore. I suffocate.'

'Your husband has any addictions?' asked Mrs Lal, her lips twitching.

'Arrey, no, he'll be all goody-goody now. Give him two more years, and then he'll show his true colours.' Mrs Nath said.

4

Moushumi

Jasmine was applying ruby nail varnish to her toenails.

Moushumi stole a glance at her own feet. They were dark and rough, used to walking in the sun, not milky soft like Jasmine's. 'Why did you marry Nandkumar? He just doesn't seem your type.'

They were sitting on the sofa in Jasmine's second flat on Southern Avenue. Moushumi had phoned Jasmine after all. She knew she'd never be able to resist the opportunity to explore that mysterious aspect of her personality. She had needed to face her guilty secret and recognise it for what it was and now they met here every Saturday. At home, Moushumi told her parents that she gave tuitions in this part of town. She wondered if Jasmine lied to her husband about her whereabouts. She probably didn't need to; she seemed to be so sure of herself.

Jasmine took her time to reply. She concentrated on applying the varnish to the last of her toes perfectly. 'I didn't have much choice in the matter. My father decided for me.' She was wearing a silk robe that accentuated her voluptuous body. Her hair, still wet with post-coital perspiration, lay flat on her forehead. She didn't look like a woman who other people could make decisions for.

'I can hardly believe that.'

'You don't know what happened.'

Moushumi found Jasmine's sudden flashes of temper very attractive. It made her want to throw herself into Jasmine's arms, knowing the power and passion she would unleash on her.

'You can tell me. I'd like to know why you stick with your husband if you don't love him.' She held her arms out towards Jasmine, who ignored the invitation and walked into the kitchen. Moushumi slumped into the armchair. It was so hard to get anything out of Jasmine. Yet, she wanted to know everything that had ever happened to her. Know every pore of her body, every cell in her brain. Jasmine returned with a bottle of chilled wine and two glasses.

'Wine? At three in the afternoon?'

'Draw the curtains then,' Jasmine said and settled on the sofa again. 'Make it look like night, if that helps.' She checked to see if her nails were dry. 'Any time is a good time for a lovely glass of Chardonnay.'

'I'll pass; I have to leave soon. My mother thinks I give tuitions on Saturdays, so can't go home smelling of booze.'

'Fine. If you don't appreciate it, I'd rather not waste it on you.' Jasmine poured herself a glass then returned the bottle heavily to the table.

'Maybe I should leave then,' Moushumi said, gathering her dupatta and handbag. 'I'll leave you to savour your *wine*.' She walked towards the front door, hoping that Jasmine would stop her. But equally, the thought of misleading her parents was not favourable. How long would she have to keep up the lies? She couldn't face her mother, especially when she fussed over her after she returned home from her 'tuitions'. She had begun avoiding her parents, taking refuge in excuses of needing to plan her lessons for school or watching Bengali TV serials that she had not bothered with before. At the same time, she craved these exquisite moments with Jasmine. The discovery of her body, the pleasure it could get, and give was immense. Her days, hours, minutes were all consumed with this passion.

'Stay. Don't you want to hear the story?'

'Only if you want to share it.'

Jasmine took a long sip of her wine. She slipped out of her robe and walked to her wardrobe running her fingers through the array of clothes displayed neatly on the rack. Her body, in spite of the gym sessions and a personal trainer, was beginning to show signs of age. Ever so tiny, but they were there. Faint stretch marks splaying across her thighs. Deep blue veins crisscrossing her calves. Jasmine picked out some clothes and put them on quickly, transforming into her formidable, beautiful self.

'I had a boyfriend once,' she said, her voice a whisper. 'Ajay. We went around for a year, in college. Secretly. My father was very strict.' She lay back on the sofa and screwed up her eyes as a wafer-thin shaft of sunlight touched her face.

Moushumi walked up to the window and shut it out.

'I fell pregnant,' Jasmine said.

Moushumi sucked in her breath. Instinctively, she looked at Jasmine's taut belly. The silver stud peeked out of her navel. 'Did you tell him?'

'Yes, the coward. He ran away to the US. A rich man's son, he didn't want his future spoiled—'

Jasmine poured herself another glass. Moushumi reached out to touch her, but she leaned away.

'So I went running to my mother. I thought my parents would have the power to snare Ajay for me. But no, my father had other plans. I had to have an abortion. Seventeen was too young to have a baby, they told me.'

'How did Nandkumar figure in all this?' Moushumi asked.

'Nandkumar was just coming up in his business. He did a few jobs for my dad, like building bits on our Lonavala bungalow. He approached my dad for a loan. Seems my dad said to him, instead of a loan, I can give you a dowry.'

'No way! Why did your father do that? You could have had an abortion, and moved on in life.' Moushumi could never imagine her father selling her off like that. But then she had never gotten herself pregnant.

'My father had his ways of taking revenge,' Jasmine's mouth curled into an ugly snarl. 'He didn't approve of me. Said I was too much of my mother's child, and he couldn't stand her wilfulness, her celebrity status.'

'You didn't protest?'

Jasmine threw her head back and laughed. 'He said he'd kill me if I didn't listen to him. No one ever disobeyed my father, so how could I?'

'Poor thing, you must have been shattered. First, that bastard dumps you, then you have an abortion. You must have been a wreck.'

Jasmine heaved herself from the sofa and walked to the window. She slid open one curtain and looked out in the street below. Something made her smile and she watched a little longer.

Moushumi went over to look. A litter of puppies were pulling a bit of rope. They scampered about, making high-pitched yelps, while their mother looked on indulgently. 'Sweet little things. Maybe we could rescue the weak one. You could take him home?'

26

'I called the municipality yesterday and complained,' Jasmine said. 'Bloody idiots, letting stray dogs breed in this area. We pay bloody taxes to ensure this street stays well maintained. It's a respected area, not a place for rabid dogs.'

Moushumi stared at her. 'But, I thought you empathised...'

She didn't continue. Jasmine was right, of course. Stray dogs and stray people had no place here, yet a few feet away, poverty tumbled out of its restraints and advertised itself on the streets.

'No, I have the power to destroy them,' Jasmine said. 'So I will use it.'

'Surely, you can't?' The puppies yapped and jumped over each other, rolling and tumbling all over the pavement.

'Why? No one really cares about them. When they grow up, they'll be a menace. They won't remain sweet and cuddly all their lives.'

'Perhaps you are right. We can't save the whole world.'

'Nandkumar's alright,' Jasmine said, returning to her perch on the sofa. 'He doesn't interfere in my life and I don't in his. And I get to spend his money.' She looked up, her eyes shining like the diamonds she wore on her fingers.

'And will you be happy to continue like this forever?' Moushumi asked.

'I don't know. I live each day one at a time. But honestly, Mou, after meeting you, I actually look forward to the next day.'

Moushumi blushed. 'I'll try to make you happy, Jazz. You know I will. But doesn't he want to have a baby? An heir?'

Jasmine laughed out shrilly. The sound made Moushumi go cold. 'Of course he wanted an heir. Wants an heir for all his fortunes.' She walked up to her and pushed her down on the sofa. Her breath was sharp. She pressed her lips to Moushumi's and forced it open with her tongue. There was a roughness in the act that Moushumi did not like. It didn't arouse her. She tried to push her away, but already she was pinned down with Jasmine's hands all over her body.

'I won't let him have that baby,' Jasmine whispered. 'This is my revenge. To both the men in my life. And you, my love? I will fuck you and every time we do it, will be a spit on his face.'

Moushumi struggled to get out of her grasp. 'No, that's not right. I don't want you to use me.' Yet knowing, even as she said it, she wouldn't be able to stop. She let Jasmine rake her nails into her shoulders. She let her cry out in pain or pleasure, she was not sure what. And when she was done, they lay there, entwined and spent. All the arguments in Moushumi's head were warning her against this affair. Yet all the arguments pushed her firmly back to Jasmine. She no longer cared if her parents would worry about her returning home late. She no longer feared the marks of passion displayed on her skin. She stroked Jasmine's arm and wiped her tears. She helped her drink water and called for the driver to take her lover back to her husband's house. She picked up her handbag and dupatta and headed towards the door, already craving for the following Saturday.

Jasmine lay down on the sofa, her eyes drooping. She wrapped her arms around a cushion and brought her knees up to her chest. 'If I'd have had a baby, I'd never have had you,' she said.

5

Dipali

Dipali stood on the balcony of her new flat, watching the clouds gather in the horizon. The palm trees swayed below her. If she leaned far to the left, she could see the dull grey sea from behind the tall buildings. A lone boat bobbed uneasily until it disappeared from her view. Below, children were playing cricket in the compound. A tennis ball occasionally swerved into the air and over the wall, followed by shouts from the players. Usually some hurrying passerby stopped to pick it up and throw it back into the compound.

The bhelwala shouted past. Immediately a gang of children accosted him, demanding bhel and sev puris. Dipali wanted some as well. The bhelwala at her mother's place always kept an eye on her house whenever he passed by. She'd signal to him and he'd come over and make up a packet of spiced rice puffs for her. He knew how she liked her bhel – not too hot, not too sweet, with extra servings of tamarind chutney and crisps.

The telephone rang and Dipali hurried inside. It was her mother, who had taken to calling her often, especially at this time of day – before Sunil got home from work.

'What have you cooked for dinner?'

'Nothing,' Dipali said. 'Sunil's taking me out tonight.'

'Don't call your husband by his name, doesn't he mind?'

'No.' Dipali went back to the balcony to observe the bhelwala. 'Sunil doesn't mind. He doesn't believe in being old-fashioned.'

Her mother talked on, but Dipali only half listened. She watched the children stuff bhel into their mouths and giggle. She glanced at her watch and leaned against the door.

'Well, I don't approve, but what can I say?' Her mother was saying. 'It's only the first flush of marriage. They all change, men do. You must be on their correct side. What he says today won't stand true for tomorrow. Just follow the tried and tested ways, they always work.'

Some of the boys had finished eating the bhel and had carelessly flung the crumpled paper bags on the ground. The gurkha ran after the boys, waving his stick and shouting at them to pick up the rubbish.

'Ma, please,' Dipali said. 'Just because your husband didn't turn out right doesn't mean mine is faulty.'

There was silence on the line. Dipali rolled her eyes. She had gone too far, she knew. But marriage had given her confidence, a licence to speak her mind.

'You have a lot to learn. But take it from me, go easy with him. Don't use up all your freedom in the first year; you have a lifetime to go with him,' her mother said.

'He's not like Baba.' Dipali said. 'Ma, I'm sorry Baba didn't treat you right. He was too harsh on all of us. But that—'

'I don't want to talk about the past now. It is your future I'm concerned about.'

'That's the problem. We never talk about the past, but it's always there, just below our skin. Always itching to come out.'

30

Dipali imagined her mother pacing around the room, raking her fingers through her hair. It was an image she was very familiar with.

'I hope you don't discuss your father with Sunil,' her mother finally said. 'Don't waste your time talking about those days. Go out and enjoy your dinner tonight.'

'Don't change the subject, Ma. I think it is better to talk about it. Even you should let it all out of your system.'

'I'm old now. I've done my duty, marrying you off. Sunil's a good boy, I know it. Keep him happy, Dipali, and you will be happy.'

ॐ

'My mother is complaining,' Dipali pouted over her tandoori chicken. 'The teacher's are complaining. Tell me, do you really not mind?'

He was chewing on the chicken bone, its red juices dripping from his fingers. 'Mmm, this is good.' Sunil looked up to Dipali's disapproving glance and wiped his chin. 'Who cares?'

The restaurant was walking distance from their house. Sunil preferred it as he could drink his whiskeys without worrying too much. Sunny da Dhaba, said the pink neon lighting on the door. A six-foot tall turbaned Sikh watchman, hopeful of generous tips, saluted everyone who entered.

Dipali clicked her tongue in exasperation.

'Huh?' Sunil paused chewing. He had forgotten what they were talking about.

'Look at you eating. As if I never feed you at home.'

Sunil laughed. He reached out and pinched her cheek. 'I bet your mother has been complaining! Not cooking for your husband, huh?'

Dipali drained her glass of pina colada. The festive blue umbrella and tinned cherry looked rather subdued next to her bright orange tandoori chicken. She picked on it, not wanting to taste its greasiness. The other customers were enjoying their food, gnawing on tandoori legs, Sunny da Dhaba's house special: top tandoori in town.

'No, everyone says I shouldn't call you by your name,' Dipali said.

'Why?' Sunil asked. 'Whose name should you call me by?' He scanned the restaurant. 'Perhaps you can call me by his name?' He pointed to a Sikh man on the opposite table in a pink turban. 'Pinky?' Sunil said, his face serious, but eyes crinkling. 'You want to call me Pinky? Or Pappu?'

Dipali giggled. 'Shut up, Sunil. They say I should call you shuncho, or sunte ho. Something like that. My mother called my father that.'

'Why, was he hard of hearing?' Sunil asked.

Dipali laughed. 'No—'

'—Then why did your Ma say "hey, listen up", every time she addressed her husband?'

'Shut up, Sunil. That was a serious question. It's tradition.'

'Dipali,' Sunil put a bare chicken bone down on his plate. He cleaned the gravy off with the last piece of roti and stuffed it in his mouth. Dipali waited for him to finish. He chewed slowly, as if he was contemplating a very important idea.

The waiter hurried in with the menu cards. 'Dessert?'

Sunil ignored him and leaned forward. 'When we are having sex, my dear wife, would you prefer to say "Ooooh Sunil, almost there", or would you like to say, "hey listen up, keep at it, I'm almost there"?'

Dipali jumped back in embarrassment. She glanced at the waiter to see if he had followed their conversation. But he looked benign as he thrust the menu card towards her. She waved him away. 'Sunil,' she hissed. 'What if he heard?'

'Forget him. Answer my question.'

Dipali covered her face and cackled till she noticed the other diners were staring in their direction. 'You'll find out tonight, my dear husband. Now let's get out of here.'

6

Moushumi

Two women from Diamond Harbour district of twenty-four Parganas have committed suicide after their 'marriage' is shunned by families.

Moushumi stared at the television news reporter. He was standing among a crowd of villagers, shouting out the report over their chanting. The camera then zoomed on the faces of the two women's mothers. They were wailing and beating their breasts, claiming their daughters were innocent. They had been victims of black magic. There was an inset, a rather dated photograph of the deceased, then probably in their teens, with ribbons in their hair and toothy grins.

The lovers, both from farming communities, had grown up together in their tiny village near Falta. They had secretly married each other, when their parents started looking for prospective bridegrooms, by exchanging garlands and promises in a Shiva temple. When one of the women's fathers went ahead with wedding preparations, the two came out and confronted their parents.

They were then beaten by the families. A tantric was

summoned to drive away the spirits that had possessed them to take such action. An ojha was performed and one of the women was forcefully married off to an old man. Her lover immolated herself at the time of the wedding. Hearing this tragedy, the other woman escaped from her husband's home and drowned herself in the river. She left a note for her family saying that if the two had been allowed to live together, they'd all be happy and alive.

The reporter looked straight at the camera as he finished his report. Moushumi looked away. She realised she had been so caught up with listening to the news, she hadn't noticed her father had been watching as well.

'Sensationalism,' he exclaimed from behind her. 'They will report anything in the media nowadays to get attention.'

Moushumi looked up. 'But Baba, surely must be something genuine to report this, or why would they? They were very brave to face the world.' She watched him for his reaction.

He sniffed and reached for his cup of tea.

'Ma, did you hear about this?' Her mother was juggling a spatula and a spoon while stirring the dal and frying the fish. She wiped the sweat that ran down her neck and strained to hear above the splutter of the fish sizzling in the pan.

'Utter rot,' her father mumbled and opened the newspaper again. 'What is the world coming to? Chee chee. Desperate village bumpkins. How can the TV news report such filth, I fail to recognise.'

Moushumi flinched, ashamed. She was indulging in something her father found filthy. 'It's quite normal in the Western society. It is becoming accepted there.'

Her father glared at her but said nothing. He turned to the sports page and cursed about Mohun Bagan losing again. He was clearly not interested in continuing on the topic.

'What were you saying, Mou?' her mother asked, joining them in the sitting room. The air was smoky with all the deep-frying. The smell of the fish had seeped stubbornly into the mattress on the divan and the cushions and the curtains. But it was a comforting smell, not the artificial rose and lily room freshener that Moushumi had to adjust to on Saturdays in Jasmine's flat.

Her father left the room and Moushumi decided that she could still try out her mother. 'Two women committed suicide because their marriage was not accepted in society.'

'Oh,' her mother said. 'Hindu women?'

'Perhaps.'

'Did they marry Muslims or what?'

'No, Ma. They married each other. The two women married each other.'

Her mother stopped tidying the cushions and stared at her. 'Two women? Why on earth?'

'They said they loved each other.'

'But how will they have children? Who will look after them?'

Moushumi felt better. At least she was curious and asking questions. At least her first reaction was not that they were filthy. 'Does that matter? They loved each other.'

'What fools,' her mother replied. 'They've ruined their families' reputations. I hope they haven't left behind any unmarried sisters, or that will be the end of the road for them.'

'You think so?'

Her mother busied herself with putting right the newspaper. 'Stupid naive girls, did something under the influence of filmy romance, I suppose.'

Moushumi felt betrayed. Her mother was not on her side. How could she ever tell them if the time came?

Wiping her hands on the end of her sari, her mother said, 'Anyway, I don't have time for all this nonsense. I still have to finish cooking lunch. How would you like your fish? Mustard sauce or tomato?'

CR

'Silly girls,' said Jasmine, grimacing at the newspaper-cutting Moushumi thrust into her hand. 'No brains, these villager types.'

The news of the two women had found a little space in the local newspaper. Moushumi had cut it out and kept it in her handbag. She wasn't sure whether this was to remind her that this sort of thing was not accepted, or to reassure her that this was not her fate, yet. She had hoped that Jasmine would take up their case, get angry, and promise her that such things didn't happen in big cities. Instead, Jasmine had just laughed about the whole situation. 'You too, Jazz? Don't you believe in their love? Wouldn't you have backed them up?'

'For what, Mou? Be sensible. You are living in a fantasy world.' Jasmine switched on the television. The theme song of *The Bold and the Beautiful* filled the room. She tucked the sheet under her chin and watched idly.

'But it is accepted in the West,' argued Moushumi.

'Then go and live in the West. Find yourself a lover there and make a home for yourselves. Don't keep harping on about it and spoil my mood.'

'But we are lovers, Jasmine.' Moushumi shot back. 'Like those two girls. We do the same thing, and yet you reject their bravery in wanting to live together?'

Jasmine increased the volume of the television. The air-conditioning started to whir noisily, adding to Moushumi's distress. She wanted to shut everything off and shake Jasmine hard. Make her listen to her. Answer her questions.

'We can't live together, surely you know that? Or go public,' Jasmine said finally, during a commercial break.

Moushumi nodded. She was not stupid to have such hopes.

'Then why the entire headache?' Jasmine asked her. 'You will eventually have to get a man to marry you and then we could continue meeting.'

'But, I don't want it like that,' Moushumi said. 'I want to have a truthful relationship.'

'A truthful relationship? Which world are you in, madam? Just enjoy yourself and stop complaining. You're lucky with what you're getting.'

There was truth in every word of what Jasmine had said. How could they have an open relationship? What name would they give it? Moushumi thought of those two village girls. Did this kind of love mean being confined in a bedroom, once a week, having sex? She realised she was lucky that Jasmine had another flat for them to hide in, to indulge themselves in. What about the rest of them? Where did they go? What did they do?

'It's useless, Jasmine. This whole thing is a waste of time.' Moushumi slid under the sheets and held Jasmine's hand. 'Why do I bother to come?'

Jasmine turned around and stared at Moushumi for a long time. Her gaze softened, and when the commercial break ended, she didn't turn back to the television. 'I'm so glad you do come, darling. So don't spoil things with miserable realities. Okay, let's get out of this place. You'll have to tell your parents a very big lie, mind.'

Moushumi nodded. At that moment, she didn't care very much. She would do anything for Jasmine. She clung to her, trembling, waiting for Jasmine to touch her. Soothe her nerves. They kissed quietly, and Jasmine stroked her hair, murmuring into her ear. Moushumi calmed down.

At last they were going to venture out of this flat. They were going to do something fun.

ॐ

They walked down the lobby in their party clothes. Moushumi had never been to a five-star hotel before. People walked up and down the lobby, talking in hushed tones, their shoes clicking politely. Moushumi tugged at her backless choli that she had borrowed from Jasmine's wardrobe, pulling it down as it hitched up her breasts. It was a Rajasthani patchwork sari blouse, with its cuts made to highlight the curves. It was covered in mirror-work embroidery, teasing people to have a look at her assets. A smartly dressed woman stood behind the reception desk. She looked up with smoky eyes. Jasmine winked at her and walked on. Moushumi's stomach lurched. The woman glanced at Moushumi before returning her attention to the computer screen.

Anyone would think they were just friends, going to a nightclub to meet up with other friends. No one would guess they were lovers, that they'd share the dance space together and then go home to each other's arms. If her mother saw her in these clothes, she would die. If her mother knew of the other things, she'd not only die but go straight to hell for giving birth to such a devil. Moushumi was thankful that no one from her part of the world would inhabit five-star hotels. She was safe here.

The door opened and immediately the music and the darkness engulfed them. The smoky nightclub was packed with sweaty bodies gyrating. Moushumi's eyes stung as she wove through the crowd to the seating area. The strobe lights flashed, showing shining faces in a trance, arms waving, vacant smiles and blurred eyes.

Jasmine pulled her down on her lap and kissed her fully on her lips. She laughed as Moushumi struggled in her grasp.

'Jasmine, stop. People are watching.' She slid out of her arms and stood up, wobbly in her high heels. She felt cold in spite of the muggy air.

'Relax, babe. Don't be scared. Whatever happens here stays within these walls.'

'I don't see any women kissing,' she pointed out to Jasmine.

Jasmine tossed her hair back and went towards the bar. Moushumi followed her, still trying to get used to the tiny bit of cloth covering her breasts.

'Oh, stop fiddling,' shouted Jasmine over the throbbing music. 'You look sexy.'

Moushumi blushed. 'You too.' She admired the way Jasmine had dressed so simply in a chiffon tunic and leggings and yet managed to stand out in the crowd.

Jasmine leaned forward to ruffle her hair. Moushumi kissed her neck tentatively and moved closer. They pushed their way towards the bar. God, she needed a drink, maybe two if they were going to get down and dirty in the nightclub.

'Sweetheart,' Jasmine said as they sat back and sipped their drinks. 'Don't be so caught up with this lesbian-label. You are a human being, for God's sake, and you have a right to enjoy yourself.'

'I know,' Moushumi argued. 'But this is all very strange to do in public. What if we spot someone who knows us? Aren't you afraid that your husband will find out?'

Jasmine didn't reply. She finished her drink in one gulp and rubbed her eyes absently, smudging her mascara. A man appeared and called out to Jasmine. Her face lit up in a fake approximation of joy as she allowed him to peck her on both the cheeks. Moushumi gave her a see-what-I-mean look. Jasmine turned away to talk to the man. He looked at Moushumi and waved. She waved back. He went back to the dance floor and joined another man. They held each other and danced. Now Jasmine gave her see-what-I-mean-look and laughed.

Moushumi studied the crowd. There were teenagers, lavishing it out on their parents' money, downing drinks recklessly and dancing like there was no tomorrow. There were couples kissing and embracing like there was no tomorrow. There were people drinking like there was no tomorrow. In fact, the whole place seemed to have a sense of urgency. Desperation to get things done before the end of the night.

Moushumi and Jasmine danced with an urgency she had never realised before in her life, like everything depended on this moment. People bumped into them, she felt their damp bodies press against her and she moved closer to Jasmine. She smelt her citrus-laced sweat. Her mind went pleasantly blank. She was floating high above the nightclub, her heart throbbing to the beat of the music. Her arms and legs were moving to their own accord. Perhaps this was what drug-taking was all about, Moushumi thought. Being on an absolute high. Never wanting to touch earth again. What bliss. The music changed to a romantic number and arms encircled lovers within them.

Jasmine held Moushumi close. She rested her head on her shoulder, but she was not light-spirited. Her weight dragged Moushumi down. When she looked up, she had tears in her eyes. Moushumi kissed the tear that fell to her cheek. Jasmine shook her head and moved out of her arms. She led the way out of the nightclub. She tipped the doorman and waited for her car to be brought up to the entrance. Jasmine drove away from the disco until they reached a narrow lane. She parked in a gap between two crumbling buildings. It was dark, except for the street lamp that was flickering intermittently. Just like the disco, thought Moushumi. There was a muggy stillness and so Jasmine turned the air-conditioning up high and it drowned out the sounds of the night. She reached out and pulled Moushumi to her and, somewhere in the car, Moushumi lost her choli and her inhibitions.

7

Dipali

It was close to midnight, but there was no sign of the Diwali party winding down. People hung about the bar, nursing their drinks. Some of the women sat on rugs, smoking and chit-chatting. The men discussed politics and cricket. They talked about the rumours that a mosque would be demolished soon to make way for a temple in Ayodhya. Another group played cards, as was the Diwali tradition. Dipali could see Sunil was bored. He wasn't contributing to the conversation, just holding his drink and laughing once in a while. But this was his regional head's party. They'd have to stick around a bit.

Dipali walked to the balcony and sat on the cane swing. She rocked slowly, trying to enjoy the music. Daler Mehndi wasn't her style but his music definitely suited the occasion. She looked out to the sea. It was a moonless night. The street lamps glowed orange and the promenade was busy with people out celebrating. Youngsters and older people alike waved sparklers around, creating light lines in the air. Showers of sparks flared up from tubris, accompanied by laughter and cheers. Fireworks fizzed like popcorn in the sky.

Rockets exploded leaving an acrid smell lingering, the horizon hazy with sulphuric smoke. It was late, but still children were up on their terraces, bursting 'chocolate bombs', their deafening bangs ripping through the air. She jumped every time one went off. The wine made her groggy. What a waste of a Saturday. She'd rather have spent the evening back on *their* terrace, bursting crackers with the neighbours and their children, and then chilling with her husband in front of the TV with a bottle of wine.

She thought back to her conversation with her mother earlier that week. As always it ended with her suggestions, either in hints or now more blatantly, that she was looking forward to having a grandchild. She had been married two years and the pressure was on. Why couldn't she enjoy her life? Surely she deserved a bit of peace? She had lashed out. Her mother had cried.

Dipali's stomach rumbled. She hadn't eaten since they had arrived. She shouldn't have been so harsh on her mother. Anyway, Sunil didn't want a child now. He wanted a promotion. He wanted to buy a flat. But she hadn't the heart to tell her mother that. She slipped into the kitchen to find that most of the food had been eaten. There were a few soggy dhoklas on the table, but Dipali ignored them. She had been drinking on an empty stomach, and that gave her a headache.

Out of the window, she could see the late-night hawkers on the street below. They were roasting corn on the cobs, or selling hot peanuts. People were buying ice creams too. She craved for a kulfi. Her head started to spin. She caught Sunil's eye. 'Fancy a walk?' she asked him, she asked him, snatching the car keys from his hands. His breath was sharp with alcohol and Dipali puckered her nose.

'Not really. Where do you want to go?'

'I'm starving, Sunil. Let's just get something downstairs. Peanuts, ice-cream, anything?'

'Let's walk to Chowpatty,' Sunil said. 'I'll buy you the best kulfi in town. Then we'll walk home.'

'You're not serious!' Dipali shouted over the music. 'We're miles away. Hey, Sunil, wake up. We're in Bandra. We live on Peddar Road, if you haven't forgotten.'

'I'm quite high,' said Sunil, pulling her close. 'I shouldn't drive all the way. There'll be a nakabandi on the roads for sure and the cops will catch us. Plus, it will be a romantic walk, no?'

Dipali laughed and wrestled him. The watchman looked at them and turned away. In the distance, a stray dog began to bark.

Sunil laughed with her. 'I'm serious, babes. Do you want to drive?'

'Sunil, darling, the cops will catch me right away. Even when I'm sober, I can't drive in a straight line. Anyway, I'm quite drunk too.'

'You shameless woman,' Sunil said. 'How many pegs did you have? I'm impressed.'

Dipali did a mock bow and stuck out three fingers.

'And now you can't even walk straight. I'll have to carry you home,' Sunil shouted, chasing her.

'But I'll race you to the nearest kulfiwala,' Dipali removed her high-heeled sandals and set off at a sprint.

The road was strewn with the singed remains of firecrackers, chakris and tubris. People stared at them as they ran. It wasn't very often that women sprinted on the streets holding sandals in their hand. They entered a small dhaba and sat on two rickety stools. Dipali giggled till her eyes watered. The other customers were mostly auto drivers and some drunks. Sunil looked at them and eyed his wife uneasily. The men were leering at her. He quickly ordered some kebabs to be parcelled and pushed her out of the shack.

'Let's go home to Ma's,' Dipali said, biting into a kebab. The juices escaped and slid down to her chin, but she didn't care. 'I can't walk anymore.'

'It's nearly two in the morning,' Sunil said. 'She'll have a heart attack.'

'Oof, I have a key. We'll just slip in.'

It did make sense. Dipali's mother's house was just five minutes away by auto rickshaw.

'We'll have to be very quiet though.'

'Yes. Like teenagers. Smuggling a boyfriend into my room.'

'Did you smuggle boys in when you were a teenager? I wish you had, actually. Added some spice to your life,' Sunil teased her.

Dipali sobered up when they arrived outside her mother's house. She didn't want her mother discovering alcohol on her breath.

'My brother once came home smelling of beer. He tried to run into his room before Baba caught him. But of course, nothing escaped him. He beat him with a belt. A twenty-year-old man. Can you imagine what Ashish must have gone through?'

Sunil held her tight and wiped her eyes.

They tiptoed to the front door. The house was dark and still. The mango tree rustled. A string of firecrackers ricocheted in the distance, killing the neighbourhood peace. Dipali's head throbbed. She wanted to turn back and run. But Sunil supported her back and led her into the house. He assured Dipali that her mother would be pleasantly surprised at discovering the break-in in the morning.

℃Ջ

Dipali and Sunil visited his parents during the Easter holidays. They sped through Calcutta in a juddering yellow Ambassador, the driver honking madly and grinning from ear to ear. He evaded cows and goats and farmers with baskets of vegetables making their way to the morning marketplaces. Smog hung over this city as well, making it dull and grey. They passed the fisheries and the tanneries, each with their own distinctive stench. The driver swore at school children who ran across the road without looking. He nearly ran into a cyclist with hens in a basket. They squawked in retaliation. The cyclist lost his balance and landed on the ground and the hens flew out of the basket.

On they drove, beyond the mayhem of rush hour traffic at the seven-point crossing of Park Circus with continuous honking and lane-changing. Beyond the butcher stalls with their displays of different cuts of cow and goat's body parts hanging from metal hooks. Urchin boys and girls stood bathing near a tube well, the water creating a soapy, scummy stream down the street. Somewhere the persistent whistle of a traffic policeman was ignored while the morning got on with its business.

When they swept into the view of the Victoria Memorial it was a soothing balm to frayed nerves. The marble structure was blinding white in the hot sun, while watery mirages on the green played pleasant tricks to sore eyes. Cattle grazed where once coiffured and corseted English ladies must have walked with their parasols. Dipali breathed deeply and was rewarded with the smell of freshly cut grass and horse manure. The racecourse came into view, and through the haze, in the distance she saw the commercial buildings of Calcutta rise into the sky.

Finally, they reached their destination. Dipali leaned out to have a closer look, sure this was nowhere near her in-laws' place. Instead a structure rose in front of her, solid and pink. She leaned out further. There were long queues outside the gate. People were in a celebratory mood. Sunil had brought her to Eden Gardens. The hallowed cricket ground of Calcutta; the biggest cricket stadium in India. 'What are we doing here?' Dipali asked. 'Aren't your parents waiting for us?'

'First match, then the rest,' said Sunil.

'But what about our suitcases?' Dipali panicked. 'We can't take our luggage inside.'

'No,' he said. 'I've paid the taxi driver to drop it at my parents'.'

'What?' She swung round to look for the taxi, but it had already sped off. 'He's gone with our bags.'

Sunil took her hand in his and walked towards the gates. 'This is Calcutta, my dear. I've paid him. He will drop our luggage off. You have to trust him.'

'And what if he doesn't,' Dipali insisted.

'Then, my dear wife, you will get a new wardrobe.'

'The finals, *the finals*,' Dipali clasped Sunil's shirt and jumped up and down. 'You sly creature, you've brought me to watch the finals.'

'A bribe to make you behave decently with your in-laws!'

She punched him on the arm and laughed. The Hero Cup finals. Pakistan versus the West Indies. She recalled the air of secrecy before the trip and she now understood why Sunil had insisted she wear jeans instead of a sari when she was supposed to be meeting her in-laws. Cricket fans were chanting, singing, eating, drinking and generally having a good time as they were slowly being let into the grounds.

Dipali and Sunil joined the queue. He waved the tickets at her.

'How did you manage that?' she said, trying to snatch them from his hand. 'Oh, what an amazing surprise.'

'Better than seeing your in-laws?' Sunil gave her a sideways glance.

'If I'm going to be face to face with Imran Khan and Wasim Akram, Sunil, definitely, definitely better!'

They found a place to sit. The spectators had already opened up their picnic boxes. Out flowed samosas, fries, pakoras, chai, cold drinks, peanuts. Bottles and crumpled wafer packets and other junk littered the area. It was a packed stadium, which meant there were around ninety-thousand people about to witness the final match. The sun climbed up into the sky and the ground lit up green and fresh, ready for action. A tiny figure manoeuvred the roller across the grass. The spectators screamed out their chants and danced clumsily in their spots.

There was a roar of applause and Dipali craned her neck to see. The cricketers entered. Captain Imran Khan led his team forward and she screamed with excitement. Sunil clapped and whooped when he spotted Viv Richards in the West Indian line-up.

Dipali looked at him, her face flushed. 'Let's have a bet,' she yelled above the screams. 'I bet Pakistan will win.'

Sunil grabbed her arm and squeezed hard. 'Okay. Loser has to obey the winner for a whole week.'

'Done,' Dipali squealed. 'I'm going to win, so beware, my sweetie pie.'

QR

Later that evening, Dipali leaned back into her chair and listened to her husband as he recounted their experience to his parents. They sat at the dining table in his parents' flat in Alipore, all wide-eyed and excited. Her in-laws kept glancing at her, nodding and smiling, while she carefully arranged the pleats on her sari and added her bits of description of their day to them.

Sunil didn't tell them that he was to give in to her every demand that week nor did he tell them how after the match, they'd rushed out to buy a sari just as the shops closed. Dipali had hurriedly put it on in the fitting rooms of a dilapidated shop, with her jeans still underneath and a ready-made blouse that was too loose. What he did say was how amazing it had been to watch Malcolm Marshall bowl. He talked of how Dipali had screamed when Imran Khan picked up the trophy for Man of the Series and so her voice was hoarse now; and how amazing it had been to be part of that historic match at Eden Gardens.

8

Moushumi

Moushumi sipped her ice-cold water gratefully. Monsoon was still months away and she shuddered at the thought that she'd have to leave Jasmine's flat soon and face the muggy, unbearable heat. Her house was at the other end of the city. She did not have the comforts of air-conditioned cars to drive her back and forth. But luckily, ever since the metro trains started operating, life was much better. The first network of its kind in India, she thought proudly. All posh and air-conditioned. She'd have to persuade Jasmine to travel on it someday.

There were big canvasses on the walls of the lounge. Famous signatures featured on these paintings. She never tired of studying these pieces of art, especially the Manjit Bawa that Jasmine had recently acquired. It was a bright vermillion canvas. There were rows of cows standing or sitting, eyes half closed, as if mesmerised by the cowherd who played a flute. He was cerulean blue. The colour of Lord Krishna, God of love.

Krishna was Moushumi's family deity. Every morning, after their baths, she and her mother would dress and feed their little bronze statue of Krishna and pray for the well-being of the world. She felt uncomfortable that he was now going to stand there and witness her sins. She hoped that Jasmine would remove the painting from this flat, their little love nest. But more than that, she was disturbed that she thought herself sinning against God. Krishna celebrated his love life and was never ashamed of having many wives and lovers. Surely he would understand her feelings and not judge her actions? Maybe it was alright to have him here in this flat after all. He probably had the most liberal mind.

She felt better after reasoning it out with herself. She tiptoed back into the bedroom where Jasmine was asleep, her hair spread fan-like on the pillow, her pale skin glowing against the deep blue sheets. Their clothes were in a heap on the floor. The cricket match was on. If she made it back in time, she'd get to watch the end with her parents. Moushumi dressed, switched off the television and padded out of the room.

Moushumi cursed as she stepped onto the street. The sun scorched the tarmac and she felt the heat through her sandals. She dived under the shade of the trees, struggled to open her umbrella and then walked briskly towards the Metro station. Traffic was nonexistent because of the cricket. People flocked outside electronics shops, watching the match on the television sets displayed in the windows.

She quickly called home from a telephone booth. Using Jasmine's phone always seemed like she was calling from the scene of the crime. Her sister answered. They were all at their parents' home.

'What kind of people go for tuitions on the day of the final?' Aparna demanded over the phone. 'Come home as soon as possible, Mou. We've got the neighbours piling in to watch as well. We'll have a party.'

Moushumi hung up and hurried along.

She walked past the construction workers' washed laundry, which were hung out to dry on roadside railings. The clothes flapped nonchalantly in the breeze as if in someone's back garden. A woman was cooking on the pavement. Moushumi had to step aside, or else she'd have to jump over the tiny stove. She took a deep breath. The woman was making khichri, a mixture of rice and lentils. Moushumi's stomach growled. She wanted to eat some real food. She always had that feeling after being with Jasmine. There was only so much takeaway pizza and pasta one could have.

There were plenty of food stalls lining the opposite pavement. Moushumi crossed the road, dodging a bullock cart and a scooter. She longed to get Jasmine to these roadside places and enjoy phuchkas and egg rolls, but of course, once out in the city, Jasmine never stepped from her air-conditioned car unless she had reached a 'five-star something'. She stopped in front of a vendor. A boy was kneading expertly. She watched how he dug his elbows into the dough to make it soft and pliant. She hoped his elbows were clean. Another young man was in charge of the large iron tava, which he kept well oiled to fry up his egg parathas.

'One egg-roll,' said Moushumi. 'Lots of onions and chillies.'

The man nodded and cracked two eggs onto the tava. He then threw one rolled-out dough on top of the eggs and let it cook. He sprinkled salt and sliced onions and chillies and rolled it up.

'Five rupees,' he said, handing Moushumi the roll. She bit into it, savouring the bite of the chillies mixed in with the eggs.

It was cooler underground. Moushumi checked the arrival time of the next train. Ten minutes. She walked further up the platform. It wasn't crowded at all. There was a group of people hesitating by the top of the escalator, unsure how to go down it. Two women, their saris hitched well above their knees, were shrieking and clutching on to a young boy's collar while stepping onto the escalator. The boy looked away, embarrassed, while other commuters shouted words of encouragement from the bottom.

'Didi, don't worry. You won't fall down. Hold on to the banister.'

'Oh, Boudi, have faith. We will catch you if you fall.'

'Arrey, you useless, good-for-nothing boy, help your mother down. The train will be here soon.'

The duo wailed and cursed the government for replacing stairs for this death trap. It was a while before they finally made their way down to the bottom.

The far end of the tunnel lit up. Moushumi stood to join the others. The train swept in. She boarded, sat in one corner and took out her book, *Hamlet*. She would be teaching it next term. She wondered about Ophelia. Death, even there, was the solution to a failed love. She couldn't concentrate on reading, so she let the book rest on her knee. There were about a dozen other people in her compartment. A young couple were sat opposite, their hands not quite touching but still she could feel their excitement in being so close to each other.

She felt envious. They could show their affection in public. They could even get married. They were so sure about each other. It made her feel dirty, as if her relationship with Jasmine was impure. But how, she argued with herself. How is it impure? She's my best friend, though she does get on my nerves sometimes. We love to spend time with each other. Talk to each other. That's not perverse. It wasn't like in the porn magazine she had once found tucked under her cousin's mattress. That was in poor taste, and she and Jasmine were not like that.

Why did it seem such a dirty word? Because society had made it like that. All those magazines and films made for man's entertainment. She looked out of the window. Fluorescent tube lights flashed by. The train thundered on to the next stop. And then the next. And the next. Further and further away from her fantastical world. They emerged into the sunlight and Moushumi blinked. The city poured in through the windows. Houses, some thatched, some half-built of brick and stone, spread away from the railway tracks. Narrow lanes spiralled giddily through the gaps. Children waved to no one in particular. The train stopped and everyone shuffled to the door. The last stop on that line, furthest away from the city of Calcutta.

A few rickety cycle-rickshaws stood expectantly by the station gates. Moushumi hopped into one and the driver immediately began to pedal away. He swerved in between autos, cycles, and cars, consistently yelling and blowing the horn. The sun burned down on his bare back. He was wearing only a lungi that was hitched up to his thighs and his calf muscles bulged as he pedalled. Those were the only muscles she could see on his wiry body. Sweat coursed down his back. She thought of Raju, Jasmine's driver. Suave and so respectable in his white uniform and polished shoes. He spoke English and had a pager. He even wore Old Spice aftershave.

It smells so different here, she thought. She looked at the open drains and the pigs lolling in the sewage and grimaced. Funny, how she never even thought of such things before, while she was growing up here. But then she had nothing to compare it with. South Calcutta was even more remote than

England or Africa. Those she read about in her history books or watched on Doordarshan TV or, more recently, on all those cable channels. But what opportunities ever took her to the wealthier parts of her city? A yearly trip to Park Street to see the Christmas lights. Puja shopping at New Market, perhaps. The fanciest house had to be her cousin, Kishore's. They lived in Ballygunge and were considered very posh by the family, but she had never been to those huge flats with marble flooring and air-conditioned toilets. Now she was spending most of her time in just such a place.

Moushumi knew she'd never be able to invite Jasmine here. How could she show her that half-built house her father never managed to complete, the naked brick surface with no plastering or paint, the dark, damp passage where clothes were put to dry on wet days? The rickshaw stopped outside her house. She handed the driver a crumpled five-rupee note and he clicked his tongue in exasperation.

'Take it or leave it,' she snapped, and jumped off the rickshaw. 'Asking for new notes as if you're driving a Mercedes.'

ॐ

'Today, I want to do it my way,' Moushumi said and squeezed Jasmine's hand. Jasmine adjusted her sunglasses and stepped out of the car. 'This is the Calcutta *I* love and I want to share it with you.'

'That's nice,' Jasmine said. She turned to her driver and gave him instructions to wait for them.

Another week had passed. A sudden shower had left the city refreshed, making Moushumi adamant on venturing out of the apartment again. The river was calm, like a sheet of opaque glass. There were lots of people walking on the Strand. Couples, families, friends were out enjoying the evening. The women wore saris or salwar kameezes, men in bush shirts or jeans. There were hawkers selling peanuts, jhal muri, balloons, toys, and ice golas. It looked like a fairground. Moushumi took Jasmine's hand, but then quickly pulled away. No, it was not possible to do it in her world. Jasmine sniffed and looked around. She wiped her hands on the front of her jeans and pushed her sunglasses up her nose.

'What are we doing here?' she asked. 'What's so special about this place?'

'Jazz,' Moushumi chided her. 'This is the Strand. That is the river Hooghly. An evening out here is magical. I promise you.'

Jasmine didn't look convinced. She kicked aside a banana skin with her silver sandals. A rush of wind blew plastic straws and paper cones up their way. A wave of anger swept through Moushumi. She wasn't sure if it was directed towards the people for littering or towards Jasmine for being so critical. She took a deep breath and pursed her lips.

'How about a boat-ride down the Ganges?' Moushumi suggested. 'Come, don't say no.'

Jasmine was about to protest, but Moushumi ran up to buy the tickets. She took Jasmine's hand and led her up the stairs to the top. It was a launch boat named *Sagar Prem*, love for the sea. She bobbed prettily in the water, her railings flickering with fairy lights. Moushumi found them a seat in the front. The boat filled quickly with families and couples, all talking excitedly.

'I used to come here often,' Moushumi said. 'We'd bunk college and spend the afternoons in Scoop, eating ice-cream, and then go for a boat ride to watch the sun set over Belur Math.'

Jasmine smiled back, but didn't say anything. The couple next to them were staring at her and giggling. The engine started and the boat began to vibrate. They sailed towards the Howrah Bridge. Old temples lined the banks, their bells ringing, and the smell of incense wafted over the water towards them. People were washing themselves in the ghats, or setting afloat prayer lamps, little oil-lit flames nestled in dried leaf boats, and flower garlands. The birds were flying back to their nests, calling out as they passed overhead. The people on the boat hushed down to quiet whispers and watched the shoreline. The water lapped as the boat glided across; the lone evening star quivering in her wake.

As the sun set they approached the ancient temple of Belur Math. Its domes glittered like jewels in the orange glow.

'I come here every year with my parents,' Moushumi said. 'Have you been?'

Jasmine shook her head. 'No, I haven't. It's beautiful, I think I should.'

'I'll take you,' Moushumi said happily and held Jasmine's hand. Jasmine gently eased her hand out of Moushumi's grip. She shook her head very slightly. But Moushumi was too happy to care. She leaned closer to Jasmine and stroked her arm. A young girl sitting opposite them giggled. Her mother glared her into silence, and then she glared at Moushumi.

'Don't,' whispered Jasmine. 'You're making me uncomfortable. This isn't Venus nightclub. This is bloody middle-class public transport.'

Moushumi jerked back in shock. Jasmine locked eyes with the woman opposite, who finally had to look away. No one would dare glare at Jasmine in her tight blue jeans, red manicured toenails peeping out of silver-strapped sandals. She stood out in this milieu of middle-class people. Even Moushumi looked too roughly shod to be her companion. Belur lost its charm. The launch looked tacky, the plastic chairs sat cheaply in rows, filled by gaudily dressed sightseers. Moushumi's eyes filled. She had never realised how mediocre everything she loved was.

9

Dipali

The Rais were very different from Dipali's own family. It had been quite a shock to see her mother-in-law get up early in the morning, leave instructions with the houseboy and then drive off to work. She'd return only late in the evening, have a wash and sit down directly for dinner. Dipali's father-in-law would return home in time to dine with his wife. But he'd spend his day at the Calcutta Club. He had retired some years ago and now spent his days relishing the pampered services he received at the Club.

They lived in an expansive flat overlooking the National Library in Calcutta. Big French windows let in the balmy breezes from the grounds beyond. The floors were all marble, or granite. The dining table was teak. It could seat sixteen diners and it took up the entire dining space that went with the sitting room. The silver candle stands, shining, of course. The Spode dinnerware, brought out in honour of the newly-weds. The crystal chandelier was almost floating above the big soup tureen in the centre. Six leather-backed brass-studded chairs dotted the table. It all looked very Victorian.

Dipali looked at the ancient decor and wondered about Sunil's childhood. Did he have his meals sitting at this table? Did he ever reach up to it or did he have to sit on cushions? But he had spent most of his childhood in a boarding school in Darjeeling. He didn't have much attachment to this place.

She sat there, back automatically straight and elbows off the table. She eyed her silver cutlery nervously. She preferred using her fingers. All this fuss with fork and spoon took the joy away from eating. She wondered what they'd be served by the ancient butler. Gulabchand. A red rose was embroidered on the chest pocket of his smart white uniform. Dipali looked at Sunil and bit upon a giggle. Gulabchand was taking his name too literally. He held a large tray with two serving bowls.

He laid the food out on the table and Dr Rai thanked him. Mr Rai nodded absently. He was humming a tune under his breath, and drumming his fingers on his thigh. Dipali looked at the food in front of her. Spaghetti bolognese. A strangled laugh escaped from her throat. She hit her chest and turned it into a cough.

'Are you okay?' Dr Rai said, getting up. But she'd have to walk the length of the table to reach her daughter-in-law. She sat down again. Mr Rai was oblivious. He kept singing softly. Sunil frowned at her. Dipali quietened down.

'I'm alright,' Dipali spluttered. She bent down and collected her fork and spoon.

Gulabchand served her a big ladling of the spaghetti bolognese.

'Some extra virgin olive oil?' he asked gravely, hovering over her, bottle in hand. All this Victorian drama and then being served a pasta by a uniformed butler. She'd had no idea this was how Sunil had been brought up.

She shook her head. She was too afraid to speak. She might have had a laughing breakdown. Gulabchand moved on to Sunil. Dipali was curious to know how Sunil would react to all this. He was non-committal and just ignored Gulabchand as he served. There was no chatter, just the occasional clink of silver. Dr Rai chewed her pasta slowly. Mr Rai slurped his down, the tomato sauce speckling his chin. He looked at Dipali from time to time and encouraged her to eat, indicating with his eyes only. Sunil didn't look up from his plate. He just swallowed, his Adam's apple bobbing. Dipali ate quietly. Her eyes roved from one person to the other, but no one was interested in talking.

Dessert was custard apple ice-cream. That was served in a huge silver ice-cream cup. As soon as Dr Rai finished her dessert, she carefully wiped her mouth with a napkin. She then smiled at Dipali. 'We don't talk during meals. I should have warned you earlier. Didn't you tell her, Sunil?'

'No,' said Sunil, getting up. He had already pounced on the remote control before his father could. 'I thought you'd change the rules for your daughter-in-law, Ma.'

'Rules and rules,' smiled Dr Rai. 'You remember that, bou-ma. It comes in use when you have to run a family on restricted time.'

They retired to the lounge by the French windows. The chiffon curtains floated back and forth in the twilight breeze. The Library had been lit up for the night. Dipali stood by the windows and admired it. Sunil watched the cricket highlights on mute. Dr Rai sat down next to Dipali and took her hands in her own. Dipali found her mother-in-law's hands very spidery but surprisingly warm.

'You must find us to be very different from your family, Dipali. But you mustn't mind us. We are very work-oriented people. Or at least I am now. I am in no mood to retire.' She smiled and her dimples deepened.

Her mother-in-law was a very attractive woman, Dipali admitted. She was slim, bird-like, with very thin hands and feet. Her bones and veins stuck out, and she had a slight stoop. But what made her attractive, Dipali decided, was her attitude towards life, and her success in a world dominated by men. She was a leading cardiologist in Calcutta. She also ran a village hospital. She was well respected in her field, and was a visiting lecturer at the Calcutta Medical College. Her eyes were luminous, as if excited about the latest thing she was about to discover or do. Age fell off her face when she laughed. Light-hearted laughter, like the tinkling chandelier over the dining table. She was quite a persona. By comparison, Dipali felt inconsequential, as if she was wasting her time, wasting her life.

Dr Rai continued holding Dipali's hand. 'I hope you are happy with Sunil.'

Dipali blushed and nodded.

'We'll get to know each other in time, my dear. But remember, what you see here is all eyewash. Do you think I care about all this regalia you see in this house? I know you found it funny. I would too, but from my point of view, I cannot do away with the old. All these ancient things are my husband's heirlooms, handed down the generations. I look after it only for the next generation. I don't particularly care about it, myself, though I do respect the sentiments attached. I care about Gulabchand, who looks after the house and husband for me, and serves us a quick meal because his arthritis cannot have him standing over the stove for hours.'

Dipali noticed Sunil looking at his mother, a smile playing at the corner of his lips. He turned back to the television. Mr Rai wished them goodnight and shuffled to his room.

'My husband isn't what he used to be, my dear. Don't mind him. He's getting forgetful. It's the beginning of Alzheimer's. He was very different before. I don't know what Sunil's been telling you about us.'

'Oh, nothing,' blurted Dipali. 'I mean nothing bad.'

'Well, the one thing you should know is this,' Dr Rai said, drawing her shawl up to her chin. 'All this wealth you see around us, we've worked over the decades and accumulated it. But it is meaningless to own this money without hard work. I've put it in my will; all this money will go to the hospital and the orphanages I have built and support. You don't need it, my dear. My Sunil and you will work hard to make a life of your own. That is my belief.'

'Oh,' Dipali wasn't sure how to react. She had not thought about the money or inheritance. It hadn't seemed important to her. 'Don't worry about it. The hospital should absolutely get all the funds. And the charities. I have no problems with it.'

She wanted to ask who would inherit these Victorian heirlooms. She didn't want them either. But then thought it would be impolite to ask. She wondered when would be the appropriate time to go to bed. She wanted Sunil to herself desperately. She caught his eye and indicated very slightly that she wanted to go. They sat watching the television for a few more minutes and then he switched it off.

Dr Rai got up and stretched. 'I'm off to bed. I'll see you both tomorrow at dinnertime.' She gathered her journals and left the room.

'So, Mrs Rai,' Sunil smiled. 'A tête-à-tête with your ma-in-law?'

'Well, someone's got to talk,' she scolded him light-heartedly. 'The men in your family don't believe in talking.

And your mother's been warning me we won't inherit anything from her.'

Sunil laughed. 'So she's making her intentions clear then. Good job I believe in only action, my dear, and not silly talking. Maybe that creaky old Victorian table needs to see a bit of action?'

'You wicked creature!' Dipali squealed and raced to their bedroom. 'I'll lock the door if you don't come in now.'

10

Moushumi

Moushumi's mother was in the kitchen, singing under her breath and frying fish. 'Ah, you're back. How was your day? Did the students play up?'

Moushumi nodded vaguely. She hated these lies, these underhand methods of deceit. She looked beyond her mother, to the sticky, soot-stained walls of the kitchen. At one time, it had been yellow. She looked at the shining steel utensils stored on the wall rack. The room reeked of mustard oil and fish. Her mother looked greasy and dull. Gulping down her rage, Moushumi rushed to her bedroom, flinging her bag on the floor. Life wasn't fair. She thought of Jasmine's kitchen, made of Italian marble and granite, non-stick cookware adorning the shelves. Jasmine didn't even use them. Her kitchen was pristine – a show kitchen – she mostly ordered food from restaurants. If only Moushumi's mother could have a kitchen like that, where she could fry her fish and use the fan to dissipate the smell. Now the whole house stank. Her saris too. She wondered if Jasmine smelled the middle-classness on her.

Her mother followed her into the room. She held out a glass of lime juice for her. 'What's the matter, Mou,' she asked. 'The children give you a hard time?'

Moushumi shook her head. She drank the juice in big gulps and turned away.

'Those rich kids must be a pain,' her mother dusted the bookshelf and flicked through a textbook on the desk. 'Why can't you get tuitions closer to home? You are away all day on Saturdays, and you work hard all week. Where's the time for you to spend with us?'

'It's okay, Ma,' Moushumi said. 'I don't mind.'

'But look how dark you've become. All this travelling has made you thin too. It's not good you know. Especially now, with Baba looking for a suitable boy for you.'

Moushumi froze. It had been her father's obsession a while back. Writing up a list of possible suitors from newspaper matrimonial columns. Asking around in the family circle. Arranging meetings with shortlisted candidates. So far, she had met two, and had refused both of them. Her father had stopped then, but she knew it was only a matter of time before they'd zero in on her again. She was of 'marriageable age' now.

'What are you saying, Ma? I'm not interested in getting married.' She tried to sound casual, but her hands trembled as she put the glass down on the desk.

Her mother straightened the corner of the bed sheet, sat down and smoothed her hands on her sari. 'Oh? Why won't you get married? You are twenty-three now. You can't wait any longer than this. Your sister got married at twenty.'

'Yes, Aparna did. But she married a boy from the para, from our locality. They knew each other ever since they were babies. Anyway, I don't have to do what she did. Don't compare me with her all the time.'

67

'Mou, Mou, don't start arguing again. Aparna was fortunate to get married to such a good boy. But we will find the same for you.' Her mother grinned at her conspiratorially. 'In fact, a better prospect. He's a civil engineer. From the Indian Institute of Technology. Lives in America. You can live in America, Mou, have a good life.'

Moushumi stared at her mother. She wondered how far things had developed.

'What do you mean? Who is this man? How far have you all talked behind my back?'

'Oh, don't get angry. We've not said anything. Bula mashi just dropped in yesterday and suggested it. He's her husband's cousin's wife's sister's son. Wait, did I get that right?'

'Oof, I don't care, I'm not marrying him,'

'You haven't even seen him,' her mother complained. Then her eyes lit up. 'Have you found someone yourself, Mou?'

Moushumi shook her head. 'Oof, Ma, stop it.'

'We don't mind, Mou,' her mother smiled. 'We are very open-minded. As long as he is a good, Hindu boy from a respectable family.'

'Very broad-minded indeed, Ma. Good Hindu boy, indeed. Brahmin better?'

Her mother burst out laughing. 'Very good. Who is he? Bring him home. Is he a teacher?'

'No, Ma. I don't have anyone. But please, please, leave me alone for a while. I will marry soon. But now, I just want to work a little bit more. I want to see the world.'

'It's entirely your father's fault. Being so lenient with you.' Her mother stood up and rubbed her back. 'See the world with your husband, na. This boy lives in America. So what's the problem?'

'Why do you want to send me so far away from you?' Moushumi shot back. Emotional blackmail could stop this proposal from going any further.

'No, no. It's not that, my dear. But we can't be selfish you know. We want you to be happy. We want you to live in a decent place and have all the advantages of living in a good country.'

'Do you mean to say you are not happy here?' Moushumi asked, looking at her through slit eyes. 'Were you upset when you got Baba instead of a rich, Green-Card holder? Are you upset living in this dingy, damp house that stinks of fish and mustard oil? Are you regretting you have to live in fear of malaria or cholera every second of the day?' Moushumi realised she was shaking.

Holding her breath, her mother stared at Moushumi. She finally exhaled, and tucked a stray hair behind her ear. 'No, Mou. You've got me wrong. I've got what I deserve. I don't regret it. I'm happy with my husband. I'm happy with this house, because this house has been built by your father and me. Every drop of sweat and blood we shed is within these bricks. I'm sorry we couldn't complete it. We've been squeezed dry. I'm happy with the cooking smells because it reminds me that we have food on the table every day. I can still feed my husband and daughter fresh food after they have worked hard all day long.'

Outside the window, the crows were cawing on their way back to their nests. Conch shells were being blown three times as people in the other houses around them started on their evening prayers.

'No, I'm not happy about the diseases, you are right about that. But I have left it to the gods. I pray every day to Maa Durga to protect us, and of course, I check our mosquito nets for holes and boil our drinking water. If we still get it, it is God's will. I deserve all of this because I am not educated. I'm a simple village girl who was married off to a city man. So in that way, I too have come a long way. A promotion in my family. An uneducated girl from Mukutmanipur managed to find a husband from Calcutta. So naturally for you, my dear, I have set my sights on America.'

She looked steadily at her daughter. She then picked up the empty glass and walked out of the room.

ॐ

The doorbell announced the arrival of the 'boy's' family. Immediately, there was a flurry of activities and last-minute instructions shouted out before her father attended to the door. Moushumi stood in front of the mirror. Her mother had forced some make-up on her, and she shuddered at her own reflection. The sari felt unfamiliar to her body. Her shoulders sagged. Oh, to go through this ordeal yet again. She wondered how long she would entertain this man before turning him down.

In the front room, she heard the nervous laughter of her parents, trying to make their guests comfortable. She felt sorry for them. They were trying so hard to get her settled down. If only she could tell them the truth and free them of this headache. There had to be a way out.

Aparna hurried into the room, grinning. 'He's very handsome,' she whispered. 'Much better in person than in the photo. You shouldn't say no this time.' She frowned at her sister. If she disagreed once more, she would have a lot of answering to do.

Moushumi's mind began to work quickly. If this time, she thought, I can make *him* turn me down, I won't have to explain. She entered the living room and lowered her eyes, not because she was being demure in front of a prospective groom, but because she was guilty of carrying on this charade.

'Come, come, Moushumi, sit down next to me.' His mother cooed to her. She straightened her shoulders and sat down. Mrs Kahali smelled of expensive perfume and paan. She had diamonds on her ears and yet her mouth leaked a bit of betel nut juice from the corners. She held Moushumi's hands in her own exceptionally icy ones.

'So pretty.' Mrs Kahali lightly touched Moushumi's hair. 'Even though she's a bit on the dark side.' She gathered her lips in a pout. Moushumi edged away from her.

There was silence, in which a crow cawed rudely through the window. Moushumi's father cleared his throat and requested his wife to serve tea. Her mother jumped up, sweat running down her back. Tea, of course, of course. Hearing that, Aparna, who was listening from the other side of the door, rushed to the kitchen to fry the loochis.

'I suppose you two would like to talk to each other in private,' Mrs Kahali said. 'Wouldn't you, Upen?'

Moushumi dared a peek at the man. He was indeed extremely handsome. Any girl would be thrilled at the prospect of being wooed by him. He smiled confidently at her, his teeth unnaturally white. He stood up and allowed her to lead him to the balcony.

'Why do you want to marry me? Moushumi asked him directly. 'I'm dark, thin, not the type you'd want to show off to your colleagues in America. Definitely not the type your mother wants.'

Upen smiled, as if indulging her bad mood. 'What sort of wife should I have according to you?' he asked.

Moushumi heard giggles from below. There was a gathering of people, mostly children on the street below, witnessing the balcony scene. Obviously, word had spread that a suitor had come to see her.

'Bhalo chele, didi. Na korish na.' Someone teased her. Everyone agreed he was a good catch and she shouldn't refuse him.

'Let's go back in,' Moushumi suggested but Upen stayed there, leaning against the grills. 'Why? I think they make sense, don't you? I am a very good match, like they say. But I have only one fault. My mother doesn't want to share the information, but I think I ought to tell you.'

'Oh, what is it?' Moushumi wondered what dark secret he was hiding. Was he already married to an American, and his mother was forcing him to take on an Indian bride for her satisfaction? Was he gay? Oh, that would be ideal.

'I want a girl who speaks proper English. Not with a Bengali accent, you know. And you are an English teacher, aren't you?'

'Yes,' Moushumi said. 'Do you want to speak English at home with your wife, or outside?'

'Everywhere. My children need a good English education. Ma refused to let me marry an American, but an English teacher would be the best next option. You can quickly pick up the American accent, no?'

She saw the desperation in his eyes. Did such people really exist? But she knew she could play to his weakness and win. She grinned and fluttered her eyelashes in mock shyness.

'I am a pure Bangali gaarl at heart. I may bhi an English teachaar, but I can speak English like thees only. Sorry.' Moushumi put on a much-exaggerated accent, hoping he would get the point. Upen sprang back like he had been physically assaulted.

'You're joking, aren't you?' He looked her up and down, but her simple silk sari and garish make up only seemed to confirm that she wasn't capable of mixing with the people he wanted to be with in America.

Moushumi shook her head, and focussed on the plastic bag fluttering on the electricity pole to keep her from laughing out loud. 'Don't look here for a bride then,' she whispered to him.

'Look in South Calcutta. The women there will give the Americans a run for their money.'

Upen's shoulder sagged. Of course, he must know that. But would his English be good enough for them to say yes to him?

ॐ

'A boy came to see you?' asked Jasmine. 'What was he like? Tall, handsome? Rich?'

'You seem very happy about that, Jazz.'

She told Jasmine what he had wanted in a wife and how she had made him reject her. They laughed, swapping accents between the heavy American twang to the Bengali English accent.

'But, if he was a good guy, despite his strange demand, you should have considered him.'

The car inched forward in the Calcutta traffic. The prelude to the festive season meant one thing. Shopping. And people were out in throngs, wandering from one shop to the other, often the idea being absorbing the companionship found in the usual banter with the shopkeepers and other shoppers, checking out the latest fashions, testing the grounds before stepping into the shopping foray like seasoned warriors.

'Did you have to sing for him or make tea?' Jasmine teased her.

'No, no, I didn't do anything. I just sat there and didn't talk much to him.'

'Didn't he ask you anything?' Jasmine retouched her make up as the car turned towards their destination. Faces of young children pressed against the window, offering bunches of flowers to buy, or pirated copies of the latest American bestsellers.

Jasmine laughed. 'I wish I could have seen his face. Girls are dying to go abroad and you just did the opposite?'

'Exactly! I knew he'd reject me then and there! I made it clear to him that green card is not a magic word for me.'

'Believe me, sweetheart, a green card is more important than the man. The man can be rectified or changed as need be. Besides, he will be your ticket to the West.'

She lowered her voice. 'Where women can have open relationships, remember? Dump him when you find one.'

Jasmine instructed the driver when to be back to pick them up and got out of the car. Moushumi followed her as they weaved through the crowds to enter New Market. They walked past the old cannon at the entrance and through the narrow lanes between tiny shops that sold everything from cosmetic to shoes to cake to live hens ready to be slaughtered.

'How can you talk like that?' Moushumi felt sick. She hated Jasmine's non-committal attitude. 'Don't you love me?'

'Hush, darling,' Jasmine whispered dramatically. 'Which world do you live in? Is there such a thing called love?'

'Don't tease, Jazz. No, I want you to be truthful to me. I won't marry anyone as long as I'm with you.'

Jasmine sighed. She took Moushumi's hand and pulled her along. 'Let's buy the curtain material now. I need to send it to the tailor tomorrow.' They walked along the shops, stopping sometimes to look at the salwar kameezes and saris.

'This is my favourite market,' Moushumi said, brightening. 'As a child, I always got my Puja dresses from here.'

'That's nice,' Jasmine said, and tugged at a shiny sari draped on a plastic mannequin. 'Bhaiyya, how much is this?'

'That's so gaudy,' Moushumi said. 'Why do you want that?'

'Oh, for Sita, my maidservant. I'll take it for her as a Pujo gift. I never shop here. Lord, when will they have decent shopping malls in India? I have to go to Singapore every six months to get my stuff. It's tiresome.'

Moushumi walked on ahead while Jasmine haggled with the shopkeeper. This part of the market had burned down some years ago. Moushumi remembered feeling devastated that they couldn't go shopping here that year. She had missed her treat of cream pastries from Crystal bakery. She wondered if she should take Jasmine there and then decided against it. She'd probably say that Raju, her driver had his tea there and why not go to the Grand to freshen up instead.

The hawkers called out to Moushumi, trying to tempt her to buy their goods. She smiled as she remembered the poem she was teaching in class: Rossetti's 'The Goblin Market'.

'Come buy, come buy.'

But no, these poor men were not the goblins, enticing her with forbidden fruit. Her enticer was Jasmine; Jasmine and her heady charm. She was addicted to her.

Moushumi marched faster and faster away. She thought she heard her name being called, but her ears were buzzing. She paced to the back of the market and stepped out into the narrow lane. Here the street was lined with tiny pet shops. Dogs. Cats. Kittens. Birds. They called, piteously, excitedly, resignedly.

On her thirteenth birthday, Moushumi's father taken her to the market to buy birthday shoes and on the way they had stopped at the pet shops. He had bought her a dove. Moushumi could still feel the soft down and the warm feathers; the scratch of the feet as the dove struggled in her grasp. She remembered letting go, and the bird soaring up into the sunshine. The sound of her father's cheering as the bird escaped. Then he bought another bird and they let it go too. In all they bought thirteen birds and freed them from their cages. At the end of the day there was no money left for the birthday shoes they had intended to buy. But she remembered the wonderful feeling she shared with her father. That special bond that would break the minute he'd learn the truth about her.

11

Dipali

'The Babri Masjid has been controversial for centuries,' the newsreader stated in the early morning bulletin. 'It is claimed that Babur's commander-in-chief, Mir Baqi, had destroyed a Hindu temple and built the mosque on its site. Ayodhya, being Rama's birthplace, is very important to the Hindus. This site has seen many communal riots down the centuries...'

'What a load of bullshit,' Sunil muttered as he switched off the television. 'The politicians just used it to their advantage. A bloodbath, all in the name of religion.'

In early December, the mosque had been destroyed by a group of Hindu nationalists, 150,000 of them, and as the walls of the mosque came tumbling down, they took with it the lives and blood of innocent people who got entangled in the net of hatred and malice that spread.

It was very quiet outside. Dipali couldn't see anyone on the street below. Even the watchman was not in his place. She felt uneasy. Ever since the riots things had changed. It wasn't that evident in her neighbourhood, an affluent area of the city, but one did notice little things. The Khans, her next-door neighbours had disappeared one night, without any goodbyes. They had the money and the means to escape abroad. But her maid had not been so lucky. The slum where she lived had been burned down by an angry mob and her husband was now in a government hospital with third degree burns. He didn't have a chance of survival.

The violence of the communal riots had washed over the city like a tsunami of hatred. The city was reduced to cinder and ash, to hatred and pain. Every morning, when she rode the bus to school, she'd see loss all over the place. The big timber godown was still smouldering. Burnt cages of taxis littered the streets. Shopfronts had blackened walls and charred tree stumps punctuated the pavements. Thank goodness, the bodies had been removed.

From her tenth-floor apartment, they were able to see smoke rising from the Muslim quarters of the city. At night, they could hear the screams and the shouts and men raced, armed with scythes and swords, to slaughter their enemy. For many nights, the residents of the apartment blocks kept watch on their rooftops. Muslims had been attacked in their homes, in apartment blocks just like theirs. One by one, they disappeared. They either left the city, or moved to 'safe' areas, where the concentration of their own religion was the majority.

Schools and offices had been shut since the Christmas vacation. They had stayed indoors, glued to the television, unable to venture out because of the curfews. Dipali had been so worried about her mother, alone, and far away from her. What if they came one night with torches and sticks and destroyed her mother's house? And killed her? When the curfew was lifted Dipali and Sunil locked their doors and windows, packed whatever they could and raced to her mother's place. They stayed there for a month, wondering why all this was happening.

CR

Dipali brought out the tea and toast and put it on the table. Sunil sat reading the newspaper and swearing under his breath. He did not believe in anything the media reported anymore. March had finally brought some semblance of peace to the city. Schools were re-opened. Sunil resumed work at the office. They had returned to their flat, and tried to get as much normality as possible back into their lives.

In spite of all the unrest, Dipali had been determined that she'd get pregnant that year. But after a few failed attempts, she was beginning to panic. What if she could never conceive? Was there something wrong with her? Or Sunil? Would they have to go through treatment? She believed that this time she had succeeded. She had been feeling nauseous the last few days. Also she was four days late for her period. Her stomach lurched and cramped.

Would this be the day? She hoped for it. She prayed for it. She hurried to the toilet. She checked. But no, there was a dark brown smudge in her underwear. She stared at it, hatefully, wishing it would disappear. Not this time, either.

She returned to the dining room and flopped down on a chair. Sunil looked up at her and she shook her head, not looking at him. He sighed and went back to his newspaper.

'You could say something, you know,' she said. Her teacup crashed on the saucer and caused the tea to spill over the table.

'Yes, about nine hundred people are dead from the December riots,' he said.

'No, I mean about this. Doesn't it mean anything to you?' she snapped.

'Dipali, what can I say? I'm sorry about it. But it's not our fault. It'll happen when it happens.' He tried to look concerned, but he was too distracted with the news.

'Sunil,' she said in a high-pitched voice. 'You were not like this.'

'Dipali, you are getting too dramatic now.' Sunil leaned over and touched her hand.

'I know this is important for you. But try to understand. We are not emotionally fit to do this now. Too much stress doesn't help, you know.'

'Isn't it important for you? We've been trying for months,' Dipali lashed out. 'Why is it only me who wants a child?'

Sunil stood up and stroked his chin. He rubbed his eyes and stifled a yawn. 'It's not that. I want a child too. But let's not hurry. Let's not go crazy over the issue and put things into perspective. It's only been six months. It takes time.'

Six months? It's been three years since we've been married, she wanted to scream at him. But you've always postponed it. 'Maybe I should see a doctor,' she said.

Sunil went over and put his arms around her. He stroked her hair till she became quiet. He held her for a long time, his face buried in her hair. 'Alright. If that's what you want. We'll have a chat with the doctor. There's nothing wrong with you, or me, okay?'

Dipali held on to his arm. 'How do you know? My brother doesn't have any children either. Shikha boudi told me once they'd been trying for years. I just want to be certain. And have a baby. And be happy.'

'That will take a while. We are living in strange times now. But we'll try, and who said we are not happy, Dips? I'm still crazy about you, aren't I? Only now there are a lot of things on my mind.' Sunil patted her shoulder and went towards the bathroom. 'Get an appointment over the weekend. I have to go to the passport office soon and get the passport sorted. It still has the old Calcutta address on it.'

'So when are you going to London? Has it been finalised?' she asked.

'July,' said Sunil, turning on the shower. 'Hey, perhaps you could come too? It could be a holiday we need so badly.'

Her face lit up. Yes, perhaps taking a break would be the thing to do. Going to a different country, away from all the violence and unrest would certainly help. Perhaps she could even conceive there. 'Are you sure?' she asked him. 'What about the cost?'

Sunil smiled at her indulgently. 'Surely we can afford it. I've got that promotion, haven't I?'

Dipali nodded. Yes, he had got the promotion, finally. The one that had taken up so much of their time, made him forgetful of her and her needs. Made him so cynical, and disagreeable sometimes. Now things would change.

ॐ

'I think you are being too hasty,' the doctor said. She smiled kindly at Dipali.

'But it's been three years, doctor,' Dipali persisted. 'Surely, I could try something to hurry things along.'

The doctor shook her head. They sat wedged in the tiny clinic space. There was a narrow bed against one wall and a table and chair squeezed at the foot of the bed. Dipali sat on a stool. She had hesitated when she saw where the clinic was situated: in a tiny lane behind a vegetable market. The smell of rotting vegetables in the nearby dump filled the air. She waved flies away and stepped into the ramshackle building. It was sublet to many doctors and other small businesses.

Prosperity Consultant and Advisor, read one of the boards hanging outside. He obviously was very successful if he couldn't get himself out of this dump in the first place. *Saraswati Classes,* read another. *Express way to success. English Medium/ Semi English.* The businesses in this building seemed to be quite desperate to advertise their expertise. Couldn't they spruce up their surroundings to attract more clientele? But then wasn't Dipali here as well? Visiting Dr (Mrs) Vinodini Bhandari, gynaecologist (MD, DNB, DGO, FCPS, DFP), 100% *success, one time, every time.*

It didn't matter where people did their business. The desperate would go anywhere to find a solution. She had spotted a Mercedes squeezing its way out of the crowded lane, its shining white body standing out among the rust-ridden bicycles and autos. It made her hopeful.

'You are young and healthy,' Dr Bhandari said. 'And your husband?'

'He's healthy too,' Dipali said, surreptiously touching her wooden stool.

'Maybe we could run a few tests if you want to be sure?'

Dipali brightened up. 'Yes, that would be good.'

'And for your husband as well.'

'Oh.'

Dr Bhandari smiled. 'Well, we would want to eliminate problems from both parties, isn't it?'

'Yes,' Dipali answered. Now what? She hadn't told Sunil of this visit. He wouldn't be happy at all. He'd say she was jumping to conclusions. 'But Doctor, the thing is, even my brother has no children...'

The doctor nodded and turned to her computer. 'We need to do tests, Mrs Rai. You could make another appointment with my secretary and we can set up them up. We'll need to check your ovulation cycle. Scan your uterus to check for abnormalities. Don't worry, everything is possible these days. And please bring your husband the next time, he'll need to do a sperm count too. And a sperm health check.'

Dipali's head reeled with the information. She wondered how she could approach Sunil and convince him to do the test. She also remembered Shikha telling her that Borda had refused tests at first, considering it a suspicion on his manhood. But Sunil wasn't like that. He was the most understanding and levelheaded person she had known.

Dipali slipped into a taxi and directed it home. Maybe this holiday would work wonders. She would buy lots of vitamins from London. And lingerie. Anything and everything to help them on their way to parenthood.

12

Moushumi

'Hey, Mou,' one of the men from the youth club called out to her. 'I saw you with your friend the other day.'

Moushumi tried to ignore him and hurry on. Young Men's District Youth Club, the peeling-off sign proclaimed on the crumbling walls of the building. It was more of a two-room structure topped by a corrugated tin roof. The idea had been for young boys to have a place where they could spend time playing carom, have access to books, meet other young boys, and arrange cricket matches. Generally stay out of trouble. But what did the members of the youth club do? They were not young boys at all, but mostly unemployed men who sat on the veranda and ogled at the women passing by. Although they *did* play carom and drink tea. And, of course, the evening adda, when they'd sit on the threshold of the club, cigarettes glowing in the dark as they chatted. Conversations about life, employment or rather the lack of it, girls and the severe lack of them, frustrations (plenty) and jokes (banal).

Moushumi sniffed and held her nose high in the air.

The men talked loudly as she passed. 'I've seen her in town

a few times, with a very posh lady. Hey Mou, she your friend?'

Moushumi stumbled. She didn't turn round because she was afraid they'd see her face turn red.

'Mou doesn't mix with us gaiyyas any more. She's a city chick now.'

She swept around and glared at them. They had all grown up together in the same neighbourhood. She knew them by face, if not by name. While some of the boys grew up to be responsible men with jobs, some just stayed behind, smoking cigarettes and making trouble. And this lot facing her were trouble.

'What's it to you, hah? Mind your own business.'

'Nothing, nothing,' the man who started it spread his arms out in appeasement. 'Just thought I'd tell you I saw you. She's quite a firecracker, your friend.'

They hooted with laughter and slapped their thighs. 'Bring her over for tea sometime.'

Moushumi wished that she could go and slap them. She strode up to the club. 'This firecracker friend of mine is so because she is dutifully employed. She earns her own money to live as she pleases. Unlike you, sitting idle and getting jealous of other people's successes.'

'Arrey, Mou, why are you getting upset? Why are you targeting us poor unemployed youth?'

There was suppressed giggling at the back. The others stood behind the brave man who had decided to confront Moushumi. They jostled each other and eyed her as she stood at the bottom of the steps.

'She could hire us, you know. For whatever she does.' The young man relished the admiration from the others at his outspokenness.

'Listen, why don't you just get on with whatever you were doing and stop wasting my time?' Moushumi shouted. Inside she was afraid. What did this guy know about her and Jasmine? How often had he seen them together? And what made him speak out to her so confidently?

'Are these fellows irritating you, Mou?'

Moushumi swung around. It was her brother-in-law, Palash. She turned to look at the men again. They seemed to have shrunk into the walls of the club.

'Sorry, dada. We didn't mean any harm.' The young man retreated. 'Just asking didi here…'

'You don't need to ask her anything,' Palash said. He motioned Moushumi to follow him. They walked silently until they turned a corner.

'Why did you stop to argue, Mou?' Palash asked. 'You shouldn't encourage them. Bloody good-for-nothings. They will only make trouble.'

Moushumi hung her head and nodded. But she wasn't listening to Palash. What did they know? Would they try to blackmail her?

'What were they teasing you about?' Palash strode ahead, his bright blue rucksack at odds with his formal shirt and tie. Moushumi struggled to keep up with him. She knew his long commute to and from work made him irritable, so she didn't want to start explaining to him. Also, as he was married to her elder sister, he extended paternal-like treatment to her, and she didn't always welcome it.

'Nothing, really. Just something to do with my friends. They have nothing better to do.'

'And you were arguing back with them?' He looked at her sternly and she turned away. Why couldn't he just stick to disciplining his rascal son?

She turned towards the market, knowing it was the opposite route to his house.

'Why are you going to the market so late? Do you need anything?' Palash asked, looking at his watch. Moushumi could see him struggle internally whether he ought to accompany her to the market or go home, where a hot shower and dinner waited.

'Yes, jamai-babu, I need to buy a light bulb. Mine just blew a fuse.'

Palash shook his head. 'Don't you keep spares at home?'

'Well, the spare one got fused. You go home. I'll be fine,' Moushumi said and walked away. She was thankful that he had sort of rescued her but then she always needed to be rescued from his critical tongue as well.

Back home, Moushumi went over what those men had said to her. She tried to think of the times she had been out with Jasmine. Quite a few times to The Grand Hotel for coffee or lunch. Park Street. New Market. The nightclub. Where could he have seen her? The boat ride? Not the Grand surely, what would that loafer be doing there? Not the nightclub either. So surely it had to be New Market or Park Street. They weren't doing anything to arouse suspicion then. Just shopping. But then, Moushumi realised dismayed, the New Market episode had been too dramatic. What if he had seen her after she had rushed away, crying? Would that tell him something? Surely not?

She was sure they had never behaved in any way that would draw attention to the two of them. Jasmine always made sure of that. She was the millionaire's wife after all. And this guy from the youth club, what opportunity would he have had to move around in those circles to see them together? Perhaps he had been a doorman somewhere? Or a waiter? A shop assistant?

And so what? He was only jealous of her friendship with a high-class woman. He just wanted to show off in front of his friends. That's all. That had to be all. But still, she knew that she'd have to be careful. She couldn't let such gossip reach her parents. How would she explain to them her lies? That instead of giving tuitions, she was gallivanting around the city with a millionaire's wife.

Sleep did not come easily that night. Moushumi struggled under the sheets, perspiration dampening her bed. The streetlight flickered through her window, creating a comic shadow play on the bedroom wall. The silhouette of her shelf with books and bric-a-brac crammed together resembled a witch's crooked nose. Where was she heading to? She knew this thing with Jasmine wouldn't last. And then what? Moushumi hadn't thought of this before. Yes, there was physical closeness, but somehow Jasmine did not satisfy her emotionally.

Intellectually. Her thoughts returned to the maid next door. Still bathing in the open in this cold weather, still shivering in her makeshift bathroom. Jasmine was no better than the maid. Moushumi still felt like an onlooker in her own affair. She was merely an actress in this film of her life, Jasmine was the director all the way. And she knew it was coming. The day Jasmine would say 'cut' and the storyline would be finished.

13

Dipali

The board exams were taking place. Dipali had to invigilate, a job she did not like. It was too boring. But today was the last day, and so she was looking forward to finishing. For the Easter holidays, Sunil and she planned to take her mother for a break to the hills. Afterwards she'd have to plan the big holiday. In London.

Dipali distributed the exam papers, read out instructions and then settled down in her chair. The students sat quietly, reading their question sheets, and when Dipali asked them to start, the room filled with the sound of pen scraping against paper. She watched the students write. Most looked confident and didn't pause in their scribbling. Some were unsure, and would sit scratching their heads. She walked around the classroom once, to show that she was alert and watching them, but it was only an excuse to be on her feet and break the boredom.

'Fifteen minutes more. Please check your answer sheets,' Dipali announced.

There was a collective groan and a quicker pace to the

fountain pens. The door to the examination hall opened and the Mother Superior entered. She walked briskly towards Dipali, her jowls swinging with her strides.

'Mrs Rai,' she whispered. 'There have been some bomb blasts in the city. Nothing close by though. I'd like you to complete this examination before we tell the students. It would be bad to disrupt the Board exams, especially with only about ten minutes left. We've got the office staff telephoning the parents, asking them to come and collect their girls.'

'What?' Dipali whispered back. 'Bomb blasts? Where?'

'We're not sure yet. I've heard the Air India building. But I'd rather not say anything more. There could be rumours.'

'Yes, yes, of course,' said Dipali. She was trembling. 'More riots?'

'No,' said the Mother Superior. 'Just bombs so far. In a number of places. But please, Mrs Rai, I'd ask you to take responsibility for your students and see that each one of them is collected by their parents before you go home.'

'Of course,' said Dipali.

The students were becoming restless. They could sense something was wrong. The sirens from the fire engines and police were blaring nonstop in the distance. Dipali ran to the windows and began shutting them. She turned around and faced the students.

'Girls, you have five more minutes. Please prepare your answer papers and hand them to me.'

'What's wrong, ma'am? Has something happened again?' asked a girl sitting in the front row.

Dipali put her finger to her lips. 'No talking. Just finish this paper.'

Those ten minutes seemed like ten hours. They hurriedly submitted their papers. A few started to cry. A member of office staff rushed into the room. 'Please Mrs Rai— we need to get the students home. The telephone lines have been cut off. Some of the parents are here already.'

Dipali asked the girls to sit down and called out for those whose parents had arrived. Soon more parents rushed in and with them they brought more information.

There had been a series of bomb blasts all over Bombay that had probably not ended either. These bombs were placed in cars or scooters in various places all over the city. It looked like the violence had started all over again. Dipali looked at her watch. Sunil should be in his office now. There was no news of Peddar Road being hit. She desperately wanted to call him.

Dipali looked around for the one student she knew who lived near her. Yes, she was still there. Perhaps she could get a lift with her. But she'd have to tell Sunil first. What if he had already set off to collect her from work? She left the girls with a prefect and ran to the office.

'Sarala, can I call my husband quickly?'

'Oh, Mrs Rai, the lines are down. But if you leave me his number, I'll try and get in touch.'

'Okay. In case Sunil calls, Sarala, could you tell him to go home? Not to come here. I'll go with a student of mine.'

'Right.'

Dipali raced back to her class. The Air India building had been struck. The Bombay Stock Exchange Building had been struck. Some hotels in the suburbs. The parents were agitated and panic-stricken. What was happening? Where would the next one come? How much longer would they have to endure this?

Blood pounded in Dipali's head. She couldn't hear anything. Everything changed to slow motion. She sat down.

'Where did you say? What time?'

'The passport office. Don't know exactly. After Air India Building, I think.'

Dipali couldn't think. When did Sunil say he was going to the passport office?

Hopefully in the morning.

Was he going today?

Or tomorrow?

No, no, he's alright. He's in his office now. He'll call me.

'Mrs Rai, Mrs Rai?' She heard voices in the distance. 'Are you alright?' They helped her to a chair and offered her some water. 'We'll call him. Surely he's safe.'

She nodded, believing them. Yes, it was alright. More blasts followed, this time closer to the school. There was a bang. But it sounded like an innocent fire-cracker. The windowpanes rattled with the force of the explosion, and the smell of gunpowder wafted in mixed with the salty tang from the sea. The scent reminded her of Diwali nights. Except this time, it was making her nauseous.

All the students had left. The staff also rushed to get home. Dipali spotted Divaker, her mother's odd-job man standing outside the school gates. She had sent him there, to make sure Dipali would get home safely.

'But you should be with Ma,' she shouted at him. 'She's all alone. You go home now.'

'No, didi,' he said. 'I must accompany you home. I cannot leave you alone. Once Sunilda comes home, I'll return.'

Dipali motioned him to the student's car. They drove through Bombay, once again passing carnage. Smoke clouds hovered in the distance and people stood watching, mute with shock or disbelief. Crushed glass was strewn across the road. Fire engines and ambulances zig-zagged through the slow funeral procession of traffic. Each hesitating to get home. Each not wanting to find out who it was that would not make it back.

Three days passed but there was still hope in Dipali's heart. He was out there somewhere. She only had to find him. Once more, as the city lay smouldering, people waited to count the dead. This time, the headlines and the statistics in the newspapers were personal. Ashish had rushed to Bombay the second night. Together, they scanned every hospital they could. The government hospitals. The private hospitals. The nursing homes.

The lists. Dipali would have them engrained in her mind forever. Names hurriedly scratched out on whiteboards in the hospital corridors. The names of the dead. Her eyes would scan these lists, mind blank. Would there be a name she didn't want to read? So many names. So many unfortunate ones. But not his.

When Dipali saw a woman crying over her dead child's body, she felt glad she was not doing the same. When she saw a woman embracing her injured husband, she felt a pang of jealousy. Where was he? He never returned to the office that day. His passport, Dipali panicked. Surely it was destroyed in the blast. How would they go to London?

Ashish held her hand. They would have to visit the morgues next.

The city morgues. It was like entering straight into hell's underbelly. What Dipali would remember for the rest of her life was the smell. Chemicals. Decay. It was the smell of defeat. The stench of no return. Day after day, they visited morgues in the different city hospitals. Every time she entered one Dipali prayed that Sunil should not be found in there.

The bodies lay stacked on top of each other. Tagged with a number. They were covered with soiled once-white sheets. A mangled foot stuck out. A bloodied arm. Tattered clothes. *Sunil, Sunil*, her heart cried out. She remembered what he had been wearing that morning. A Van Heusen shirt. White with blue pinstripes. Beige pants. His socks were not matching because they were the only ones she hadn't soaked in the wash. He had been annoyed with that. His patent leather shoes. That heady fragrance of Hugo Boss that she always looked forward to in the evenings. Mingled with his sweat.

All gone now.

He lay somewhere in these piles. A number. Dirty. Ravaged. Decaying. He wouldn't be smelling nice now. Were his clothes sticking to his burnt skin? Were his shoes still on? Would she have to identify him? She didn't want to look. Ashish took her out into the sunshine. There was a throng of people trying to get inside. They all had the same expression on their faces. Shell-shocked, yet hopeful. They wouldn't find their loved one here. Somehow he or she had miraculously escaped. Then a wail would pierce through. Someone's hope had been dashed. A body had been identified.

Ashish took her back home. He insisted on going alone. Dipali didn't need to go through this. She didn't have the strength to argue. Sunil's parents had arrived as well. They had aged twenty years in the last three days. They sat silently, watching. They were the living dead.

A week later, Ashish returned home with news. Sunil's body had been found. He identified it through the help of his watch. Hearing that, Sunil's father collapsed.

'It belonged to his grandfather,' he broke down. 'It was gifted to him when he graduated. *May you have a long life, and a successful and happy one*, my father had said to him.' He shook his head and wept. His wife held his hand and wiped her tears.

'Sunil had said, *you bet, Dada, I will*. That watch was his talisman.'

Dipali took the watch from Ashish's hand. She was used to its glowing face in the dark. Of inadvertently removing it from the bathroom after his shower. Of its icy touch when Sunil's arm brushed against her skin. Now it stared back at her. Crushed. The glass cracked. The time on the watch. She tried not to think of it. The exact time of his death.

14:55:25

14

Moushumi

Moushumi sat on the terrace. Dark clouds were gathering in the sky. There were paddy fields in the distance; the flooded land reflected the burgeoning clouds. Aparna was frantically removing the washing from the lines. Her son, Poltu, raced about, chasing his pet kitten.

'Mou,' she called softly. 'Come inside. It's going to rain any minute.' She touched her lightly on the shoulder. Moushumi smelled the damp clothes and stirred. She nodded and followed Aparna downstairs where she sank into the bed.

The encounter with those youth club men had rattled Moushumi. She had begun to question her relationship with Jasmine. She'd begun to question her own morality. It didn't seem right to her anymore. She was so confused. How could she marry when she loved a woman? And did Jasmine really love her?

Jasmine was away in Singapore that week. She went every six months to top up her wardrobe. Moushumi wondered where her old clothes disappeared to, as she never seemed to repeat an outfit, ever. Moushumi had wanted to see her off at the airport, but Jasmine had said no. Her husband's driver was dropping her, and she didn't want to raise any suspicions. She had promised to bring her a gift, a peace offering after the incident at the market. But what gift could pacify Moushumi? All she really wanted was a security of some sort.

But Holi was here now. Moushumi had been swept away by the excitement and activities that came along with it. At least it helped push out her fears and insecurities for the moment. She looked gratefully at her sister, who was struggling to hang up the washing on lines that criss-crossed her bedroom walls. Moushumi wondered where Jasmine hung her wet clothes. She'd never seen any washing lines anywhere. Surely she needed them too, living in the same city?

Same city, Moushumi sighed, but not the same world.

'What is it?' Aparna asked, sitting beside Moushumi. 'Why do you look so gloomy?'

'Are some local goons bothering you? Palash told me what happened the other night. They were talking about some woman...'

'What else did he hear?' Moushumi asked.

'Mou, is there a problem somewhere? Even Ma is worried about you. You're rejecting proposals left right and centre. Do you have someone in your life?'

Moushumi nodded and covered her face. She couldn't hide it any longer. It wasn't a sin. How long could she hold out against the truth?

'It's that woman they were talking about,' she said.

Aparna ordered her son to go play with his grandmother and he ran off, taking the kitten with him. She turned back to her sister, 'What about her?'

'I love her.'

'What? You are in love with a woman?' Aparna removed Moushumi's hands from her face. 'Mou, what are you saying? Who is she? What's going on here?'

Moushumi drew her knees up to her chin and hugged them.

'Mou, you have to tell me. This is serious. How far has all this gone?'

'Didi, the damage is done. I can't look at another man.'

'What nonsense,' Aparna said, 'Nothing is too late. It's just a silly crush. It's normal, things like this.'

'Is it?' Moushumi arched her eyebrow. 'We went to the same school. Did you fall for a girl as well?'

Aparna laughed nervously. 'No, I didn't. Some girls in my class did have crushes. But they didn't add up to anything. They're all married now. Happily, I may add.'

'That's it. I'm different. I love being with Jasmine. I think about her all the time...'

'Oof, Mou. You sound like a broken record. Once you get married, you'll forget her.' Aparna turned her back to Moushumi and began fiddling with the laundry.

'No, I won't.' Moushumi shouted. She stood up and swung Aparna around. 'Look at me, Didi. Do I look abnormal to you? Is it wrong to be in love with a woman? I can't forget her. I've... We've had an intimate relationship. I can't see myself with anyone else.'

Aparna looked up at her, her eyes wide. 'Quiet, Mou. Not so loud.' She quickly shut the door and pulled the latch. 'What do you mean intimate? Physical?'

'Yes,' Moushumi said. 'Physical, sexual, call it what you want.'

'My God,' whispered Aparna. 'Mou, Mou, what were you thinking?'

'It felt so right, Didi.' She looked at her sister with pleading eyes.

'Tell me Didi, didn't you feel right with jamaibabu? You were physical with him even though you weren't married at the time?'

'But he's a man,' Aparna whispered. 'And we got married eventually. I mean, we always knew we would. It was different.'

'No, Didi. It doesn't matter if it's a man or a woman. Love is love.'

'Stop it, Mou. You are being very filmy. You need to have a husband and children, everything will be fine then, I'm telling you. You'll forget all this love-shuv. All these complications. You're a school teacher. Think about that. You need to be careful what you do. You can't live with another woman and expect people to accept that? You won't have a job, a family. And have you thought of what will happen to Baba Ma?'

'Is that true, Didi? Is it a crime to be in love with the same sex?'

'I'm sorry. I just can't get it into my head. You saw what happened to those two girls who married. They were not accepted in society and they had to die. It is abnormal. It's not right.'

'I won't ever get married.' Moushumi said, flinging herself on the pillow and raking her fingers through her hair. She stared at the ceiling fan for a while, tears rolling down the sides of her face. 'I don't need men.'

'Oh, you silly girl. You are only twenty-three. You are being hot-headed and jumping to conclusions too soon. Be sensible. Can you see yourself living with this Jasmine creature? She lives in an ivory tower, na? With a husband. And just not any husband, but Nandkumar Ghoshal. Baap re baap.'

Aparna reached out for Moushumi's hand.

'That witch cast a spell on you. Used you, my dear sister. Do you think she will care if you are here or there? There will be hundreds of others waiting to take your place. If not taken it already.'

Moushumi started to sob. She pressed her face into the pillow, trying to control herself. Had it all really been so inconsequential? Did Jasmine really not care? She hadn't even called her from Singapore once.

'Mou darling,' Aparna held her close. 'Don't ruin your life like this. Things will fall into place. You will become normal again.'

'Normal? Do you think I'm abnormal, Didi? Is that how you look at me?' She tore herself out of Aparna's embrace. 'You will never understand me. These things happen to people, Didi. I didn't choose to be this way. I've always been like this. Whose fault is it?'

'No, no, I'm not blaming you,' Aparna replied. She sat beside her sister and stroked her hair comfortingly. 'I just don't know how this happened to you. I mean, we grew up in such a middle-class way. Just school, then home. Friends in the neighbourhood. So how did you—'

'Well, Didi, I'm not an expert on homosexuality. I don't know what causes it. I just know what happens inside me. I'm not too happy about it either. I mean, just look at me. Always worried, always wondering what is it I need to do? What kind of person do I need to be? I cannot express myself, because I don't know how to. And who to?'

They sat opposite each other, not knowing what else to say. Moushumi dried her eyes and looked resolutely at her sister, willing her to say something.

Aparna avoided her gaze. She traced patterns with her finger on the bedspread. Finally she spoke. 'I suppose there is such a thing as loving the same sex. But what good will it do? It will only cause heartbreak, Mou. For you, for our family. People will treat you badly, like a freak.'

'I suppose they will, Didi. But imagine, what if I was abnormal in some other way. Like if I had no legs and arms. Dependent on you to look after me in every way. That would also cause heartbreak. People would call me a freak. Would you disown me then?'

The street lights came on, casting an orange glow on the people returning home from work, cyclists nudging autos and cars, buses thundering past while people hurried on the foothpaths, dodging cows and handcarts, carrying nylon bags full for purchases from the market. Moushumi looked down at them. All these people, hurrying home to their loved ones. Which of them had a secret they could not share with the world? Which of them was a freak like her? They all looked hungry, and tired, and impatient to get back. They all looked like normal people. She imagined herself in the crowd, leaping over puddles, pushing and shoving to get on the train, looking forward to the evening meal. She would have looked normal as well. Just like the others. Except that she wasn't.

Aparna switched on the tubelight and moved towards the door. 'I have to get dinner ready. Poltu must be hungry,' she said. 'Think about it, Mou. Sometimes sacrifices have to be made, for the good of everyone. Don't give in to those fanciful ideas.'

ରୁ

'Jasmine, when are you returning to India?' Moushumi could hear her lover's sharp intake of breath at the other end of the line. She leaned on the glass door of the phone booth, her eyes on the meter, which was leaping upwards. After the talk with her sister, she couldn't keep still. She had to make her decision, know what Jasmine's plans were.

'Not for another week,' Jasmine's voice seemed tinny over the crackling line. There was a lot of noise in the background and Moushumi couldn't hear very clearly.

'Why so long? I want you here. My sister knows.'

'Knows what?'

'About us. Jazz, about us.'

'I don't think there is an us, Moushumi. There can't ever be an us. Why don't you just get that?'

'What?' Moushumi stared at the mouthpiece and then slammed the phone back to her ear. 'I don't believe you are saying this, Jazz. What is it that we have then? Just screwing around, like freaks?'

People looked in her direction. She realised she was shouting. Her head started to spin. This was not going too well.

'I'm sorry, but I never promised you anything. In fact, I've always encouraged you to find your own way.'

'You're lying to me. I suppose you've had your fill. Now you need to fuck a new girl.' Moushumi's body convulsed violently. She wished she could slap Jasmine and ruin her salon-treated face.

'Control yourself,' Jasmine's voice rose. 'My husband knows about us too. He found out. I'm only trying to protect you.'

'Bullshit.'

'Believe me, it's true.'

There was silence on the other end. Then Jasmine erupted. 'Leave him? And then do what? Come and live with you? What a perfect fairytale, Moushumi. And what are we going to live on? Your meagre salary? Arrey, I buy shoes that are worth more than that.

There was a click and the line went dead.

Moushumi stood still, the telephone in her grasp. This was a nightmare she was having. If only she could snap her fingers and get out of it. But no, this was real. The telephone operator was asking her to pay the money. She was rummaging into her purse, looking for the cash. She was walking out of the booth, forgetting to take the change. She was walking in the darkness, not aware of anything around her.

This was real. It was too quick, what just happened. It was all finished. She couldn't have Jasmine. Her sister thought she was abnormal. She herself could not define what she wanted. All she knew was that hers was not a normal state of mind.

PART TWO

1998

1

'Come, come, Mashima. Welcome.'

Asha Devi smiled as she entered the house. 'God bless, my dear. Where's the lovely bride-to-be?'

'Inside. Getting ready for the gaye holud ceremony.'

Dipali followed her mother in. It was her cousin's wedding in a couple of days. Today was the special turmeric ceremony. Most of Dipali's female relatives were present, bustling around, laughing, teasing and chatting. Quite a few had come down from Calcutta, Bela mashi had arrived from Kanpur as well. It was going to be a big wedding. Shiuli had managed to secure a green-card holder for herself. She'd be in California by the end of the month. Dipali watched Shiuli's mother bustling about, beaming in self-congratulation at her choice of groom. She strode around, giving curt orders to the domestic staff, while smiling sweetly to the guests, offering them cold drinks and snacks. She chewed her paan with relish.

A few of her relatives were meeting Dipali for the first time since Sunil's death. Five years had passed, but still their eyes filled up like it was only yesterday. They held her close and sniffled. Dipali stared blankly into the distance. She hated all this drama. Some hadn't even bothered to call her when it had happened, so why this show in front of everybody now? She wriggled out of all the mournful arms and rushed to look for Shiuli.

The bride-to-be was sitting resplendent on a dais, wearing a simple salwar kameez. Presents were strewn all over the room. Gifts from the husband-to-be's side were arranged on the bed. Saris. Jewellery. Cosmetics. Fairness cream. Utensils. Shoes. Bed linen. Underwear. Nothing had been left out.

'Sing, didi, sing a romantic song.' The younger cousins made requests from old Bengali film songs. Dipali watched as one of her cousins stepped up to the task. It was Apu, who had sung at her wedding as well. She had such a sweet and melodious voice that it was impossible for her to stay in a room for long without being asked to sing, even a few lines, to a very appreciative audience.

Akhono tare chokhe dekhini
Akhono tare chokhe dekhini
Shudhu bashi shunechi

Dipali closed her eyes and thought back on her wedding day. How true the words of this song. She had heard so much about her husband-to-be, his achievements, his good looks, his merits, that she had felt like she knew him intimately before even actually seeing him. The others joined in. Shiuli's cheeks reddened. Soon, the elderly relatives streamed in and joined them. The smell of fish frying followed them in. They sniffed the air and clucked in appreciation. The groom's family had sent them first-class ilish maach.

Shiuli's mother hurried in with the turmeric paste.

'Come on, everybody,' she said. 'Time to apply it on the bride-to-be.'

'Long live, my dear.'

'May you be the mother of a thousand sons.'

Shiuli giggled self-consciously. All the years of beauty treatment, aerobics and public speaking classes had finally ended well. Her mother had left nothing to chance.

'May you have a long and happy married life.'

The women moved in closer. They applied the turmeric paste generously on to her arms and face. They rubbed it into her skin, making sure no exposed part of her was spared.

'Dipali,' her mother called her from the other room.

Dipali eased herself out of the crowd and went to her mother. She was sitting by herself in the sitting room, reading a newspaper. 'Aren't you going to join us, Ma?'

Asha Devi said 'Can you make some paan for me? It's in my bag. Make one for Chotodida as well.'

Dipali turned and saw her mother's aunt shuffle into the room. She sat down heavily on the divan and fanned herself.

'Oof, this heat,' she grumbled. 'Dipu, come and sit by me.'

Dipali dug out the betel nut leaves from her mother's bag and smeared it with chun. She pressed a supari in and folded the leaf into a triangular shape. She understood why she was in the room with these two women. They were all widows. And widows did not participate in celebrations. Certainly not where marriages were concerned. Nor babies. She looked at her mother and Chotodida. They seemed quite content to be there and yet not be there. They lowered their voices and gossiped about Shiuli's mother's efforts to snare such a worthy groom.

'Why are we here, Ma?' Dipali looked at her mother with irritation. She looked pointedly towards the room with the festivities. 'Why are we sitting here?'

Her mother looked up. 'Shiuli's wedding of course. It's her gaye holud today.'

'Yes, I know,' said Dipali. 'But why are we here? We're not allowed to participate.'

Asha Devi turned red. She darted a look towards her aunt, but she didn't seem to have heard. She was busy swatting at flies and cursing. 'We're here to bless her, of course. And wish her all the best in life. We can't take part in certain ceremonies, but still Shiuli's mother is broad-minded. She invited us to be here. I just didn't want you to take advantage of her kindness.'

Dipali hurried away into the courtyard. She didn't want people to notice her tears. But there was too much commotion outside as well. Dozens of workers sat around, making flower garlands and the bride and bridegroom motif to go on the entrance of the wedding hall.

Shiuli weds Romesh. In red roses and white tuberoses. Deep yellow marigolds bordering the piece. Everything reminded her of that day. Everything was the same, played out again and again, year after year, generation after generation. And yet, each one thought of their own wedding as unique, the very best.

She was aware of the curious glances cast her way. She dried her eyes and turned around. It was time to be sensible. She went back to sit beside her mother and wait until they were welcomed back into the celebrations.

ॐ

Dipali poured the puffed rice into the kadhai. She let it roast, added peanuts and chole. She stirred vigorously, so that the ingredients didn't stick to the pan. A warm aroma filled the kitchen. She switched off the gas and got the cutting board out. She finely chopped ginger and chillies and added them to the pan. She poured out some mustard oil. The smell was sharp and pungent. It caught her breath and she coughed. She mixed everything up and placed it in a big stainless steel bowl.

This was her way of escape. A bowl of jhaal muri and a steaming cup of tea could solve many problems of the world. She sat by her bedroom window and savoured the crunch of the puffed rice.

Her mother and sister-in-law Shikha had gone shopping for more wedding saris. Dipali had excused herself, claiming a terrible headache. She scooped another handful into her mouth. This time she was rewarded with a peanut. She chewed it till it released its earthy oiliness in her mouth. She didn't want to be part of the shopping spree. She didn't want to see Shikha revelling in choosing from many gorgeous saris. She didn't want to see red, blue or golden fabrics dancing in front of her, mocking her while she stood pale and nondescript in her boring whites and creams. How Sunil would have hated to see her in her widowed state. She knew he would have disapproved, but she couldn't face up to rebel against her family or society. What would she gain by wearing colourful clothes? Insults and disrespect. She certainly wouldn't get her husband back.

Dipali looked out into the garden. The mangoes were taut and green. It was the wedding season. Hot and humid. The rains would come in a month's time, reminding her of the day she was a bride. So eager to be a bride. So much in love with her new husband. It was in this house where she had dreamed of her future. She would childishly follow their horoscopes, to look into the future. How many children would they have? Would they be in love till the very end? How would Marjorie Orr, renowned astrologer have known, staring out of the *Mid-Day* every afternoon with a benign smile? She could not predict the bomb blasts. Nor could she predict his end.

She wiped her hands on her old housecoat and went to her wardrobe. Cautiously, she opened it. Her clothes were hanging, carefully starched and ironed. Her work clothes: pale cotton saris. A few salwar kameezes. Why were the colours squeezed out of them? Even though they looked elegant and smart, they were not of her choice. There was a drawer at the bottom of the wardrobe. She never opened it. But today she did. It creaked and resisted her pull. She pulled with greater force. There were some clothes inside. Dipali looked. Her saris. She had given away most of the heavy expensive saris after he died. Her trousseau was all gone. She had only kept the ones that Sunil had presented to her. He hadn't given her many, so it was easier to hold on to them. She had also kept the bandini skirt and the lovely silk top he had presented her on her birthday. And the tight pair of jeans, the one she wore to the cricket match in Calcutta. She had photographs of herself, dressed in these clothes. Looking happy. Looking normal.

She didn't have many pictures of herself after that day. She always hid behind someone or managed to escape when 'photo sessions' were inevitable. The only time she couldn't avoid a picture taken was the annual school photograph. She'd make an effort to dress as cheerfully as she possibly could for that day, for the sake of the girls. But she herself never brought a copy home.

She took a sari out. It was a crepe silk in peacock blue with a border of golden buti-worked paisley. He had presented it to her on their first wedding anniversary. With the sari, he had also given her a bracelet, but that was in the bank safe deposit now.

She held the sari to her nose and it unravelled to the floor. It still had a faint fragrance of the perfume she used to wear then. She realised she had never washed this sari. So technically, Sunil's touch still existed in its folds. She remembered him embracing her when they returned home from an evening out. Even then, this soft silky material had slipped off her shoulder and exposed her skin to him. He had made love to her right away. Then on the Kashimiri rug in the living room. Her sari struggling at her waist, her blouse undone. They had got entangled in its folds and had laughed as they tried to unravel it from their bodies.

'Careful,' she had cried. 'Don't ruin it, Sunil.' Pressing the fabric to her face now, she was glad it was intact. She inhaled deeply, hoping to catch his scent.

Dipali slipped out of her housecoat, now smelling of mustard oil. She stripped off her underclothes. She draped the sari around her, luxuriating in its silkiness. She pleated it carefully and threw the anchal over her bare shoulder.

She glared at herself in the mirror. Why, oh why, if she were a widow, why hadn't god taken away her beauty, her sensuousness away as well? She gazed at her milk-white skin, at the curve of her hips, the slight swell of her belly. Her breath became fast. It was as if she was seeing herself through Sunil's eyes. This is how he must have felt when he saw her, when she invited him into her arms. My god, how could he resist? A strangled cry escaped her lips.

She slipped her fingers under the pleats. She closed her eyes and probed deeper. How she wanted to be touched. She imagined Sunil on top of her, looking at her flushed face, lustful eyes, demanding mouth.

She hurriedly tore the sari from her body and threw it to the ground. With trembling hands, she wrapped the housecoat around herself and fled from the mirror. She was afraid to succumb to her feelings. It was a sin, even to think like that.

To have sexual thoughts after her husband's death. No, it was that damned cousin's wedding that was making her crazy. Giving her ideas. She had thought about it often. How her cousin would now have a husband. A man who would transport her away from this world. They would do everything that she was now deprived of. And it brought out the worst in her.

Hours later, her mother and Shikha returned armed with bags of shopping and laughter. She welcomed them with hot cups of tea and samosas. Her mother glowed with happiness, her betel-stained teeth flashing as she laughed. Dipali had had a shower, her damp hair clung to her scalp. Sprinklings of cloud-like lavender talc escaped from within her cotton salwar kameez, enveloping her in a fragrant cocoon she wanted to hide inside.

Shikha paraded around the room, showing off her sari. Asha Devi had bought it for her.

'Look at what Ma presented me with,' she said, thrusting the sari out at her. It was a baby pink kanjivaram, with silver zari work on it. 'But you shouldn't have spent so much on me.'

Asha Devi brushed her away. 'Nonsense, it's something very small. Wear it to the wedding. At last, there is good news from in our family.'

Dipali stared at Shikha's wide girth. She had noticed it before, but had thought nothing of it. She'd grown fatter, she had assumed. But no, she was pregnant. No wonder her mother was all over her. There was to be a grandchild soon.

The two women looked so happy in their little bubble, rummaging through the shopping bag, discussing due dates and more ceremonies they'd have to plan. Dipali's smile was frozen on her face, but in her mind she ached for that baby she never had. She sensed she was a failure in every way for her mother. And she was now being punished for all that she had failed to achieve.

Her mother had taken widowhood well. She had finally escaped from her husband's sharp tongue and violent reactions. She knew nothing of being a widow at twenty-seven, of being cheated of a married life, and so she could look forward to a wedding that would not poke barbs at her or to point out her position as a lowly widow in the hierarchy of life. And now, every time she'd hold her grandchild in her arms, she would highlight the empty womb of her daughter's.

2

The train drew up into the station. The coolies leapt in through the open doors even before it came to a halt. Moushumi leaned to one side and ignored a coolie who was trying to bully her into engaging his services. She was hot and sticky, having travelled thirty-six hours across the plains of India. The dry summer heat had rendered the landscape arid, the land looking scorched or parched in different shades of yellow brown or gold. But Moushumi had no inclination to admire the scenery. In her bag was her appointment letter, her reason for sanity, her means of escape.

As soon as she got off the train, the humid air hit her. She had never visited Bombay before, but she knew those who came to this city never left empty handed. Dreams were always realised here. She held on to her bags and stood on the platform, trying to take in the frenzied activity that was happening all around her. The coolies marched off with suitcases balancing on their turbaned heads, families racing to keep up with them. People talked, shouted, ordered, and she realised everyone was speaking a different language. She heard Hindi, English, Marathi, Bengali, South Indian languages she couldn't recognise.

Moushumi bit her lip. She should really call it Mumbai now, not Bombay. The current ruling political party had insisted on reverting back to the original name the natives used to call their city. Mumbai, named after the patron goddess, Mumbadevi. She liked that. Different names, different identities, but the spirit of the city had not changed. She too would metamorphose. She would find her destiny here, away from the family pressures back in Calcutta. She would exorcise those demons that played inside her head. She grabbed her bags and walked towards the entrance. So many Bollywood films began on the steps of this great railway station, the Victoria Terminus. The hero, a young man full of dreams, climbing down these very steps, surviving all the blows the city delivers, finding lady love, rescuing her from the baddies, a few dishum-dishums later baddies dismissed and the lovers unite to sing in the gardens or in the more recent films, dance against the snowy backdrops of Switzerland.

Moushumi felt resolute that she too would do the same. Overcome everything, find the love of her life and be happy. The past few years had not been easy. In Hindu legends, for a woman to prove her purity, she would have to walk through fire, and if she emerged unscathed, she'd be accepted by her husband, by society. It was called agni-parikha. The symbolic test of fire. She too would have to go through it, to prove to her family, to herself, to the world that yes, it was possible to love another woman, and be happy.

The roads were blocked with the rush of passengers getting into taxis or buses to take them to their destinations. It was eight o'clock in the evening, and yet the local trains were crammed with people going home to the suburbs. Moushumi was pushed and jostled as she stepped hesitantly out into the street to get a taxi. She reached into her bag and pulled out an address: 24/A Block C Krishna Nagar, Andheri East, her paying guest accommodation.

She got into a taxi and watched the city pass by. There were no empty spaces here. People were everywhere. On the streets, in the bazaars, leaning out of windows of the buildings, under the flyovers, hanging out of local trains that clattered by on the rail tracks running parallel to the roads. When the taxi stopped at a light, a young woman tried to entice her to buy her strings of gajras, waving the fragranced but slightly dry jasmine flowers in front of her. She looked away. But on the other side, there was a young boy, hand outstretched, begging her for change. The lights turned green and the taxi lurched forward.

A group of women leaned against a wall at the next traffic light. They were dressed in low cut dresses or saris, and they laughed raucously. They eyed the man in the Honda in front and made lurid gestures at him. The man said something and they doubled up with laughter. Then one of them ran towards the car and leaned inside. The lights turned green yet the Honda didn't move. The taxi driver leaned on his horn. The woman stood up and screeched abuses at him. The Honda revved and sped out into the night.

'Bloody whore,' the taxi driver yelled as he nearly ran her over. 'Get out of the way.'

Moushumi closed her eyes. Exhaustion claimed her body and her senses. What she longed for was a cool shower and sleep.

ॐ

Moushumi's new room was tiny. The pink paint was peeling off, showing a dull blue underneath. The narrow bed clung to one corner of the room and a flimsy wardrobe slanted on the other side. There was a window above the bed, one of the panes missing, and the light of a red neon sign flashed into the room.

'For seven hundred a month, it is very good,' Mrs Ghatnekar had said. 'You have to share our toilet, of course. Cannot use between eight and nine in the morning, as husband needs to get ready for work. Food, breakfast allowed. No lunch. Dinner you can bring home. You must be home by ten o'clock, okay? Cannot use phone, there is a public phone downstairs. For emergency phone, we charge five rupees per call. Incoming phone, emergency only, not after ten o' clock. Okay?'

'No emergencies allowed after ten o' clock,' Moushumi had joked with her landlady, who glared at her in return. And no peeing between eight and nine o'clock, she finished off in her mind.

Moushumi lay down and hugged her pillow. Her thoughts, always on a loop: her mother, her father, her sister giggling and chasing her son down the stairs. Jasmine. Her mother crying. Her father shouting. Jasmine laughing. It went on and on until she forced the pillow down on her face and begged her mind to shut off.

But she couldn't avoid thinking. Her father's curses still rang in her ears. He had called her *filthy*. *A pervert. Where had she learnt to indulge in such dirty things? What a shame to the family.* When her mother tried to calm him, he lashed out at her. She was to blame, for spoiling her daughter, giving in to her every demand. Her mother had suggested going to a doctor. *It could be cured*, she had wailed. *It was a disease. She had contracted it from that woman. Perhaps they could do a puja and clean her mind of these evils?* There was a solution: *She could marry a man and forget her sins.*

But Moushumi had stood her ground. Did they want her to do a blood test? An MRI scan? Would lesbianism show up in the results? *If at all*, she had screamed, *it was their fault. Her parents fault, for giving her the defective gene. She was not diseased, she was not insane. She was a lesbian, had always been so, but didn't realise it until she found a woman to express herself to. It was normal. Some people were born like that.*

Hijra, her father had screamed at her. *Eunuch. How dare you blame us? We are respectable, middle class people. I have worked hard to feed this family, and you blame us? Is your sister the same? Look at her, married with a son. How dare you call yourself normal? You belong on the streets, begging for money, like a hijra. I fed you, educated you, loved you and this is what you give in return? It is better you die than destroy our family. Your sister's family.* And he spat on the ground and left the room.

At some point she must have fallen asleep, only to wake up with a start to find the red light blinking in her face. She panicked, unsure where she was. The bed was hard and unfamiliar. Somebody was snoring in the other room. The stray dogs were barking consistently, and an old Hindi song reached her from a battered transistor somewhere below.

She hugged her knees to her chest and waited. Sleep would not come. But the tears came.

What was she doing in a place like this?

The Ghatnekars were middle-class Maharashtrians. The husband, Ramesh, worked with a local courier company. The wife stayed home and cooked chapattis. She would get up at four in the morning and start rolling out five hundred of the flatbreads, which she would then distribute to the various agents who provided dabbas or lunchboxes to the many offices around Mumbai. Her kitchen was covered in white flour and oil. Moushumi shuddered every time she entered to make her morning cup of tea, she would have to lean over the bent Mrs Ghatnekar, pounding dough. Mrs G, as Moushumi nicknamed her, would finish making the chapattis by seven, and then a teenage boy would come to collect them and scoot off. She'd make breakfast for her husband and her daughter after that. Moushumi would rush to finish her cup of tea and claim the bathroom before eight o'clock. She was glad that the husband smoked, as that meant she could sneak a fag in the toilet without giving out her secret.

She would then dress and run out of the house before the fish frying started. A bus would get her to school, but most days, she struggled to be on time.

Weekends were the worst. She couldn't bear to be sitting around in that cramped flat with the rest of the family. The daughter, only seven, studied in the bedroom she shared with her parents. The father sat in front of the television and flicked channels relentlessly. Moushumi noticed he wouldn't watch anything for more than two minutes. At nine o'clock, the daughter was brought in to watch *Fawlty Towers* to get an English education. Moushumi would wince as she watched the family watch the antics of Basil Fawlty with a straight face and then get their daughter to speak with an English accent.

'I know,' Lakshmi would drawl self-consciously, trying to imitate Sybil Fawlty, and Moushumi would stuff her face in the pillow to muffle out her laughter.

3

Soon, the wedding season was washed out by the monsoon. Mosquitoes. Overflowing drains. Unending traffic jams. Dipali set off to work with purpose every day. Ashish and Shikha returned to Delhi after Shiuli's wedding, taking Asha Devi with them for a couple of weeks. It was their duty, Ashish was clear to mention, to look after mother. But of course, Dipali knew it was more for her help around the house while Shikha lay nauseous in bed.

Dipali welcomed the break, reading paperback romances and eating crisps in bed. Most nights she ordered Chinese from the local takeaway, or her neighbour sent her thick stuffed parathas, smeared with pure ghee. As a result, Dipali found it hard to fit into her clothes.

As usual, the teachers complained about the workload, the disobedient girls, and the non-teaching duties they had been assigned. But they were glad to be back. No more haranguing mothers-in-law, or absconding maids, or irritating husbands to deal with for the term-time at least. They could complain and gossip and support each other once more. Dipali looked around the staff-room. Nothing had changed. No one had changed either. Only the desk next to her was empty, as the English teacher had retired last term.

The school bell rang and the teachers rose, still chatting, to attend the school assembly. As they filed out of the staffroom, a woman rushed in, panting and flustered.

'Staff Room C?' she asked.

'Yes,' Dipali nodded. 'Are you okay?'

The other teachers milled around them, curious to see the new teacher. Mrs Nath stared at her sleeveless blouse, pointedly showing her disapproval. Dipali nudged her to one side, away from the teachers' prying eyes.

The new teacher had already rushed inside to find her desk. Dipali showed her where to sit.

'I'm Mrs Rai,' she introduced herself. 'Dipali. I teach history to the middle school.'

'Hi, I'm Moushumi Dutta. I'm the new English teacher.' She held out her hand to Dipali. Her books slid out of her grasp and landed heavily on the desk. 'Sorry, I'm so clumsy. And late. I didn't know it took more than an hour in this traffic to get to school from Andheri.'

'You're not from Mumbai?' Dipali picked up a couple of the books that had slid onto the floor and handed them back.

'No, no,' Moushumi said. 'I'm from Calcutta. New to this city, but not new to teaching. You're Bengali, aren't you?'

'Yes, but let's go now. You don't want to be late for assembly. Not on your first day.'

Dipali lead Moushumi to the assembly hall. They exchanged some information about each other on the way, and Dipali decided that she really liked this new teacher. She wasn't like the other teachers in the staffroom. There was something different about her. In the middle of singing the Lord's Prayer she smiled to herself. She knew she was going to enjoy her time in school from now on.

CR

'There's a shed at the back of the staffroom,' Dipali said quietly as Moushumi settled down next to her. They'd taken to eating lunch together in the staffroom, sharing a desk to spread out their lunchboxes. Usually Moushumi ordered something from the school canteen. Sometimes they'd even go to the local Udipi and eat a thali. Their friendship had made great strides, mainly because of their common language and culture. And also because they could speak in their mother tongue to make jokes about the other teachers in front of them.

Moushumi raised an eyebrow but said nothing. They both had a free period before lunch and were doing their marking in the staffroom.

Dipali leaned closer. 'The teachers are beginning to suspect, so I thought I'd warn you.'

Moushumi rummaged in her handbag and pulled out a packet of Marlboro Lights. 'You mean these?'

Dipali nodded. 'It's against the school rules. So it would be best if you stopped. But if you can't, then there's the shed.'

'They'll be here any second to interrogate you, since this smell has started only since you've come.'

'Hmmmm.'

The bell rang out and soon the other teachers walked into the staffroom. Just as Mrs Lal and Mrs Nath entered, Moushumi sprang out of her chair, hand theatrically on her chest.

'Goodness,' she said loudly. 'Did you get that awful stink in the toilet? Does it ever get cleaned?'

Mrs Nath cleared her throat and looked at Mrs Lal. 'Oh, we were wondering the same—'

'Disgusting,' Moushumi exhaled. 'We should do something about it.'

'Yes,' Mrs Lal said. 'It smells of cigarettes.'

'Does it?' Moushumi asked, fluttering her eyelids. 'Oh, I wouldn't know. Do you smoke, Mrs Lal?'

Mrs Lal sputtered. Dipali gave out a strange sound and stuffed her sari anchal into her mouth.

'No, no,' Mrs Nath came to her defence. 'Of course she doesn't smoke. Her husband does, in the toilet. I think it's that Ashok, the peon.'

Moushumi wagged her finger at Mrs Lal. 'Tell your husband it's bad to smoke. Especially in loos. It's the others who suffer.'

Mrs Lal nodded vigorously and rushed to her seat.

'Oof, that stink,' Moushumi repeated, and reached for her handbag. 'I could do with some fresh air.' As she turned to leave the staffroom, Moushumi stroked her handbag in an exaggerated manner and smiled at Dipali.

CR

'That was such a fun film,' Dipali said as she and Moushumi stepped out into the hot afternoon. 'I haven't been to a cinema ever since—'

Though they had become friends quickly, still there were those spaces that were best left unsaid. Moushumi smiled at her, understanding, for she too was wary of filling in the gaps.

'We should do this more often,' she said. 'That way, I'd at least stay out of that rubbish hovel.'

'You should look for another place,' Dipali suggested. 'Somewhere closer to school.'

'I am looking,' Moushumi said. 'But Mumbai is so expensive. I had no idea.'

'Oh yes, you do now,' Dipali laughed. 'I saw your face when you paid for the movie tickets. It's cheaper in Calcutta, na?'

'Everything is cheaper,' Moushumi said. 'And tastier. The fish is vile in Mumbai.'

'That's because you have that stinky fish your landlady cooks. Have you tried the rui?'

'Where am I supposed to get that?'

'Come to our place. My mother cooks the most amazing fish. Fish in mustard sauce. Steamed hilsa. Oooh, the taste! I used to eat at least three pieces at one go.'

Moushumi stopped at looked at Dipali. 'Used to? Don't you eat fish anymore?'

Dipali shook her head. 'No, not since... Not since, you know... Sunil died. Our family is very strict about keeping the traditions and all.'

'Really, Dipali? But honestly, do you believe in all that, in this day and age?'

Dipali looked away. It was such a difficult question to answer. Of course, she missed eating fish and she missed wearing fashionable, colourful clothes. But she didn't have the confidence to break the rule or challenge her brother about it. Instead, she thought of Sunil, saying: 'He was not meant to die.'

Moushumi took Dipali's hand in hers. They walked towards the train station. What had happened to them both had not meant to be. But here they were, both scarred women, holding hands, trying to make things right.

Dipali got off at Khar station. Moushumi managed to squeeze next to an elderly woman. The women talked in high-pitched voices. Moushumi tried to listen in to some of the conversation. They talked of what they'd cook once they got home, they gossiped about their mothers-in-law, husbands, neighbours. They discussed television serials with great sincerity. Eventually Moushumi's attention drifted off and was lost in her own thoughts. It was not a pastime she enjoyed particularly, for it meant replaying the hurtful events in her head in a constant loop. Her parents. Jasmine. The screaming. The accusations. She leaned back on the seat and tried to think of other things. The film. Dipali. Laughing with her.

When she opened her eyes, they fell upon a poster on the wall of the train. Hanging on between a poster about rabies and another about Pearl abortion clinic, was an A4 photocopy proclaiming, *'If you are gay, why should you pay?'* Moushumi could not read any more over the heads of the crowd until a station came into view and the women streamed out. Then she edged closer:

'Condemned? Assaulted? Insulted?
You don't have to take it anymore. Join us, an ever-growing movement of gays and lesbians into finding our own path in life. Call on:'

Instead of the phone number, in a dark marker pen that left an indelible mark, PERVERT was scratched over the paper.

Moushumi scanned the compartment for other such posters, but they had either been torn out or the person hadn't had the guts to display another one. But here was hope. Someone had made the effort to reach out to her, and she was going to find her.

❧

Moushumi walked down the Colaba streets. The sun slipped behind the buildings, leaving a red sky behind. Muslim women, covered in their black burkhas, herded their children towards the old British-built apartments. They reminded her of blackbirds homing in to roost. She passed the street stalls selling jewellery and clothes, the fabric shabby in the artificial lights.

She had heard that this was where she could find one of her kind. One of her kind, Moushumi thought cynically. Like she was a vampire. So where did gay people meet under the shadow of the night? The nightclubs of Colaba? As darkness fell, another group of people swooped down to claim the streets. Youngsters, brash in their cars with music throbbing out of the windows lined up outside the clubs. Flashy clothes, shiny hair, pockets flush with money. She had seen their kind in Calcutta too, when she moved in the same circuit with Jasmine. Drug pushers and abusers jostled in the alleyways, hookers whispered a price to a prospective client.

Moushumi walked into Leopold Café. The ground floor was an Irani restaurant, with its trademark red-checked tablecloth and black wooden chairs. The ancient fans rotated high above the clientele, promising little respite. She wasn't interested in the menu the waiter handed to her. She saw the narrow stairs in the corner, leading upstairs to the nightclub. Leo's.

She was nervous to go into the club alone. She climbed up the steep and narrow steps to where the ground shook with the intensity of the music. Inside, the space was bathed in a dim blue glow. It was tiny, very narrow with a single row of tables hugging the outer side of the wall, and a dance floor the size of a bathroom, where people obstinately tried to move their bodies.

A waiter came up to her. Immediately, she said she had friends at the far end of the room. She edged her way inside. It was eight o'clock and the crowd was mostly teenagers.

Young girls whose parents didn't know their daughters had been out dancing since the afternoon. If only they saw their children in this hellhole, Moushumi thought. Drinking. Groping. Dancing. Some of the boys didn't even have a proper growth of facial hair, she noticed. They were all kids. Disappointed, she elbowed her way out again. The adults would come only later at night, when she had to be back in her prison, Cinderella with her ten o'clock curfew. She bought a kathi roll from Bade Mia's. It was just a little cart behind Leopold's, but with the best kebabs and rolls one could ask for in the city. So licking the juices from the kebabs that oozed out of the thick flatbread onto her fingers and chin, Moushumi made her way back to the station.

Another day gone. And still, she was the only lesbian in the city of Mumbai.

4

Ram Vilas stood in a lane, which once was quiet and shady, but now had become the main route for the auto rickshaws to go to the railway station, by-passing the Khar market. Named after Dipali's grandfather, he had built it slowly, with a lot of love and pain. Her bedridden grandmother had told her the stories over and over again in her childhood.

Those windows you see, she would say, pointing a bony finger towards the grilled windows in her room, *they were procured after selling two of my gold bangles*. Dipali would nod, not understanding the sacrifice made. Those windows were really quite ugly. If she had sold jewellery, couldn't they have got better window grills? Now, just repairing the leaks and joints of the house made her wish she had enough gold bangles to sell. She would use the money left behind by her in-laws time and again to repair the house, rather than ask her brother to contribute.

Every time her mother mentioned the leaks to Ashish, he would snort over the phone and complain that he couldn't repair the toilet in his house, and they put up with it. And now with the baby coming, she ought to start thinking of putting aside for her only grandchild. Asha Devi didn't mention it again. And the kitchen ceiling turned soft and pulpy, big pockets of damp threatening to burst open over their heads. Dipali had asked for a quote from a plasterer, and she had haggled with him till he came down to her price. She meant to get the work done before her mother returned from Delhi. A New Year present for her.

Prices in Mumbai were always escalating, but the quality did not appear to respond to the price. She'd have to supervise the repairs the whole time. She thought of Moushumi and her complaints of her living quarters. Such a high price for that shit? Dipali studied the newspaper ads, hoping to find her friend a decent paying-guest accommodation within the budget. But no such luck. Moushumi continued to live with the Ghatnekars. And the leaks continued to slither down the kitchen walls.

CR

Three things happened in the new year. The kitchen ceiling in Ram Vilas was repaired. Moushumi found a new place to live. And Asha Devi had a healthy grandson.

'A palace,' Moushumi beamed at Dipali. 'A real good deal.'

'I'm so happy for you,' Dipali said. 'Where is it?'

'Much closer to school. In Parel. An old Parsi lady is letting out a room with attached bathroom, did you hear it? Attached bathroom with geyser. Hot water showers will be possible again, imagine that. She needs someone in the house to look in on her. I get to use her kitchen too. And the telephone. But I have to pay the telephone bill.'

Moushumi danced around the staff-room.

'That's fantastic. When do you move in?'

'Next weekend. No more toilet curfews. No more nighttime curfews. Only, no smoking.' She made a face.

'Well, you can't win them all. It's a good thing. Will help you kick the habit.'

'Nah, no chance.' Moushumi dismissed her. 'I can hang out of the window and smoke.'

'I'm very happy for you. I don't know how you survived in that place. The stories you told me were horrible.'

'No more strange and horrific stories, Dipali.' Moushumi said in an exaggerated tone. 'From now on, only sweet Parsi ladies and flush clean toilets and lagganu custard aromas will exist in my life.'

'I hope so. By the way, lagganu custard is made only at weddings. Whose wedding will it be served at?' Dipali teased.

Moushumi bent down close to Dipali's face. 'Yours,' she whispered and turned away.

'How can you say such a thing?'

'Shh,' Moushumi held her finger to Dipali's lips. 'Don't say anything. Yet.'

'I meant you,' Dipali said. But something stirred inside her. Could it be possible?

'I'll never marry,' Moushumi said, gritting her teeth. 'But we'll have to think about you.'

That night, those words played on Dipali's mind. She was still young. Why hadn't anyone thought of that before? She swayed between hope and guilt. Did this mean she didn't love Sunil. But of course she did. But he was gone. And she was alive. What would they have expected of him, had she died? He would have married again, or at least, there would have been talk of it. She was not even thirty, and yet it was taken for granted she would live her life alone forever. Was that being fair?

Dipali tossed and turned in her bed. She heard her mother groan and then snore. She thought of her brother and his wife.

And their new born baby. She dreamt of a sweet baby boy. Hers. The baby looked like Sunil. His tiny petulant mouth pouting, dribbling.

☙

Moushumi heard the shouts and abuses from outside her door. It was becoming more frequent. Mr Ghatnekar was coming home drunk more often. She tried to drown out the noise by turning the volume up on her walkman.

Lakshmi burst into the room crying, 'He'll hit her.'

Moushumi didn't know how to react. She didn't want to meddle in their affairs. She was leaving in a matter of days. Sure enough, the wife's screams changed. Lakshmi buried her face in Moushumi's pillow and blocked out the sounds. Her body racked noiselessly. They stayed that way, mute and frozen, till silence prevailed in the outer room. There was a bang as the bedroom door shut. The television was switched on and Basil Fawlty was at his incoherent best. Lakshmi smiled at Moushumi and slid out of her room. Moushumi shut her eyes. Just two more nights. She'd have to bear with this for two more nights and then, bliss.

5

Valentine's Day. Moushumi grimaced at yet another TV advertisement for jewellery. Chocolate. A gift for someone you love. Why was it in India that Valentine's Day was meant only for lovers? It's supposed to be universal love. But no, yet again another ad, fairness cream to look beautiful in the eyes of your man. What shit, Moushumi thought. She flicked off the television and reached for the phone.

'Hey, Dipali,' said Moushumi. 'Let's celebrate Valentine's Day together, shall we? Go out for a few laughs?'

'I don't know—' Dipali didn't want to acknowledge any special day meant for couples.

'Yes, we can,' Moushumi insisted. 'It's not meant just for lovers, how these media people like to portray it. You can give your brother a Valentine's card, if you like.'

'No, thank you,' Dipali said. 'I'd rather not.'

'Okay, okay. Don't then. How about me? You can't sit and mope at home. Let's go out and have fun. You suggest where we ought to go. Where you'd feel comfortable. I don't want to sit around at home with my Parsi landlady and share her Rippon Club dhansak with her.'

Dipali took a deep breath. She looked across the room at her mother, who was watching a Bengali cooking programme

134

on television. Dipali wondered at the absurdity of her mother watching intently as the chef cooked mutton curry. She wouldn't touch meat now, yet her mother religiously watched its preparation on television every day.

'Let's go,' she said. 'I'm sick of hating Valentine's Day. Let's go and get it out of the system.'

They met at the train station. Dipali had decided to dress up for the occasion. A pale yellow churidar kurta and high heeled sandals. She'd left her hair loose and wore dangling earrings.

'Oh, look at you,' Moushumi whistled. 'Didn't know what was hidden behind that drabness, Dipali.' She caught Dipali's waist and gave her a brief hug.

'Stop it,' Dipali giggled. 'You haven't done too bad yourself. I love your dress, very stylish.'

Moushumi pretended to act coy. She fluttered her eyelashes and they both burst into giggles. She took Dipali's hand and they walked out into the road.

'Who knows, I may find that 'someone special' tonight,' Moushumi said.

'I hope you do,' Dipali laughed. 'I'll help you find one.'

They went to a restaurant in Bombay Central, well known for its Gujarati cuisine. The teachers in the staff room had ardently declared it the best in town, and Dipali was curious to try it out. And it was vegetarian as well. The place was packed with young Gujarati couples out to celebrate their love. There were families too, waiting impatiently for a table. Children were crying. Their mothers shouted shrilly at them to shut up while they perspired in their heavy saris. The men wore mostly wore safari suits and marched around importantly, yelling at the waiters to hurry and give them tables. Yet, every time the door opened to the restaurant, the divine aromas would lull even the most irritating child into a trance.

'How long do we have to wait?' Moushumi asked the manager who hovered by the door, struggling to write down the names of diners in the correct order of their arrival. He studied his long list and guessed at one hour.

'Good Lord,' Moushumi gasped. 'Is this your idea of a romantic Valentine meal?'

Dipali stared, disappointed. 'I didn't know this would be such a popular place.'

'Come on,' Moushumi pulled Dipali's arm. 'Let me take you somewhere else.'

They got into a taxi and Moushumi instructed the driver to take them to Haji Ali. Dipali winced. It was close to her flat in Peddar Road. Often Sunil and she would drive down to Haji Ali's famed fruit juice stalls in the middle of the night.

'Haji Ali's amazing juice to get us started on our culinary adventure tonight,' Moushumi announced as they approached the juice centre. Fresh fruit was displayed on the glass counter and hung from hooks above. Dipali scanned the menu. Mango, apple, sweet lime, orange, ganga jamuna (orange and mosambi mix), ganga jamuna sarswati. She frowned. What was that? Pomergranate, New Zealand cherry, New Zealand grape, New Zealand apple, New Zealand kiwi... they didn't have these when Sunil was there. Cocktails, Rooh Afza, Falooda— oh, the list was endless.

'I'll have a Ganga Jamuna,' said Moushumi. 'And you?'

'I'll try a New Zealand kiwi,' said Dipali. Anything that would not bring memories rushing back to her mind.

They sat on the wall of the promenade, facing the old mosque that was built on a rocky outcrop further out into the sea. A queue of people made their way to or from the mosque.

It was lit up, making it stand out against the dark grey of the sea beyond.

Dipali sipped her drink. It was sharp. Her faced screwed up, and she had to request for more sugar. 'The Haji Ali mosque was built in the fifteenth century,' she told Moushumi. 'Isn't it amazing how it is still so beautiful and has withstood the force of the sea?'

Moushumi nodded.

'It's five hundred metres off the coast. On a little island. And it gets completely cut off from land at high tide.'

'Have you ever been there?' Moushumi asked.

Dipali waved her hand and shook her head vigorously. 'Never. I lived so close by once, passed it every day on my way to and back from school. Never thought of visiting.'

They finished their drinks in silence and split the bill.

Moushumi took Dipali's hand and pulled her off the ledge. 'Come on.' She led her towards the entrance of the mosque. 'Ah. this is the place for doomed lovers to seek peace. An apt place to visit on Valentine's Day. Maybe, we'll be absolved of our tragedies today, you think?'

Dipali couldn't answer. She let Moushumi lead her through the entrance. The walkway leading up to the mosque was narrow and up to a kilometre long. She looked on either side where the waves caressed the white rocks. There was a busy stream of people going either way. Beggars clamoured for attention and the devotees dutifully handed out alms to them. There were people from all walks of life, not just Muslims. Dipali watched men in white collars and ties hurry up the path. She saw women holding on to their errant saris that played up in the wind walk along with women in burkhas and scarves. There were many children who found the journey more exciting than the destination. They hung on to their balloons or other toys bought for them from the hawkers that lined the entrance to the path.

The sun had set behind the structure, leaving a black silhouette of the mosque against the orange sky.

'Beautiful,' Moushumi whispered, tightening her hold on Dipali's hand.

Dipali walked on silently. She enjoyed the sense of activity on this narrow bridge. She turned to look at the city behind. Mumbai was lighting up for the night. The neon adverts flashed bright reds and blues, while the sulphur orange streetlights adorned the curve of the bay, resembling a bejewelled necklace. They finally reached the main hall. It was supported by marble pillars that were intricately decorated with coloured mirror work. The smell of incense wafted in the air. They were hurried along by the surging crowd till they reached the tomb.

'The tomb of the saint Haji Ali,' whispered Dipali. She was not sure what she ought to pray for, but it seemed right to bow her head in reverence. The tomb was covered in with a red and green sheet. An image came to her mind. Another body, covered with a white sheet. Those images had seared themselves into the backs of her eyes.

'I pray— I pray for release,' she said to herself. She wiped away the tears and looked at Moushumi. She was shocked to see her eyes were watery as well.

'Funny what some places can do to you.' Moushumi said, rubbing her face hard.

Dipai nodded. 'Let's go somewhere else. I'm not ready to do this right now.'

Moushumi squeezed her arm. 'I'm sorry, Dipali. I should have realised.'

6

'Why did we have to meet here?' Dipali whispered, looking around. It was nearing the end of lunch hour and the restaurant was full of men shovelling biryani or drinking beer. All eyes had been on them as the two women had walked in and were seated by the window.

Moushumi raised an eyebrow. 'Does it bother you? They're not even interested in us.'

Dipali settled down in her chair and forced herself not to look around. How could Moushumi not notice the glances coming their way? The waiter slapped down a laminated menu card on the table and disappeared.

'You know, I'm worried about you,' Dipali said. She picked at the peanuts that were remaining in the bowl.

Moushumi ground her cigarette into the ashtray. She poured herself more beer, tipping the bottle so that every single drop fell into the glass.

'This beer is excellent. You sure you don't want to try?' She smiled at Dipali, who screwed up her nose. 'I tell you, on a hot day, nothing satisfies like a bottle of chilled Kingfisher. Aaah!' She sipped and licked the froth that lined her upper lip.

'You sound like a beer commercial. But you can't sell your pitch to me.' Dipali firmly pushed the bottle away from her.

They sat quietly together. The air-conditioner blasted icy air directly into their faces, relieving them from the scorching heat outside. Soon the customers finished their lunch and marched out, back to their offices. A few continued to sit around and enjoy their drinks. They spoke loudly and laughed even louder at regular intervals. The waiters carried piles of plates and beer glasses to the kitchen. There was a peculiar smell when air-conditioning mixed with beer. Dipali winced as it always reminded her of her days with Sunil. She didn't tell Moushumi that she knew exactly what Moushumi had meant when she had praised the qualities of chilled beer on a hot day.

'So what is holding you back, Moushumi? Would you like to share it with me? Something is worrying you.' Dipali fiddled with her napkin and then smoothed it on her lap. Moushumi drank deeply from her glass.

'Well,' Moushumi said, wiping her mouth with the back of her hand. 'It is a difficult story to tell.' A small burp escaped her lips and she laughed. 'Not very sophisticated, am I?'

Her red eyes belied her attempts at cheeriness. Dipali hoped she hadn't made things worse for her by asking. Moushumi had rung her early in the morning. She had sounded hysterical. She needed to talk, she had said. Could they meet in town? Her behaviour worried Dipali. She knew Moushumi had problems that she didn't like to talk about. She had had a family crisis and had cut off ties with them. It was, most probably, a love affair gone wrong. Her boyfriend had married someone else, or her parents had refused to let her marry him.

Moushumi fumbled to light another cigarette. At last, after a deep drag, she seemed to get control of herself. 'I'm making it quite dramatic, aren't I?' she said.

Dipali shook her head. 'No, take your time. I just thought you'd feel better by sharing. But if you don't, I can understand.'

'No, it's alright.' Moushumi said. 'What I am really afraid of is losing my friendship with you.'

'What do you mean? I don't understand.' Dipali grabbed the table in alarm. She felt the oiliness of the tablecloth and hastily moved her hands away.

'Well, I'll leave it to you to judge and make up your mind what you think of it. It has not been easy on most people, I know. It's like this.' Moushumi leaned forward, her face veiled by a stream of cigarette smoke. 'I come from a conservative family background. Very middle class. Just me and my sister, and of course my parents. So far so good, huh?'

Dipali nodded and leaned forward to listen. Moushumi continued her story. 'Everything seemed quite normal, till I fell in love.'

'Isn't that always the case? Parents never agree.' There, she had been right after all.

Moushumi scratched her forehead. 'Yes, you could say that. Mine certainly couldn't believe it. Okay, let me get it out straight.' She sat back in her chair and looked straight at Dipali. 'Dipali, I was in love with a woman.'

Dipali lurched back and spilt her iced tea on the faded tablecloth. A waiter hurried to their table and started to mop up the accident. Dipali wrung her hands together and kept apologising to him, who kept assuring her it was alright. Moushumi smiled at her through the smokescreen.

'So, would you like me to continue, or would you rather leave?'

Dipali's face was burning. Maybe she ought to buy another iced tea so that she could hide behind it. 'No, no. It's fine. You must understand, Moushumi, this is the first time I've ever heard of it. I mean, I know of it... from the newspapers and magazines, but not from a live person. You understand? It's difficult. But I don't mean to...'

Moushumi laughed. 'Stop babbling, Dipali. It's like a déjà vu. There aren't too many people who I've talked to about this, but they all had the same reaction. Well, almost the same. Only my parents went ballistic. Their darling daughter so carefully and lovingly raised and educated to be delivered safely into the arms of a suitable groom. All their dreams were shattered. My mother suggested I visit a psychiatrist. Can you imagine that? They thought it a kind of mental illness. She sobbed for days, and did all kinds of puja at home, to drive away the demons from my head. I saw my father cry for the first time in my life.'

'I am sorry about my behaviour.' Dipali leaned forward to hold Moushumi's hand, but stopped. Would that mean something else? Instead, she awkwardly pretended to brush off some invisible remnants of iced tea from the tablecloth.

'Just give me some time to realise what you have said. It is natural, for a woman to be infatuated with another woman. Isn't it? Especially, in schools and colleges. In our school, we have quite a few attractive girls, so I can see...'

Moushumi waved her hand in the air in dismissal. 'No, that's not what I'm about. Yes, I had such tendencies when I was in school and college too. But then, it grew on me. I've never been attracted to men. And no, I haven't been a slut: sleeping around with every woman available either.' But her eyes wavered. She looked down at the stained tablecloth. Her hands were trembling. 'Or maybe I have been one—'she barely whispered.

Dipali turned away and stared out of the window until the sunlight blinded her. When she looked at Moushumi again, she saw her through a kaleidoscope of dancing colours – a

142

soft-filtered heroine in a sixties Hindi film, surrounded by starburst. Moushumi had transformed into another being. There was something dangerous and exciting about her, and Dipali sensed this feeling profoundly now. 'No, Moushumi, tell me what happened? Has something happened recently? You've changed all of a sudden.'

Moushumi looked up startled. 'You noticed?'

Dipali nodded. 'You've become so withdrawn. And look at your arms, you're breaking up into some kind of rash. Is it stress? Or what? You're not too well.'

'Last week,' Moushumi said, lowering her voice. 'I... no, a woman... made a pass at me on the train. I was sitting opposite her and she kept staring at me. And when it was time for me to get off, she followed me to the door.'

'How do you know she was making a pass at you?' Dipali asked. She couldn't believe such things happened in the open. In local trains, where all she had ever observed were middle-class women rushing home from work to their families, harassed mothers, college girls chattering in high-pitched voices, old women dozing on their seats. Bangle-sellers, beggars and snack-sellers. She had never thought that any of them could be a lesbian. And yet, when Moushumi travelled on the train, she was one, and nobody could tell.

'She whispered in my ear and rubbed her body against mine,' Moushumi said. 'She asked if I'd go to Razzmatazz with her. That it was unofficially gay nights on Fridays. They hired out rooms by the hour.'

She was breathing hard. She scratched the welts on her arms till they stood out fiery red again.

Dipali reached out and took her hand. 'Stop,' she whispered. 'Don't do that to yourself.'

'I felt so cheap,' Moushumi said. 'How did she pick me out

from the crowd? Why did it have to be just about sex? Did I advertise myself to her that I was available for just about anything?'

Dipali didn't know how to respond. Such things had never even crossed her mind. She had considered herself a close friend of Moushumi's and yet she never figured out what was behind her cheerful exterior. A lesbian? She looked closely at Moushumi, trying to find some sign, something different in her that would mark her out as one. Nothing. Opposite her sat a vulnerable woman with tears in her eyes. Looking like she needed help, not judgement. She forced herself not to think further but to concentrate on the situation in front of her. Concentrate on Moushumi's trauma. There was no way she was going to lose this friendship; it was all she had now.

'It could have been a coincidence,' Dipali suggested. 'Maybe she just took a chance on you. It could have been me. Maybe she was randomly trying her luck, you never know.'

'Maybe, but it wasn't a good feeling. If it had been a straight woman, she would have shouted, picked a fight. But I just kept quiet; I let her feel my skin. I felt I was party to her overtures. I couldn't push her off, even if I wanted to. I know I want someone, but not like that,' Moushumi covered her face with her hands. 'Sometimes I don't know what I want from life anymore.'

'Who does?' Dipali said. The walls were breaking down, but they were beginning to reveal perhaps more than Dipali could handle. Moushumi looked at her and shrugged.

'I didn't want to face you after the incident. I felt so dirty. Her touch – I can't get her touch off my skin.'

'You'll ruin your skin if you keep scrubbing, rubbing, whatever you are doing to it. The answer is not there, Moushumi, where do you think the answer lies?'

'What is the question, Dipali?' Moushumi asked. She rubbed her eyes tiredly and pressed her temples. 'Sometimes, I feel I have lost the question.'

'So, Mou,' Dipali said slowly. 'Did you have someone in Calcutta?' She was beginning to understand the reason why Moushumi had moved away.

'Jasmine.' Moushumi whispered, cupping her chin in her hands. 'For eighteen months, we kept it a secret. People thought we were the best of friends. She's quite a dynamic woman. You've probably seen her on the society pages of the *Times* or in *Femina*. She's married to a very famous builder. You know, Nandkumar Ghoshal? You may have heard of him. He's building all these five star hotels in Calcutta.'

Dipali nodded. 'But how did you meet her? This celebrity? I mean, how did it all start?'

'Well more of a socialite, really. You really want to know? You sure you won't faint on me or wreck this place by spilling things?'

'No, I'm over the first shock. Nothing can unfaze me now.'

'Amazing,' said Dipali, when Moushumi finished. 'It's amazing how women always seem to be treated in a second-hand way. Whether it comes to love or the lack of it, whether you gain the love of a woman, or lose the identity of your husband, a woman always has to lose.'

'Being homosexual is a criminal offence in this country. Section 377 of the Indian Penal Code make sexual activities between men illegal. It doesn't include women, though.'

'Why not?'

'Because,' Moushumi stressed, 'women cannot do these things. Queen Victoria was shocked when Macaulay's Law suggested that female homosexuality be addressed as well. She couldn't believe such ghastly acts were committed by women. So technically, I am legal!'

145

Dipali smiled, but her mind was far away. How was she any different from Moushumi? She too was edged out into the border of society. There had been a law that stated widows should burn on their husband's funeral pyre. Women stopped being human beings after the death of their husbands.

Dipali looked at Moushumi, sitting across from her. 'In a way,' she said, smiling. 'We are kind of similar, no?'

Moushumi raised an eyebrow. 'How?'

'Widows and lesbians. Both are hanging on to the edges of society, begging to be recognised. And both don't have the presence of men in their lives.'

Moushumi threw her head back and gave a full-throated laugh. Tears fell on her cheeks. Dipali joined in. The waiters looked at them, startled out of their afternoon reveries in the sleepy lunchroom. Then Moushumi collected herself. She hiccupped into the chequered napkin and wiped her streaming eyes. 'No, Dipali, we are not the same.'

'Why not?'

'You have a choice.'

'Meaning?'

'You can get married again. You have the choice. I don't.'

There was silence between them. Moushumi finished her beer and Dipali her iced tea. Outside, shoppers struggling with their shopping bags, negotiated with taxi drivers. A hippy couple with blonde dreadlocks studied a map, but still looked very lost. A one-armed beggar pestered them for change. A white-uniformed driver spat betel juice in a wide arch on the stone building wall. The juice splattered when it hit target, bright as blood and it dripped down the wall. Dipali watched and wondered how much that building must have endured. It had been standing there since the British Raj, and indeed seen enough bloodshed of the real kind.

'As you were saying, Moushumi, about Jasmine, please continue.'

Moushumi opened her mouth to say something and then let it go. Those memories still stung. She had always known that it would never work, and yet she had continued, and allowed herself to get hurt. She couldn't explain. 'Jasmine was very special to me,' she said finally. 'She gave but when she took, she hacked me down.'

'That's awful. Why did you let her?'

'No one has the answer to that one.'

'Did you tell her of your attraction that very first night?' Dipali asked.

'Oh no, not at all. She dropped me home after the drive, and said she would like to see me again. I was delighted. We met many times after that. At her place, or the cinema, at cafés. The Grand Hotel was her favourite haunt. She'd take me there for coffee or high tea. It was fun, really. I went to art shows with her.'

'And her husband didn't know? I mean, didn't he ever suspect?'

'Her husband never had the time for her. You know, Jasmine was so proud of the fact that she was using his money and cheating on him. It was a little game for her.'

'Was there ever a future for the two of you?'

'Where would we go? How is it possible in our society? So many suicides, women killing themselves in despair for having to give up their love. And then I found out about the other woman. It was her hobby, actually, seducing women and then dumping them for fresher ones. An adventure. Just like that. I called. I cried. She threatened to send her husband's thugs after my family. That he'd finish me for good. She just seemed so casual about it. That's what hurt most. The love that was so important to me, was such a vital part of my life, whoosh, gone. She made nothing of it.'

'Is that why you left Calcutta?'

Moushumi lit another cigarette.

'I haven't seen my parents for years now. I feel so unclean in front of them. My mother found me on the floor that night when I had confronted Jasmine on the phone. She had heard every word. She couldn't believe it, refused to believe it. She said Jasmine was a witch, had cast a spell on me.' Moushumi hesitated, trying to control her feelings.

'My father's words still burn my ears. My sister confessed that I told her earlier, but she didn't want her family involved. It would be too much of a scandal. I had to leave.'

Dipali reached out and held Moushumi's trembling hands. But she didn't know how to comfort her. It was good that she was talking. She felt privileged that Moushumi trusted her with her deepest secret.

'And then another woman just wanted me for her pastime. It's never for a serious relationship. I want to have a happy life. A normal life.' Moushumi sighed. 'Well, normal under the circumstances. A relationship. Wake up in the morning, have breakfast together. Go to work. Spend the evenings cooking, talking, arguing, what normal couples do.'

They walked out of the restaurant. The street had fallen silent. People were back in their offices. A few cabs cruised around, waiting for the stray passenger. A dog barked out of sight, shattering the silence of the lazy afternoon. In another hour, the scene would break up into one of rapid movement and hurry, as on Saturdays most offices worked half-day.

When Moushumi left in a taxi, Dipali walked towards the railway station. There were a few women already travelling back home. She studied them as they sat around her, either reading or chatting or just simply spaced out. She wondered which one of them could be a lesbian. She stared at the young college girl in tight jeans and tank top. She looked bold and the sort who could be adventurous. But if she dressed like that, it would attract boys, not girls. Dipali sighed. Who knew, maybe even girls. Another woman boarded the train and sat down opposite her. She was dressed in a pink, chiffon sari, and silver anklets on her feet. She smelled of a mixture of fading perfume and cigarette. Dipali sat up. Could she be a lesbian? Moushumi looked and smelled like that.

The woman smiled at Dipali, who dropped her gaze and then looked away. Goodness, the woman was making a pass at her. Was it the same woman Moushumi had picked up before? Dipali's throat scratched. She pulled her dupatta more securely over her shoulders and crossed her arms. She was getting paranoid. She was being silly. She glanced at the woman again, but her face was hidden behind her book. Dipali peered to look at the cover. It was a Mills and Boon. No lesbian would want to read about tall, dark and handsome men with hairy chests. When the woman looked at her again, Dipali smiled back.

7

The photography gallery was quiet that Sunday afternoon. The air-conditioning was on full, making Dipali shiver underneath her cotton sari. She glanced at the big, black and white prints and walked slowly towards the first photograph. So contrived, she thought harshly. So stereotypical. The subject was a young girl, maybe four or five. She was looking straight at the camera. There was blankness in her gaze. In the distance behind her, out of focus, was a blaze. Dipali peered in closer. It looked like a car was on fire. She then read the caption on the photograph: 'My father was a taxi driver'. It dawned on Dipali then. This girl was witnessing her father burning to death in his taxi. Maybe she hadn't realised it just yet. Maybe her mother was beyond the frame, screaming. Who knows? The photographer knew. She turned to look at him. Gandharv Mallik. She could make him out, standing with a camera in his hands. He was talking to Moushumi, their shared friend.

She moved to the next photograph. It was a scene at a railway station. All the people in the photograph stood crushed against each other. As if they all wanted to be in the frame. There were arms, legs, hands, and feet everywhere. The mouths were open, spewing out rancid breath, abuses and wails. The eyes wide – fear, anger, desperation. The people were all trying to get into the train. A baby was frozen in mid-air. Someone had just flung the baby high when the camera snapped the action. The baby was meant to go into the train. But into whose arms? There was no face in the compartment who was seeking that baby. No arms uplifted to catch the baby. What happened after the camera clicked?

Gandharv had his arm around Moushumi They were laughing at something he had just said. Suddenly these pictures disturbed Dipali. Gandharv Mallik didn't seem to be affected by his subjects. He was laughing in this air-conditioned art gallery. Drinking chai in a glass. Flirting with her best friend. But what happened to that baby? Did he know? Did he care to know? She would ask him.

Moushumi brought her over and introduced them. 'Dipali,' she gushed. 'I'd like you meet Gandharv. I knew him in Calcutta. But then he ran away to Mumbai to become famous!'

Gandharv rolled his eyes at her then offered his hand to Dipali. 'Not the best of introductions, I'm afraid. But Mou has always been like that. Nice to meet you, Dipali.'

Dipali smiled and shook his hand stiffly. It was warm in spite of the freezing room. 'What happened to the baby in that picture?' she asked, motioning to the photograph with her hands.

Gandharv turned to look. His smile vanished. He studied the picture quietly, and it seemed like he was transported to that moment when he had shot the frame. 'The baby vanished inside the train,' he said. 'I don't know if it survived. I was nearly crushed in that mob, and I had to escape.'

'It,' she stressed, 'was a girl.' She pointed to the little ribbon tied to the hair. Then she turned to the other photograph. 'Did the girl understand her father was burning inside that taxi?'

'No, that taxi in the background isn't her father's.' Gandharv walked over to the photograph and read the caption. 'Her father's corpse is actually below the frame. Covered in a white cloth. But I didn't want to show that. I wanted the metaphor only. And the blankness in the girl's eyes.'

Dipali nodded silently. 'It's the '92 riots, isn't it?'

Gandharv nodded.

'My husband was killed in the bomb blasts that followed,' Dipali stated, looking straight at him. 'I wish a photographer would have caught his last moments, before he died.'

The air-conditioning hummed loudly. Then Dipali walked over to see the rest of the exhibits. A eunuch, standing by the Bandra Station traffic lights. It was a close-up of the eunuch's face, lined and unshaven. He had flowers in his hair, but they were drooping. His eyes were wet. A black streak was running down his uneven cheek. In the reflection in his eyes, Dipali could see flames. There was such beauty in the photograph. Such a horror of what the people of Mumbai had been subjected to. The terror. The sorrow. The resignation. 'It's a very telling photograph,' Dipali said, turning to Gandharv. 'You are very good, I must say. You bring out the emotions of your subject very well.'

'Thank you,' said Gandharv, somewhat subdued. He didn't apologise for Dipali's loss and she was thankful for that. She was tired of having to respond matter-of-factly to her greatest tragedy when people, strangers even, tried to grasp her hand and proclaim, I'm so sorry, and then continue with the conversation like nothing had happened.

'Do you always take such sad photographs?' she asked.

'Are they sad?' Gandharv asked. 'They are reality.'

Dipali looked at him, eyebrows raised. 'Why, it's all death and destruction. How can it be anything else?'

'But that is reality. There's nothing happy or sad about reality. Things are just how they must be, given the situation. It is how we perceive them, happy or sad.'

'So how can this photo of the girl above her father's corpse be anything but sad?' she challenged.

'Not happy, I'm sure. But that's how I translated the picture. The reality is that maybe it turned out better for her. He used to beat her. She escaped that.'

Dipali flinched. She knew that feeling. 'She told you so?'

'No, but the neighbours did. They said it could be a blessing in disguise.'

'And where is she now?'

'She's with her step-father. And she's a happy young woman.'

Dipali looked up, surprised. 'How do you know?'

'I visited their house again. The neighbours told me.'

'You went back?'

Gandharv nodded, but he looked very embarrassed. 'I was just interested to know...'

'Do you have any happy photographs?'

Gandharv nodded. 'They are at home.'

'Oh, I see.'

'They mean happiness to me. They may not mean anything to you.'

Dipali needed to get away. She didn't want to be standing close to him any longer. It felt too intimate, inhaling his scent and arguing with him. Moushumi jumped up to follow her.

'No, you stay,' Dipali commanded. 'Catch up with your friend. I just need to be alone.'

CR

Dipali looked at the fading light outside her bedroom window. How life had changed over the years. She had spent her childhood in this room, left it only to become a wife. Then she returned a widow. The bed was the same. The walls still bore testimony of her girlhood boredom in the sly graffiti hidden in dark corners. The mango tree still cast the same shadows across the room. But she was a different person.

This evening with Gandharv had been so refreshing. Of course, Moushumi's friendship was what had brought a new meaning to her life. But today she realised how much she missed a man's presence. He had been so interesting to talk to and in spite of her accusatory behaviour, he had been very patient in answering all her questions. She sat back on her bed, thinking of his photographs. Thinking of his eyes that witnessed the atrocities he had recorded. Thinking of his fingers that froze the images forever. Was Sunil a subject in a photographer's film? His torn body? His bloodied face? His Longines watch?

Dipali went to her wardrobe. Her hand shook as she tried to fit the key into the lock. Why was she doing this? She wondered. Punishing herself? What good would it do to go through the pain again? She stopped, her head was throbbing. She knew the answer. It was because she had to remind herself that she belonged to someone else. Being with that.

With renewed force, she swung open the safe. She felt around its dark corners for the box. Gandharv today had made her forget her misery for a few moments. It made her feel guilty that she had enjoyed his company, their conversation. She needed to punish herself for finding that pleasure. She couldn't relax until she held the box. Even now its cold metallic touch made her fingers jump as if it was burnt. She took it out. It shone in the fluorescent light. She opened it. The watch lay inside. She touched its shattered glass. Her fingers ran down the silver strap. Still gleaming. The numbers were stylish. The hands pointed solemnly to the time. Other hands pointed to the date: the 12th of March, a Friday.

She remembered the day well. But how she longed to forget. If only there was a pill, to make one forget. Most of all she could remember her screams. Screams that shook the walls. Screams that wanted to reach him, wherever he was, to let him know that he had deserted her. She wanted to forget her anger. Her anger towards his betrayal. Her anger for him dying on her like that.

Dipali closed her eyes. Her breath came in short gasps. She sank to the floor, still clutching the watch. It slipped out of her grasp and fell on the floor. Dipali fell beside it, drawing up her legs to her chest. She shivered and cried noiselessly. It was like the dam breaking. The walls that she had carefully constructed brick by brick, stone by stone over the years came crashing down.

She longed to feel Sunil's touch on her body. His breath in her ear. She covered her face with her hands. The warmth of a loved one in the same bed was what she wanted. That night, she wanted Sunil as she had never wanted him before. But her arms were empty, and the bed was cold. There was a world out there where women sought pleasure in the arms of another woman. Who was the unfortunate one? They, who never experienced the love of a man, or she, who had had it snatched away from her at its peak? Dipali fell asleep at last, unable to find any answers.

They were in a garden. Flowers of all colours and fragrances filled her vision. Stone statues sprang from the grass. All in classical poses, of dancers, musicians, lovers, their bodies in motion, hands and feet moving. Long fingers strumming on lutes. Voluptuous bodies entwined in passion. She was dressed in pink. A chiffon sari that barely stayed on her. Her footsteps tinkled as she walked. The silver anklet glistened in the moonlight. He was waiting for her by the pool. He reached for her, and she came to him easily, her body moulding into his. He kissed her and she wanted more. She moaned, arching her body at the touch. Such yielding lips. The smell of roses overwhelming her.

She stretched out her hands, wanting to press him to her. But dark eyes looked back at her. Where was Sunil? Who was this? He had gone, and in his place was another silhouette. His curly head bent down to kiss her. It was Gandharv.

Dipali jumped up, her body clammy with sweat. She looked around frantically. She was alone. Yet, her body was tingling. Her stomach was taut. Her lips twitched. She ran her fingers through her hair. Her scalp was damp. Slowly, her breathing returned to normal. A dream, she thought. It's only a dream.

She got out of bed and walked to the window. The moon had disappeared. The streetlight shone on a beggar sleeping on the pavement. All the houses around were quiet. She sipped some water from the carafe. The silence was broken by the thwack of the night watchman's stick. Jagte raho. Stay alert; he called out his daily slogan. That was his duty, patrolling the streets and reassuring the dozing citizens that he was awake, so they could rest peacefully. She couldn't see him, but his shadow stretched long and angular on the wall.

Jagte raho, Dipali whispered. She walked back to her bed, and adjusted the sheets. Jagte raho, the watchman echoed into the night. She closed her eyes and slipped into a dreamless sleep.

8

He called her. Dipali held the receiver tightly with her sweating hands. He sounded nervous, because he had asked Moushumi for the number, and he wasn't sure if Dipali would feel offended. She stammered, No, it was fine. She wasn't offended. Instead, she felt euphoria mixed with dread. He had called her. What did he want? What did she want?

Over the past week, since they had met, she hadn't been able to stop thinking about him. His voice, his profile, his laugh. She had never expected him to call.

He asked if she'd like to have coffee with him. He said they had left their conversation incomplete. She said yes, she had felt the same way too.

Dipali was shocked at her answer. Did she seem desperate? She hoped she sounded sane and not over-excited. What should she wear? What should she talk about? She didn't sleep that night, tossing and turning as dreams of her spilling coffee on him, while he looked on helplessly haunted her. He hadn't invited Moushumi. So was this technically a date?

They met in town. Dipali insisted on it. She didn't want him picking her up from home, her mother meeting him. He was dressed in a khadi shirt, jeans and open-toed sandals. He beamed at her when she stepped out of the train. She smiled back and panicked. There was no way back now.

They walked across the maidan, the grass mown with precision and springy to the touch. They passed by Rajabai tower, a replica of Big Ben built during the Raj, which precisely at that moment, rang out its five o'clock chime.

'Did you know that the Rajabai Tower was named after a blind Jain woman?' Gandharv said. '—Premchand Roychand, the man who founded the Bombay Stock Exchange, funded the entire construction of this tower. On the single condition that it be named after his mother.'

'He must have really loved her.'

'She was a blind woman. And being a staunch Jain follower would always eat her meal before sunset. The chimes from the Rajabai Tower helped her know the time, and she never had to depend on anyone for that.'

'Wow, he must have been super rich to build his mother such an exclusive alarm clock,' Dipali smiled.

He laughed and Dipali got goosebumps all over. Keep calm, she said to herself. Concentrate on what he says. Don't make a fool of yourself.

'So you are a photographer full-time? If Dipali kept talking, or better, kept him talking he wouldn't realise how flustered she was. 'And a historian by hobby? You seem to know a lot of Mumbai trivia.'

'I'm a creative director at Moonworks, the ad agency. I quit Hindustan Thomson Calcutta and came to Mumbai. You see, Jehangir Art Gallery accepted my work to be exhibited five years ago. I was on the waiting list that long, can you believe it? So I thought, why not make a career move?'

'But the pictures in the exhibition don't really come within advertising work, do they?'

'No, of course not. But that's my passion. Photography. But it is an expensive hobby. I take photos for money to pay for my photos for passion. One day I will switch over, when I have my portfolio ready. This exhibition is the big opportunity, you know. And the history bits I looked up to impress you.'

They manoeuvred themselves onto the footpath again, squeezing past people and speeding cars to get to the other side of the road. Gandharv guided her across, not really touching, but she could sense his hand behind her back.

'But,' he continued, 'I'd really like to get to know you, if you don't mind. I really enjoyed our – little argument, shall we say?'

'I suppose so. Don't get me wrong, Gandharv. I'm a little awkward around people... men. I never went out with anyone except my husband.'

'I'm truly sorry about what happened, Dipali,' he said. 'The loss of an innocent life. How shameful for this country to allow such things to happen.'

'You've seen a lot,' Dipali said. 'You know what I appreciate about your photos?'

He waited for her to answer. 'It's that you never took photos of the dead. Or the dying. We never see the indignity of their death. Or their suffering. We see those who are left behind. Their pain. Because we can relate with that. One doesn't have to look at hands sticking out of the rubble or charred bodies lying unattended on the streets. That is also much appreciated. Thank you.'

'You're welcome Dipali,' he smiled. 'Do you know why I called you up and asked you out so quickly?'

'No,' Dipali said. Don't be disappointed. He wants me to be his subject.

'I'm sorry if I've been too forward. I wanted to get to know you better. I'd like to see you again, if that's alright, because life's too short to go around in circles.'

‌CR

Moushumi poured two cups of tea. Miss Lalkaka, her landlady, was sitting in her planter's chair, feet propped up on a low stool. Often, Moushumi had tea with her after school. The old lady had no relatives. Some women from the agiary would visit her at the weekends and pray with her, gossip and guzzle tea and Parle-G biscuits, best dipped in tea for a melt-in-your-mouth experience and denture friendly too. But weekdays she was all alone. Her mind was fading, so sometimes she forgot who Moushumi was. Other days, she chatted with her lucidly. Talked about her younger days in Surat. On the days when her mind was elsewhere, Moushumi talked to her about her life in Calcutta. It was easier that way. Listening to her own voice telling her story was comforting. She was reliving those days with her parents.

There was a telephone in this house. She could use it any time. But would they respond to her? She was too afraid to test it out.

After meeting Gandharv, Moushumi found herself getting depressed more frequently. He had known her in Calcutta. He'd been to some of the parties she and Jasmine had attended as a couple. He knew. He wasn't judgemental. But he didn't ask her too many questions about her life here. Was she with someone? How was she after the break up?

The telephone. Moushumi stared at it. Just ten numbers and she would be able to hear her mother's voice. Or father's. She excused herself and went towards it. If she didn't call, she wouldn't know. They could be ecstatic to hear her voice.

Forgive her, rejoice in her calling and ask her to return. Or not. She hesitated. If she didn't call, they wouldn't be able to reject her. Wouldn't that be safer, not knowing?

She dialled the numbers and waited. Someone answered immediately. Moushumi jumped at the shrill sound from the other end. 'Hello? Helloooo?'

She smiled. It was Poltu, her nephew. She listened to his voice, longing to caress his unruly hair. She could see him jumping up and down with the phone in his hand. There was laughter and the chink of cups and saucers. 'Poltu?' She whispered.

'Who is it? Give me the phone,' Moushumi's heard her father speak.

'No, Dadu, it's for me,' Poltu said. 'I want to talk, I want to talk.'

'Now, be a good boy and give it to Dadu.'

'But she said my name,' Poltu argued.

'Who did?' Moushumi's mother's voice came through.

'Moumashi.'

Moushumi's heart pounded. Would her father take it?

There was a silence on the other end. Then her father's voice. 'You mustn't talk to strangers, Poltu.'

There was a click and a buzz. He had disconnected her. Moushumi placed the receiver down carefully. Mrs Lalkaka was smiling at her, nodding her head from side to side with biscuit sludge sticking to her chin. Moushumi forced a smile and returned to her seat.

'Now, where were we?' She asked the old lady. She wiped her running nose and nodded to the chattering woman but her hands were shaking too much to hold her cup to her lips.

CR

'Have you thought of marrying again?' Moushumi asked Dipali casually, while eating bhel outside the school gates. Teachers did not usually stand in the open eating from roadside hawkers. A few students giggled and pointed at them. A couple of teachers gawked and then shook their heads with disapproval.

Dipali concentrated on her spicy bhel, sweat beads forming on her forehead, as the sea breeze blew in towards them, sending their saris fluttering at their feet. She had never considered it, even when her mother-in-law had gently hinted that she should have that as an option. But now, both were dead, and her brother was not going to give her away easily.

'You should, you know,' Moushumi said, and licked a stray puffed rice from the side of her lip.

They finished eating in silence and then paid the bhelwalla. They usually parted at the gate, Dipali taking the school bus home and Moushumi riding her scooter back to Parel. But today Dipali didn't hop on to the bus after the snack. She lingered behind Moushumi.

Moushumi led her to her scooter. 'Come on, sit down on my racehorse. I've called her Dhanno, the horse who saves women from villains, aka, men in *Sholay*. Let's go for a drive.'

'She suits you to a tee,' Dipali giggled and stroked the pink scooter. 'She's a fine breed.'

'Chal, Dhanno, chal,' shouted Moushumi, kickstarting the scooter. 'Drive away from this maze of cars. Save your mistress from the clutches of men.'

They laughed hysterically as Moushumi edged and pushed her way through the numerous cars that had bottle-necked the narrow lane outside the school.

'Oh, these rich kids,' she fumed. 'Everyone has their own

air-conditioned car to pick them up. The school ought to have rules as to how many cars can wait outside. It's a crime.'

They drove out into the main road. It was like a tributary joining the main river. Except, this river was not going anywhere. The cars stood still, the harsh sun bouncing off their tops and there was no gentle gurgle of water, only a loud din of horns blaring, drivers shouting, the useless traffic policeman whistling and children squealing and shouting. Moushumi put her hands to her ears dramatically. She let out a silent scream.

'I wonder what Edvard Munch would have thought of this?'

'Who's that?' Dipali squinted in the sun. 'Another artist friend of yours?'

This would take a while. She balanced on the back seat, gathering her sari close to her and holding on to Moushumi, whose helmet was lopsided and Dipali reached out to adjust it.

'No, silly. He was an artist alright. But he died years before you and I came along. He's famous for *The Scream*, you know, like I just did.'

'Oh yes, that terrible ghostly face in a swirly whirly landscape?'

'Yes, that's the one. Though it may have been a one-off in his country, that's the expression most of us have in Mumbai every day.'

Dipali nodded in agreement. That seemed to be her permanent state.

'See what I have to face each day?' Moushumi complained. 'Saala gaandu, seedha chal!' she yelled to the driver in the next car, who was trying to edge his way into her lane.

Dipali cringed at Moushumi's choice of words, but she had a mischievous smile on her face. 'Saala gaandu,' she repeated, savouring the sound of the expletive. 'Mou, only you can say it with absolute class!'

She turned to look at the driver it had been aimed at. His mouth was hanging open. He couldn't return the abuse, even if he wanted to, because his very angry madam was sitting at the back, shaking her fist at Moushumi.

Moushumi blew her a kiss and laughed. The woman looked away, muttering.

Dipali tried to hide from the woman's vision by ducking away. 'Really, Mou, you should control yourself. You'll get into trouble one day.'

Moushumi carried on beeping and manoeuvring her way out of the traffic. They drove towards Jogger's Park. Whenever Moushumi gave Dipali a lift home, they'd sit in Jogger's Park for a while and chat. It was a ritual to have fresh coconut water by the gate and look through the crowd to spot any film stars. There were a couple of regulars, and by now, the two had lost interest in the glamorous people that dotted the well-known celebrity spot.

The sun was still quite strong at four o'clock. There were very few people in the park at this hour. The children usually came after five, the office-goers after six or seven. Now was the time for lovers to hide in the bushes and snatch a few embraces. Or for the college students playing truant, to laugh raucously and embarrass the poor lovers in their leafy retreats. A few maids would sun themselves before their babas and babies got back from school to bully them. But mostly the park was empty, as one had to pay to get in, and it was too hot to pay money and sweat it out here. The cinema nearby was air-conditioned, and tired salesmen tended to make their way there to sleep through the afternoon.

Moushumi located a parking space easily. They went in and found a bench in a nice, shady nook.

Dipali soon broke the silence: 'I don't think I can marry

again.' She fidgeted with her handbag, and tried to avoid looking at the lovers reclining on the rocks by the shoreline.

'Why not?' Moushumi asked, as she popped a Chiclet in her mouth. She offered another chewing gum to Dipali, carefully prising it out of its plastic bubble packaging. 'You are still young, you know. You don't have to go through life all alone.'

Dipali nodded. 'I know what you are trying to tell me. But I can't, Mou. It's too soon.'

'Too soon? What's holding you back? You know someone is very interested in you.'

Dipali blushed and looked away. Yes, she too was attracted to him. But this was not the time to flirt with a man and see if it worked out. She was a widow. She had to be sensible.

'You know Gandharv likes you. You shouldn't shut him out,' Moushumi persisted.

'What makes you think he wants to marry me?' Dipali asked. 'We've only just met. He's younger than me as well. He can surely find women closer to his age.'

'True, true. I'm not jumping to conclusions. It could be him or anyone else. My question is, have you thought of marrying again?' Moushumi asked. 'Gandharv is only the first step.'

First step to what? Moushumi wouldn't understand. Dipali was not good at making choices. At first, her father decided on her life. Then her brother Ashish chose a husband for her. Later she relied on Sunil to show her the way. And now, back to Ashish. She was not used to thinking about her priorities, her needs.

'Tell me the truth, Dipali. Do you want him?'

Dipali looked at her, helplessly. She didn't know what to say. Of course she was attracted to him. She loved it when he looked at her. She loved the shape of his hands and the way they moved when he was talking. She loved his photography. His delicate fingers. His perfect fingernails. She loved it when he absently moved a hair away from her face. She could feel the touch of his finger on her forehead hours later. She loved his voice. She loved it when he took the time to explain something she wanted an explanation to. Gandharv was the reason why she now took care in how she dressed. Or how she smelled. Was she attracted to him? God, yes. 'No,' she said simply. 'It's too soon.'

'You're such a liar, Dips.' Moushumi ran a finger down Dipali's arm. 'Just thinking of him gives you goosebumps. I wouldn't blame you. I guess he has that effect on most women.'

'That's just it, Mou. He can have any woman he wants to. He has that power. That... that sexuality thing. He's just too sexy for words. And he has all these beautiful women he has to deal with. His models. His clients. All these high-society babes. So why would he even bother with me?'

'You are right, you know,' Moushumi said in mock seriousness. 'He could have anyone. Then why does he ask me about you? Why does he show up in places where you are present? Why did the two of you find yourselves a cosy corner at the last two art launches we went to?'

Gandharv did make her feel very special in those few times they had met. But maybe that's a game he played with women, till he conquered them.

But it hadn't felt like that at all.

Lately, Dipali felt like a thief in her own house, waiting for her mother to retire into her room so she could smuggle the telephone into her room and wait. Gandharv called at night, when he was in bed too, she imagined. They'd talk about photography; Dipali realised it was his life. He loved to debate about the brain drain in India. Half the people they knew lived in the States. She talked about her work, Moushumi, never of her marriage. He talked about photography, his experiences in Mumbai, never about his childhood.

'Anyway,' Dipali shook away the thoughts. 'I don't think my family will approve of him. I am responsible for looking after my mother.'

'Dipali!' Moushumi shrieked. 'What is it with you? Are you trying to play Mother Teresa or what? You are no saint, I can tell you that. Your brother is just treating you like his bloody servant. To look after your mother. So that he and his wife don't have to do it and can enjoy their lives. And that's the truth of it.'

'Mou, it's not easy to break away. You did it, but I could not. I've always obeyed, or had to pay the price for my freedom.' Dipali turned away to face the sea. How she wished she could scream out her frustration. But she spoke in a controlled voice, one she had learned to use since she was a child.

'You didn't have a didactic father or brother. Every single command I couldn't disobey. Sunil changed all of that. He made me feel special. Or rather, normal. Not under someone's thumb all the time. But he died. The hero died, not the villain. So the damsel in distress remains so. Back to being ground under the brother's thumb.'

'You sound like a TV serial, Dipali,' Moushumi replied. 'I'm not buying into it. You don't have to be a doormat, especially now. You are young, you deserve a full life. Not just fading away in your mother's house, babysitting and all that while your brother washes his hands of all responsibilities. You are the perfect scapegoat for him.'

'Easier said than done, Mou. You don't know what it is like

to not be considered a worthwhile person. Especially if you've been brought up like that.'

'Then break away from the chains. Gandharv is the perfect opportunity. Do it. Let us go away somewhere for the weekend. To hatch plans.' Moushumi's eyes turned to slits and she licked her lips. 'To plan your escape into the big, wide world.'

9

'Would you like some tea?' Gandharv asked. 'I thought we could just enjoy this evening outside before we have to go in.'

He led Dipali to the theatre's outdoor café. The gulmohur trees canopied above, their red petals floating down to the ground. Pink bougainvillea creepers climbed the walls, showering pink petals. There was a heady fragrance of roses merging with the earthy aroma of coffee beans. The sun dipped behind the trees, leaving an orange glow on the horizon. The crows returned noisily to their nests. By now the café was filling up. People stopped for a quick drink before going inside. Women in elegant saris and coiffed hair walked beside men in kurtas or crisply-ironed shirts. Teenagers loped past in scraggy trainers, shoulders drooping. Groups of young girls giggled and eyed young men from over the tops of their tall Irish coffees. These young men preened; their muscles straining under their tight black t-shirts.

'It will be packed to capacity,' said Dipali, breaking the silence. Gandharv nodded. 'It's a popular play.'

'I hope you didn't mind me asking you to come?' Gandharv said. He reached inside his kurta pocket and drew out a pack of cigarettes. 'May I?' he asked. 'I won't get a chance to smoke inside.'

Dipali nodded. 'I'm so glad, actually, that you did. I've never been to the theatre before.'

'No?' Gandharv asked, astonished. 'Never? C'mon, you must have, sometime.'

'Never. My husband was a movie buff.'

'But what about in college? With friends? Family?' Gandharv lit his cigarette as the waiter brought the bill. There were enough people waiting to occupy the tables, so sitting around was not encouraged. Gandharv ignored both and took a deep drag of nicotine.

'I— I didn't go out much in college. My father was very strict.' Dipali said. She coughed, embarrassed, not wishing to talk more about herself. But Gandharv leaned forward, and waited for her to continue.

'What do you mean?' He asked. 'You weren't allowed to go out to the cinema even?'

'No,' Dipali said; she sipped her tea quietly. 'I did not have a very memorable childhood. That's all. I had to do whatever my father said I should do. He was very strict.'

'How strict?' Gandharv asked. 'Or is it too painful to talk about?'

'No, no. I mean, yes. It was quite painful. He had problems. Very violent temper and all that. But it's okay. My husband, you know, Sunil— he helped me get over the issues I've had about my childhood. I'm okay.'

'You sure?'

Dipali nodded. She hoped she wouldn't start crying now. Mentioning her father or Sunil were surefire methods to become tearful, and she didn't want their first serious date to be ruined.

'We'll talk about it another time, Gandharv,' she said. 'Tonight let's just enjoy this play. I always wanted to be an actress. I've

170

performed so many brilliant acts in front of the mirror, but never watched a real play. Did you ever do any acting in college?'

'I did, in fact,' said Gandharv. He laughed. 'My acting skills weren't recognised though. But my friend, Jeet, is a star. He is in tonight's play, by the way. He's just amazing. Come, I think we should go in.'

They walked into the theatre. At the door, two young women ran towards Gandharv. One was in a short denim skirt and a black top. A necklace with enormous opals hung round her neck. The other was more of a classical beauty. She had thick dark hair, right down to her hips. Dipali felt quite inadequate in her simple chikan churidar kameez and oxidised silver earrings.

Even though Gandharv was dressed simply in a kurta and jeans, he still looked very desirable. 'Hello ladies,' he said to them. 'Meet Dipali.'

'Hi, Dipali,' the mini-skirted girl's pink gums showed when she smiled. 'I'm Dia.'

'And I'm Lekha, Chitralekha,' said the other.

'We're his colleagues,' they both said together and burst out giggling. It was clear they had massive crushes on him. 'We're in creative too. Work experience at the moment.'

Gandharv looked embarrassed at their silliness. 'I think the play's about to start,' he said.

'Yes,' said Lekha, adjusting her sari. 'You guys go ahead. We'll be there in a bit.'

'You didn't say we had company,' Dipali said. 'I wouldn't have come then. I don't want to intrude.'

'What are you saying, Dipali?' he said. 'Of course they're not here with us. They're here on their own.'

She felt so foolish, trying to claim possession of him. 'I'm sorry, Gandharv. I really am. I'm just really nervous.'

He gently squeezed her elbow. 'Don't worry about it,' he said, leading her to their seats. 'Don't let these silly girls bother you. I'm all yours tonight.'

It was a very poignant play. Only two characters and their letters, spanning five decades of their lives. There were no props, just a few boxes that divided the space or opened it up, whatever the actors decided to do with them. Gandharv's friend was the male actor. He was tall and pleasantly handsome. Not the Bollywood hunk at all. Rather thin and wiry, like Sunil. The woman was fiery and tactile. Ready with her sharp tongue and passion for the hero. Opposite personalities, thought Dipali. But they moulded so well together.

They were seated on wooden steps, as this theatre was not of the traditional type. If they wanted to, the people on the last step could reach out and touch the actors. The ceiling was covered with little pinpoints of light. Like starlight. Dipali shivered and instinctively Gandharv put his arm around her. 'You're cold,' he whispered. She nodded and moved in, closing her eyes. She listened to the actors read out their letters of passion, of hurt, of consolation, of love for each other. She liked the timbre of the man's voice, so comforting. As if he was reading it out for her ears only. She leaned her face on Gandharv's chest. She could feel his heart beating. His breath fell on her hair and he gently caressed her arm. Dipali felt a rush of goose bumps on her skin. The actors were now far away, talking as if in another room. She held his hand. Not caring about anything else in the world. The dark theatre gave her the confidence to reach out to him. They watched the rest of the play this way and Dipali moved away only when he bent his head to reach for a kiss.

10

The cinema opposite Moushumi's room showed C-grade Hindi films. Usually horror films, an excuse to show the heroine with bared breasts cringing from a monster. Or action thrillers, the heroine with bared breasts, cringing from a serial killer. It amused her to see the queues lining up to watch these films. They were almost always men. Sometimes women accompanied these men, probably forced to view the films with their boyfriends or husbands. There was an Irani restaurant flanking the cinema. It served a good brun pav chai special. And kheema parathas. A treat for the waiting crowds to chomp on the mince-stuffed flatbreads or sip the sharp masala tea and crisp rolls.

As Moushumi sat down for her evening cup of tea, she heard a commotion from the streets. She ran to the window. A group of women stood outside the cinema, waving rolling pins and chanting.

'We want equality, down with pornography.'

The posters on the walls of the cinema featured a buxom woman clad in a wet white sari, full lips half open. She leaned against a man with a bushy moustache and broad shoulders. The name of the film was *Ek Raat ki Kahani* (The Story of One Night). There were several smaller pictures surrounding the larger one. The woman lying on the ground, a man pulling off her sari. The woman, dancing in front of leering men. All the while, she was barely dressed, her big breasts pushing out of her blouse, thighs exposed.

The protesters then started to hit the big poster frames and tear the pictures with their nails. A policeman tried to stop them but they pushed him aside. A few women got very agitated and shouted at him in Marathi. The constable retreated.

A few men gathered, smirking and enjoying the scene. A bell rang within the interiors of the cinema hall and soon a crowd trickled out. The women pounced on them, hitting them with rolling pins.

'Perverts,' they screamed.

'Rapists,' yelled another woman holding up a hockey stick.

The men who emerged from the darkness blinked, their pleasure immediately wiped out by the raging women. They cowered. Some ran, a trail of women and sticks and stones following them. A police jeep screamed into view. Many police constables jumped out, waving their batons. The women scattered. Some remained to argue with the police, who threatened to arrest them.

Moushumi watched, at first with amusement and then with growing concern. She didn't know with whom to side. The women, who self-righteously claimed that the film was degrading women. Or should she side with the film, which, by being a means of release for these men, possibly prevented them from committing sexual crimes in reality. They probably jerked off in the cinema, giving vent to their sexual frustrations. She was in a quandary. Would these women lunge for her throat if they knew she was a lesbian. Instead of fighting against the men and their entertainment, they ought to fight for their sexual expression and freedom.

She thought of Jasmine, as she often did when she was alone. Was she sleeping with someone else? When she lived in Calcutta, she'd scan the newspapers to read anything that mentioned Nandkumar Ghoshal or Page Three parties. She had seen Jasmine's photographs in the papers a few times. There was always some woman close to her. Moushumi could tell they were in a relationship. How could her husband not see what was happening? Those pictures always made her feel ill.

The shouts from below brought Moushumi back to the present. She looked at the vandalised posters scattered on the pavement. The woman with the torn clothes was now ripped to pieces, her body parts flying in different directions in the wind.

Her thoughts went back to Jasmine. The cruel one. Who taunted her and taught her all the same. And then to the woman on the train who had propositioned her. What had she said? Friday nights at the Razzmatazz? She ran to the telephone and found the phone number. She punched the buttons and waited for the call to be answered.

'Gandharv?' she said urgently. 'What are you doing tonight?'

ଦ

Gandharv and Moushumi pulled up outside the nightclub at about nine o'clock. They walked across the gravel driveway, which was lined with rooms on either side. Can be rented by the hour, Moushumi was told at the reception when she asked. She glanced quickly at Gandharv who looked the other way.

'Why are we here?' he muttered.

'Please,' Moushumi begged him. 'I couldn't come here alone. Call me a coward, but I simply couldn't. And I couldn't think of anyone else to help me out.'

Gandharv shook his head. 'You'll get yourself into trouble one day, Mou.'

'No, I won't. I promise. I need some questions answered, Gandharv.'

'And you will find them here?' He spread his hand to point out the place to her. It was not like the posh nightclubs she visited in Calcutta. This was seedy. They entered and were immediately assaulted by the loud trance music. Disco lights flashed across the floor, baring UV-lit teeth and eyes like ghosts and vampires. The space was engulfed in cigarette smoke. There was a stage. Moushumi looked. There were men dancing with men. Some were dressed casually, others in drag. They pressed their chests together and gyrated groin to groin.

'What is this?' Gandharv muttered. 'A gay night?' He clung to the walls of the nightclub, trying to avoid any kind of physical contact with the dancers. 'What are we doing here? Moushumi, answer me.'

But Moushumi was oblivious to him. She was scanning the room. Round and round, her head turned, looking, and searching out. But she could only see men. There were women too, but usually in the arms of other men. Mostly though, it seemed that all the gay men in town had turned up. They sauntered to the bar, they gyrated on the stage, they simpered in their lovers' ears. She clutched Gandharv's clammy hands and looked nervously at him. He frowned at her.

She dragged him to a corner and held him close. 'Will you listen to me, Gandharv?'

He nodded.

'A couple of weeks back I met... I mean, a woman asked me out,' Moushumi gulped. Gandharv didn't stir. 'She mentioned this place.'

'So you've come here?' Gandharv asked.

'She said she comes here on Friday nights. Gay nights.'

'Mou, is this what you want?' Gandharv asked. 'Looking for a lesbian lover in the dark? In a nightclub?'

'What else can I do?' Moushumi pleaded. 'I don't know where I can find someone.'

'Well, certainly not here.' Gandharv dragged her out of the nightclub. 'Please Mou, get a grip on yourself. We can talk about it, you know.'

She was crying now. Once again, her father's curses rang in her ears. When would she be freed of her demons?

Gandharv led her to the lawns of the nightclub. Deck chairs and round tables were scattered around the garden. A few people were sitting drinking, talking in hushed tones, and breaking into laughter occasionally. They chose the furthest table and ordered a bottle of rum. 'Come on Mou, pull yourself up. Let's talk about it for once.' He held out a cigarette for her.

'I'm so tired,' Moushumi said finally after taking a few deep drags of the cigarette. 'All I want is to have a proper relationship. Is that so hard to find?'

'It is, Mou. And what makes you think it's difficult just for you?'

'What do you mean?'

'Look at me. Have I found anyone?'

'Don't say that to me. There are women literally falling over each other to offer themselves to you.'

'What makes you think that, Mou?'

The waiter arrived with their drinks and a bowl of soggy chips. Gandharv poured the drinks and handed Moushumi a glass.

'It is obvious. Don't fool me.'

'Maybe, Mou. But have you wondered? Do I really want them? I too want to love a woman, but I haven't met the right person yet.'

Moushumi raised an eyebrow. Gandharv sipped his drink and looked down at his glass. He pulled out two cigarettes and offered one to Moushumi.

'Well, anyway, we're here to talk about you, not me,' he said.

'Yes, so what are you trying to tell me?'

'I'm saying, it doesn't matter if you are straight or gay, one still needs to find the right person. That doesn't mean I go sleeping around to find the right person or trawl through nightclubs or whatever. You've got to be patient.'

Moushumi clicked her tongue impatiently. 'But that's where you don't get it. See, there are women everywhere. You need to be lucky to find Miss Right. But there aren't lesbians everywhere. How do I know if one is first of all a lesbian, forget Miss Right?'

'You will find her. You found Jasmine once.'

Moushumi winced and Gandharv reached out and touched her hand. 'You will find the right person. Just have patience, and don't jump into crazy things.'

She finished her glass and poured herself another strong drink. 'I need to get drunk tonight, solid drunk,' she said and smiled at Gandharv. He laughed and sank into his chair.

'Fine, I'll just get comfortable then.' They finished their drinks simultaneously and then Moushumi started on the next. She asked Gandharv about his feelings for Dipali, but he evaded her questions. This night is about you, he repeated. She teased him, asking what if Dipali became her lover, would he feel bad?

Gandharv looked away, and didn't answer her. He drank steadily with her. They watched couples stagger out of the club. There were women leaning heavily on their partner's arms. Some tottered to the rooms and shut the doors. There were men too, who came out on the arms of other men. Some shouted and whooped with joy, hugging their partners tight. Some came out stealthily, looking furtively before disappearing into cars. It was close to midnight. Nearly closing time.

Moushumi staggered to her feet and held out her hand. 'Gandharv, just humour me once,' she said. 'Let's have just one dance before we go.'

They went inside. The mood was mellow now. The music had softened to romantic Hindi numbers and slow ballads. Couples held each other close and danced. Moushumi led Gandharv to the dance floor, but her eyes were still searching beyond him. Would she be there? Could she spot her in the thinning crowd? The woman who had propositioned her.

Moushumi's head swam with the effect of the alcohol and cigarettes. She leaned on Gandharv and let him take the lead. They barely moved, only his breath in her ear. She wondered then, what was it like to be loved by a man. What did Dipali have in the past that she missed so much? She put her arms round his neck and pulled his closer. Gandharv resisted, but she tried harder. Perhaps if she tasted what a man had to offer she wouldn't go after a woman again? Isn't that what her sister kept saying to her? Isn't that what kept Jasmine going? A man was required. A man. A man. A man. And here she was, in the arms of a very desirable man. She shut her eyes and imagined his lips on hers. 'Kiss me,' she whispered to Gandharv. He stiffened. She leaned on her toes and brushed his face with her lips.

'And what's that supposed to mean?' He asked. He stepped back and looked at her.

The spell was broken. 'I'm sorry, I just felt— I'm so wasted.' Moushumi muttered with embarrassment.

'I feel you have a lot of thinking to do,' Gandharv said, but he didn't let go of Moushumi. He held her close and stroked her hair. 'You seem to be very confused, Mou.'

Moushumi struggled in his grasp. 'Oh no, I'm not confused.'

'Are you trying to experiment then?' He let go of her. 'Did you want to experiment with me?'

Moushumi lowered her eyes. She felt a bout of nausea rush up to her throat. She staggered and clutched his arm. 'I want to go home.' A sharp sob escaped her, and she covered her mouth in case she retched.

They lurched out into the fresh air and Moushumi collapsed on a plastic chair. Gandharv left her alone and went into a restroom. She wiped her face and tried to calm down. The doors had now opened and people filed out. The nightclub was officially closed.

A group of vociferous people came out, laughing and leaning on each other. Moushumi blinked as she thought she recognised a familiar face. She was leaning on the shoulder of a man, her face animated and happy. Moushumi stepped closer, trying to place the woman. She gasped. It was the woman on the train. She peered through the darkness, trying to gauge who she was leaning on. Again she gasped. For it wasn't a man, but a woman. She was dressed in a golf t-shirt, jeans and running shoes. A thick gold bracelet shone on her wrist in the lamplight. They held hands as they walked down the driveway.

Moushumi realised that she was staring with her mouth open. The woman's partner hailed an auto that was cruising, looking for passengers. She got into an argument with the driver and the woman turned. She looked straight at Moushumi and her eyes narrowed. She leaned forward, as if to get a better look and her eyes lit up in recognition. Moushumi hesitated, unsure whether to respond. The two women got into the auto and it sped off. The woman leaned out of the auto and gave a wave. Moushumi turned away, not wanting to acknowledge her. She didn't want to be propositioned again if they met on the train.

She saw Gandharv coming towards her and felt embarrassed that she had made a pass at him. He must really think of her as a fool. But he came to her and kissed her on the cheek. He rubbed her back lightly and sank into the chair beside her. 'I saw her,' she said to him.

'Who?' Gandharv asked, and then yawned.

'That woman on the train. She was here with another woman.' He didn't react. He played with her fingers and looked up at the sky. Then, suddenly, Gandharv pulled her towards him. He kissed her full on the mouth. Moushumi froze and then slowly she let herself go limp in his arms. It was beautiful, his warmth, his touch. She closed her eyes, feeling his tongue in her mouth. The lazy way he kissed her, deep and slow, was enough to make her knees wobble. But it didn't feel right. Kissing a man felt wrong. And he belonged to her best friend. She pulled away.

'What was that about?' she gasped.

'That,' Gandharv smiled and pecked her on the cheek, 'was something for you to think about long and hard. You wanted it, didn't you? Now you know. Make your own decisions. But don't rush into things with your eyes closed.'

Gandharv dropped her home. Before she disappeared through the main gate, he stopped her. 'And Mou,' he said. 'No need to mention tonight to Dipali, okay?'

Moushumi nodded. 'Of course not, Gandharv. I'm sorry I used you in this manner.'

Gandharv shrugged and lit a cigarette.

'No, I really am. And I promise I will make it up to you.' Moushumi pecked him on his cheek, and then turned towards the gate of her building.

11

'Dipali, you've got to say yes,' Moushumi breathed excitedly down the phone.

'Yes to what?'

'Don't spoil the fun now, say yes.'

'Okay, yes, but what is it?'

Moushumi smiled at her little plan. She would get those two together, no matter to what lengths she'd have to go. She'd seen it in Gandharv's eyes, his feelings for Dipali. And she knew Dipali was attracted to him as well. It was all these blasted complications that got in the way. And she had to make up with Gandharv.

'Cool,' laughed Moushumi. 'Pack your bags, girl. We're going on a holiday.'

She hummed the Cliff Richard tune, which made Dipali giggle even more. They were behaving like a couple of teenagers.

'Where to?'

'Alibaug. A cosy hut right on the beach. Authentic Maharashtrian seafood, um, food in general. Glorious sea. Beer. Fags. Swimsuits. Think about it.'

'Stop it, Mou,' Dipali laughed. 'For how long?'

'That depends how long you are permitted by your mother to stay out,' Moushumi teased Dipali.

'Oh, shut up,' said Dipali. 'My mother doesn't tie me up to a post at home.'

'Hmm, I wouldn't be surprised. So, how long can you make it for?'

'Three days?' Dipali ventured, already trying to think up excuses she'd have to give her mother.

'Bah, too short,' Moushumi exclaimed. 'I'd like five whole days to loll on the sand, float in the sea... not to mention the drive.'

Dipali burst out laughing. 'Drive to Alibaug? Who's driving?'

'The bus driver,' Moushumi said. 'We'll hang out of the window, breathing the non-polluted air. It will be an adventure.'

'I'll be sick on the bus.'

'Bloody hell, Dipali. It's only a couple of hours away. I'm not taking you to Kanyakumari or something. Stop making excuses.'

Dipali's mind went back to another time, when her husband had surprised her with an adventure. A surprise visit to Calcutta for the Hero Cup finals. The thought saddened her. Five years ago, they had been planning another adventure, a trip to the UK. They never made it. But she did get a surprise. A nasty one. She didn't like surprises or adventures anymore. She just wanted an ordinary, safe life.

'Hey, Dipali, are you there? Hello? Hello?'

'Yes, I'm here,' she said. 'Sounds like a plan. Who else is coming?' Dipali asked. Why did she ask that question, she wondered. She was hoping for too much.

'You and me, and the wind and the sea,' Moushumi sang off-tune into the phone.

'Okay. Listen, you book the place. I have to manage my

mother,' Dipali giggled. 'But promise me, you won't sing in the bathroom.'

☙

There was a chill in the air and, already, the Christmas buntings and decorations festooned every inch of the reception area. The resort was designed like a village, with bungalows or cottages scattered in front of the sea. There was even single accommodation in the main building, along with a restaurant and bar.

'The sea, the sea,' Moushumi took a deep breath as she peered out of the cottage window.

'And the stink of the fish drying on the mainland,' Dipali said, wrinkling her nose.

'All natural smells, girl,' Moushumi said. 'No city stench. Oof, I can't stand the stink from the garbage dump outside my flat. Give me the stench of fish any day.'

'Even your previous landlady's fried fish?' Dipali asked slyly.

'Aaarrgh, why did you have to remind me of that?' Moushumi charged towards Dipali, pretending to grab her throat. Dipali laughed and ducked out of the way.

Their cottage had two bedrooms and a lounge. The rooms were gaudy, but they didn't mind. There was an old television set which seemed to have only Doordarshan channels on it.

'Unbelievable,' Moushumi exclaimed, battling with the remote. 'We've paid so much money but no channels on TV other than DD?'

'Good, na, who wants to watch TV? I'm going to sleep on that hammock all day,' Dipali pointed to a lop-sided hammock tied between two stunted palm trees.

'No, I'm going to complain to the manager,' said Moushumi. 'Bloody hell. I want my money's worth.'

'Mou, leave that stupid TV alone. What shall we order for dinner?' She studied the menu. 'God, look at the seafood menu. There's practically no vegetarian food out here.'

'Duh, if you live by the sea, eat from the sea. Do in Rome as Romans do,' said Moushumi.

'Weren't there any veggie Romans?' Dipali asked.

'Dunno, don't care,' Moushumi said, flinging the menu away. 'Come Dips, don't be so morose. Let's enjoy ourselves. Let's go for a walk.'

They strolled the length of the beach. It was low tide, so the sea was quite far out, leaving behind little pools where excited children splashed and explored the marine life. Families sat together on the sand, picnicking on sandwiches or samosas. There were many young couples, dressed in brightly coloured Bermudas, looking more like Siamese twins than lovers.

Dipali and Moushumi walked slowly, taking in the salty breeze, the promise of a fantastic sunset and the companionship they both craved for.

'You know,' Dipali finally said, 'We went to Goa for our honeymoon, it was so beautiful.'

'This cannot compare to Goa,' sniffed Moushumi, untangling seaweed from her toes.

'No, actually, I don't remember much of Goa,' Dipali tried to evoke images of that place, but it felt very distant. 'I was so obsessed with my new husband, I didn't look beyond him.'

'He must have been really cool,' Moushumi took Dipali's hand.

She nodded. 'He was. One couldn't really figure him out. At one moment, he could be so intense, you'd be afraid to talk to him. And another moment, he'd be playing the fool and you'd be horsing around with him too. He was very funny.'

'You poor thing, you were dealt a very harsh card in life.'

Dipali turned to face Moushumi. 'Tell me, Mou, don't you think you too have been dealt a harsh card?'

'What do you mean?'

'I mean, you can't really express your love easily. If you were straight, you'd perhaps be married with kids, not worrying about finding the right woman for you.'

'I see what you mean. No one has it easy, Dipali, no one.' Moushumi stuck her toe in a hole in the sand and teased out a tiny crab. It scuttled away sideways and disappeared into another hole. She ruthlessly chased it from one hole to another for a while. 'I tried, Dipali,' she finally managed to say.

'Tried what?'

'Dipali, please don't get me wrong. I have something to tell you.'

She attempted to make light of the matter. Moushumi told her it was just an experiment for her to see if she could be attracted to a man. But Dipali's thoughts became confused. It's okay, part of her said. He helped her out of a situation by doing that. How dare she? Why use him? How could he? Could he do that to anyone without feeling for that person? Said another. He touched her. He touched her. Maybe this was a cue for her to stop thinking about him.

'I'm sorry,' Moushumi said. 'I didn't know what I was thinking.'

'Why did you tell me?' Dipali asked.

'I didn't want anything to come between our friendship,' Moushumi said. 'I wanted to get it out in the open so that it doesn't come between you and Gandharv later.'

187

Dipali turned to her angrily. 'Come between us? What is there between us? Nothing. Why do you keep pushing him on to me? I don't want him. I don't.' Her voice cracked and betrayed her. The sun silently slipped beyond the horizon, leaving the sky a fiery red.

12

'Hello there.'

It was a voice she recognised. Dipali turned around and looked across the restaurant. And there, framed by the doorway, was Gandharv. He smiled and walked towards their table. After a long and restless night, Dipali and Moushumi were eating a late breakfast. They hadn't talked a lot and Dipali had a headache from thinking too much.

'You planned it,' Dipali said between gritted teeth. 'You knew he was coming here.'

Moushumi hid her face behind her hands. She managed a tiny wave to Gandharv. 'Hello, fancy seeing you here,' she said, but it sounded lame.

'Figured I'd get the best company here,' he said, but he was looking at Dipali.

She looked away. She couldn't stand it any longer. She was so mad at him, at Moushumi. And yet she couldn't help notice his shining eyes, that shy, eager smile and it was hard to feel cross anymore.

'We're shooting here for three days,' he explained to Dipali. 'And Moushumi thought it was a great idea to holiday out here as well.'

'How convenient,' she said sarcastically. 'I'm sure we'll all have a great time.'

At that moment a woman charged into the restaurant, notebook in hand. She had several bangles on her arm that jangled her arrival. She was followed by two almost identical young women, both in t-shirts and hot pants. They struggled with the heavy bags on their shoulders.

'Ah, there you are, my darling,' the woman clucked, walking towards Gandharv. She kissed him on both cheeks. 'So nice to see you again... Girls,' she screamed, and everybody jumped. 'Stop following me around. Take these bloody bags to my room.'

'But we don't know where your room is,' stuttered one of the girls.

The woman glared at them and they fled.

'Gandharv, honey, shouldn't you be getting ready for the shoot? Alisha will be ready soon.'

'Oh, Shilpa, come here, relax,' he laughed. 'Moushumi, Dipali, meet Shilpa, the dragon-lady, with a heart of stone.' He massaged her shoulder muscles and she visibly relaxed.

'Hi, I'm not a dragon-lady, but I have to put on this act or else those imbeciles won't move their arses. I really should retire from this showbiz nonsense, I'm getting old.' She charged out of the room again, yelling orders as she went.

Gandharv smiled at them. 'Welcome to the ad-world.'

The shoot was for a whiskey brand. As advertising alcohol directly was prohibited by the government, the advertising agencies created ads that merely suggested 'the moment' or 'the sensations' rather than the actual product. So in this case, the couple were to be seen playing in the waves with the rain in their faces, perhaps later to get back inside and share a moment of warmth and intimacy with a drink in hand.

The morning flew by. Dipali and Moushumi watched from the sidelines as the crew set up the equipment for the outdoor shoot. The assistants unfurled big reflectors and silver umbrellas. Gandharv instructed them where to place the deck chair – right in the water, with the waves lapping around the legs. The model, Alisha Chopra, Miss Mumbai, sat under an umbrella, while the make-up artist touched up her face.

Finally Shilpa yelled again, and everybody snapped to attention. She was the shoot manager and she played the role like a military officer.

Alisha stepped out of the shade and dropped her bathrobe. Both Moushumi and Dipali gasped. This girl was like a panther, dusky and long-legged. She wore a fire-engine red two-piece swimsuit, a thin gold chain adorned her waist. She had natural make-up on, only her lips were highlighted with pink shimmer. She slunk over to Gandharv and said something. He smiled and showed her where she should go. She posed. Someone called out a light metre reading. Gandharv adjusted his camera settings and clicked.

'She's wearing a handkerchief that's shrunk in the wash,' Dipali said.

'She's gorgeous,' Moushumi said. 'Look at her body.'

'I'm not sitting here all day looking at her body.' Dipali dropped her sunglasses over her eyes. 'I'm going for a nap.' She strode off to her room, shocked by the display of bare skin and how comfortable everyone seemed to be around the model. She was irritated by Shilpa's presence as well. Somehow that woman intruded into her private space with her loud mouth and her jarring bangles. Why was Gandharv so touchy-feely with her? She felt sick in her stomach. That's what all these creative people were about, she thought bitterly. Semi-naked models. Men ogling and taking advantage. She had seen the

SUSMITA BHATTACHARYA

make-up man brush his fingers against the model's breast, and Alisha hadn't even blinked. She thought about the make-up man's effeminate behaviour and those two girls who were so alike with the drug-induced look in their eyes. Perhaps they were not gay or drug addicts. She was being unfair to the lot, judging them before she'd even said hello. But the thought of Gandharv's hands on Shilpa's shoulder, and his easy way with her unnerved Dipali.

Moushumi sauntered back around mid-day. Her eyes gleamed with excitement. 'Why did you come back, Dips?' she said. She swung herself on the twin bed next to Dipali. 'It was so much fun. The model's bikini came off in the water, and everyone got an eyeful.'

Moushumi quickly added: 'No, no, Gandharv didn't see. He was yelling at his assistant about something – I don't know what – and then he shouted at Alisha Chopra to cover up and behave like a professional. Imagine talking to Miss Hottie like that!'

Dipali snorted. 'All eyewash.'

'Hey, why don't we join them for lunch?' Moushumi suggested, fiddling with the television remote again.

'No,' Dipali said. 'You go ahead, if you want to. I don't think I can be friendly when I don't want to be.'

Moushumi sat up and took Dipali's hand. 'Okay, we don't have to have lunch with them. Let's go somewhere quiet. We need to clear the air between us. Boy, you gave Gandharv some real icy treatment. Let's find a nice little shack that serves chilled beer and fried prawns.'

Dipali glared at her.

'And some veg pakoras?' Moushumi added.

They walked in silence, watching the fishing boats far out at sea. The sky was leaden and the wind smelled of fresh rain

192

coming in from the south-west. Little crabs scuttled over their feet in their rush to safety. Broken shells added a crunch to their footsteps.

'You know you should make the most of this situation.' Moushumi jerked her eyes back towards the hotel.

Dipali grimaced. 'What do you mean exactly, Mou?'

'You know, get to know Gandharv. Intimately. You'll have all the time in the world. Go, explore, see if things happen.'

'Don't you advise me what to do,' Dipali snapped. 'I don't want us to fight over this, so let's just leave it. Let me enjoy this break the way *I* want to.'

They sat at a table outside a tiny restaurant. Moushumi ordered a beer for herself and Dipali a Tango. The waiter promptly brought their drinks to them and a bowl of peanuts.

'Is he always like this?' Dipali couldn't help asking. 'All touchy-feely?'

'Look at you, getting jealous, ha?' Moushumi laughed. 'He's alright. He's worked very hard to get to where he is now. Okay, he's a bit of a flirt. Nothing major. But it's different with you, Dipali. I can feel it.'

'How?' Dipali asked. 'Why is he different with me?'

'He gets all secretive. Doesn't like talking about you,' Moushumi said. 'And that generally means he feels differently about you.'

'Thanks a lot,' Dipali said. 'Why doesn't he have a girlfriend if he's so good?'

'I don't know,' Moushumi turned to the menu cards. 'Why don't you ask him yourself?' She studied the menu carefully. 'I think I'll have the prawns. What about you, Dipali?'

Dipali stared blankly at the menu card. She didn't care what was there to eat. She was not enjoying this tussle with her conscience. 'Yes, I'm sure he is a good man. If only I could respond to him. But I think of Sunil, every time Gandharv tries to come close to me.'

'That's natural, isn't it?' Moushumi said.

Dipali nodded. She was afraid to tell Moushumi that Sunil's face was a blur now. She didn't keep any photographs within her sight. But sometimes, a sudden waft of aftershave or the smell of a freshly ironed shirt would conjure up his memory. Or this cold beer, with the condensation trickling down the sides. She could picture his Adam's apple bobbing as he gulped it down.

'But don't you think you ought to move on, Dips?' Moushumi asked.

'Sometimes, I'm not very sure if I do. It's safer where I am.'

There was a shout from the other table. A child began to wail. Dipali and Moushumi turned around to look. The child had dropped her ice-cream into her mother's lunch. Another woman hovered around them fussing.

The woman met Moushumi's gaze. She smiled apologetically as she gathered the wailing child in her arms.

'I saw you at the photo shoot this morning,' Moushumi called out. 'Everything alright?'

'Yes, yes,' she said. 'Just the usual with kids being difficult.' She patted the little girl and placed her on the chair. The ayah took over, wiping the ice-cream off her dress.

'You're from the advertising team, aren't you?' Moushumi asked.

'Yes, I'm Neha. I'm the account manager. This is my daughter, Shreya.' The child was still sobbing, as she watched her ice-cream melt into her mother's fish curry. 'I think we need to buy some more food.' She looked at the mess and stood up.

'Why don't you join us,' Moushumi said, jumping up to make space for them at their table.

'Let me buy Shreya an ice-cream.'

'Oh, don't worry,' Neha said. 'I can—'

But Moushumi was already striding into the restaurant. Neha shrugged sheepishly at Dipali and glared at her whimpering daughter. 'I don't usually bring her along for shoots,' she said. 'But circumstances left me no other option. I've got her ayah along. Her father had to go away on an emergency. He's a surgeon, you see.'

Dipali nodded. 'Yes, it must be quite difficult with two professionals in the family.'

'Yes. Quite,' Neha said.

Moushumi returned balancing a big pink ice-cream cone. 'Whoa, there you go, Shreya,' she laughed. 'Mummy will help you eat this one.'

Shreya broke into a big grin. The ayah took over, fussing over the girl and spooning big scoops into her mouth. Moushumi invited Neha to join them, but she declined.

'Some other time,' she said. 'I have to go back to the team. We'll meet up after the shoot, perhaps?' She left the child with the ayah and walked towards the hotel.

'She looks troubled,' Moushumi said.

'I guess so. Imagine having to drag her child along with her to work. Dealing with naked women and anti-socials, oof. No wonder she's steering clear of the rest of the team during her free time.'

Moushumi laughed and fed a big spoonful of ice-cream to the gleeful child.

13

The bonfire crackled on the beach, the crew surrounded it. Someone was strumming on a guitar, old Beatles songs, with the clone girls singing along to 'Hey Jude'. Bottles clinked. The aroma of roasting potatoes mingled with the wood smoke and enveloped them in a warm, buttery air. Dipali and Moushumi walked towards the fire where Gandharv had invited them to join the group for drinks. At first Dipali didn't want to go, but Moushumi insisted. She seemed quite taken by the glamorous people present, especially the model, Alisha Chopra. Dipali hugged her shawl tighter against the evening chill.

Gandharv was sitting next to Shilpa who was talking animatedly to him. Shilpa was much older; her hair was streaked with grey, and in spite of those jarring silver bangles on her wrists, her wrinkled hands betrayed her.

'Hi,' Moushumi waved to Gandharv.

He leapt to his feet and walked up to them. 'Hi, come on, join us.'

'Would be such a shame if we didn't.' Moushumi said. 'You guys look like you're having a lot of fun.'

Gandharv rolled his eyes. He leaned towards them and said, 'This is the brand manager's idea. He wanted a vacation with Alisha. So the agency designed the ad to be shot by the sea.'

'Ha, really?' Moushumi giggled. 'So where's the big boss?'

They spotted him next to Alisha. He was a middle-aged man with a belly he seemed to keep sucked in most of the time.

'He's not any competition at all,' smirked Moushumi. 'See who wins her over.'

Dipali watched Moushumi strike up a conversation with Alisha and the Creative Director. Alisha looked at her with bored eyes and gave a tiny yawn. Moushumi offered the model a cigarette, which she took gratefully.

'How old is she?' asked Dipali. 'She looks like a kid.'

'Yes, about nineteen, I think.' Gandharv walked away from the bonfire and Dipali followed him.

'What is it with this generation of kids? She is so comfortable wearing almost nothing, and smoking – it's like her second nature.' Dipali was amazed at how different her surroundings had become. Her best friend was a lesbian. She was attracted to a sexy photographer in the ad industry, and here she was with these creative people, on a holiday, watching naked models strut on the beach. What would her father have said? What would her brother say?

They sat on the bench of a restaurant shack. The waiter came out and put a lantern by their table. Mosquitoes buzzed near their ears and Gandharv successfully swatted the one on his arm. 'A beer?' he asked Dipali, as the waiter hovered around while scratching his armpit.

'Oh no,' Dipali said quickly. She flushed with embarrassment. 'I don't actually drink alcohol, anymore…'

'No worries. How about some tea?'

She nodded silently. He ordered two teas and they sat listening to the waves break on the shore. He put his feet up on the plastic chair next to him and tilted his head back. She watched the smoke spiral into the night.

'The answer is money,' he finally said. 'Being Miss Mumbai is no small achievement. She's made it in life. Has men dancing at her feet. Has more money than she can handle. Now she'll get roles in films, have affairs with hot film stars perhaps, be written about in magazines.'

'What about her parents?' Dipali protested. 'I'd just die of shame if my daughter cavorted semi-naked in some magazine ad and slept around with men old enough to be her father.'

'Maybe you wouldn't,' Gandharv said, closing his eyes. 'You'd be too jaded by then to care. Or maybe the lure of fame and money would have rubbed off on you as well.'

'I don't think so,' Dipali said vehemently. 'I wouldn't accept that.'

'Yeah, actually I don't really care. She's not my daughter.'

'How can you say that?' Dipali persisted. 'Actually, I know you don't care. You didn't care that you kissed Moushumi. It was just a kiss. Do you do that often?'

'I don't, actually,' he said, holding her gaze. 'Does that make you mad? Me kissing Moushumi?'

Dipali turned away. She didn't know how to respond. She wanted to scream at him, saying yes, it made her mad. She didn't want him touching any other woman, lesbian or otherwise. She didn't want him near Shilpa or Alisha or Moushumi. She gathered her shawl closer and tried to control her hair from flying wild in the breeze.

'I must be honest with you, Gandharv,' she finally said. 'I'm upset because you didn't mention it to me, and Moushumi did. I wish you had.'

'I'm glad you came, Dipali,' Gandharv said. 'I don't like playing games with people. I don't like being messed about with either. Moushumi used me. I'm not saying I'm so dumb I didn't realise. I kissed her while I was fully in my senses. I assume it helped her make up her mind. That's what she said, anyway. I like you, Dipali. I wasn't sure when to mention it to you. There didn't seem to be an opportunity.'

Dipali hid behind her hair. 'You can have anyone, Gandharv. Look at the fan-following you have.' Dipali bit her lip.

'Hey, I'm not the one asking women to flirt with me,' he laughed. 'It's a job hazard, you could say. They want to please me, that's all. So that I recommend them for the next job. And the next.'

'You don't mind flirting back.'

'No. It's all in the game. But there is a limit. I don't sleep with them, if that's what you're implying.'

'You're too blunt,' Dipali said. 'You are embarrassing me.'

'But I'm speaking the truth. Isn't that what you're suggesting? Aren't you thinking, should I get involved with a guy who sleeps around?' Gandharv swung out of his chair and walked towards the surf. 'Dipali, if you want to be with me, you've got be straight with me.'

'Do I want to be with you?' Dipali lashed out. 'Did I say that?'

'That's the problem,' Gandharv said. 'You don't say it. But I can feel it. Dipali, I'm attracted to you, and I know you are to me. So why play games with each other?'

'Gandharv,' Dipali said. 'It's not so easy. It's not all black and white. I have issues, baggage, problems, whatever you want to call them. Do you think my family will encourage me to romance a man? You haven't met my brother, that's why it's easy for you to say.'

'And my argument is this: how can you jump to conclusions before even trying it out? How do you know it will click between us in the first place if we don't try? Maybe your brother will be glad to get rid of you, who knows? I feel you should let go of your inhibitions and take a step forward.'

The wind changed direction and music drifted towards them. They looked towards the tiny speck of flames flickering in the distance. People were dancing around the bonfire.

'Look, they are enjoying themselves,' Gandharv said. 'Alisha will definitely sleep with that old man tonight. Shilpa will try to hit on me, like she always does. Her assistants will get high on dope. But no one will judge them. They'll continue life like they always have.'

'And what do you want to do?' She asked him.

Gandharv reached for her hand. 'Do you want a polite answer or the truth?'

Dipali blushed, glad the darkness hid her face. 'The truth,' she said.

'Polite answer, I'd like to get to know you better. Truth is, I'd like to kiss you now.'

Dipali scuffed him on his arm. 'Shut up! You're teasing me now.'

'No, you asked me, I told you.'

The moon shone on the water, lighting up the plankton that glittered and fizzed on the surf. Dipali moved closer to him, mesmerised by the moment. 'Yes, I suppose you're right. I don't intend living like a nun all my life.'

'I hope not. You look cold. Do you mind if I hold you?'

She laughed. 'No, stop being sarcastic, Gandharv. You were just telling me you want to kiss me, so now why ask my permission to hold hands?'

'Then can I ask your permission to kiss you? Because I've been dying to do that since I saw you sulking at the breakfast table.'

Dipali sucked her breath in. 'Oh, I… I, Gandharv, be serious.'

'I am— May I?'

'Yes,' Dipali moved into his arms. 'You may.'

14

The following night Dipali and Moushumi joined the advertising group again. They had reconvened at the restaurant bar, where three large tables had been joined together to accommodate them. Every inch of the tables was covered with food and drink. Dipali at once spotted Shilpa sidling up to Gandharv and felt a prickle of irritation run through her. Didn't she have any shame? She watched as Gandharv leaned closer to Shilpa and passed the bowl of cashew nuts to her.

Moushumi waved enthusiastically at Alisha – who was ensconced in the creative director's embrace – and was pointedly ignored. The assistants got up and pulled two chairs to their table. Dipali found herself sitting next to the clone girls, in one corner, while Moushumi squeezed herself near Alisha once more. Neha sat down next to Dipali and whispered that her little girl was fast asleep with the ayah watching over her, so she could sneak out. 'Where's your friend?' she added.

'She's trying to flirt with Alisha, who of course isn't interested at all,' Dipali replied, rolling her eyes.

Neha's eyes widened. She leaned forward to look at Moushumi, who was laughing a bit too loudly. The creative director had his arm possessively around Alisha, who in turn looked stoned from whatever she was smoking.

'These creative types,' Neha whispered. 'All crazy. All fake. I hate them. I know I'm a part of them, but yet, I'm not. Well, I hope I'm not!'

'Of course, you have a family to go back to. Most of these guys don't,' Dipali said. 'It must be hard for you, putting up a shield in front of your daughter. You don't want her to be a part of this.'

Neha shook her head and sighed. 'Of course not. But I don't have a choice. My husband is away, and I don't want to compromise my job.'

Dipali raised an eyebrow.

'I mean, I don't need to be working,' Neha said hurriedly. 'But this is my freedom, my life. I want my own identity.'

'Of course,' Dipali said. Everybody wanted to lead their life their way. Wasn't that why she was here? Trying to find herself. She sought out Gandharv in the crowd and blushed as their eyes met. He raised his beer can in response.

'She's a lesbian, Moushumi?' Neha asked. 'You two are together?'

Dipali coughed. 'No, not at all. No, no.'

'I'm sorry, I thought since you guys were sharing a room—'

'—We're good friends,' Dipali stressed. 'That's all. There's nothing more between us.'

The music was loud and jarring. There was a lot of alcohol on the table: Vodka. Beer. Whiskey on the rocks. Cocktails. Bloody Mary, with the salt still clinging to the rim of the glass. Pina colada, with its festive paper umbrella now bent and drooping to one side. Not a single glass of water; no wonder the mood was buoyant. Cashew nuts and peanuts were strewn around.

Dipali wanted to yell at this group and tell them to clear

up the mess. The waiters would have to do it after closing hours. The tandoori chicken looked orange and artificial. She nearly gagged with the smell of the alcohol and the meat. But the sound of Shilpa's drunken laugh as she rested her head on Gandharv's shoulder was the worst. Dipali slipped away. She was sure no one was bothered that she'd gone but, as soon as she turned the corner, she ran. Her sandals slapped against her feet as she sprinted across the sand. The sea was invisible, having merged with the dark sky. Only the white breakers fizzed and frothed onto the beach.

She lay down on the hammock, her body tingling with the memory of last night. How could she even think of another man in her life? But he was there, and she wasn't doing anything to stop him. In fact, she was pulling him closer to her, and together they were getting into it deeper and deeper.

She thought of their kisses, gentle at first, but increasing in urgency and desire later. When she saw the creative director embrace the model, she had wanted that for herself. She had wanted to have a drink and join with the merriment. She had wanted to pull Shilpa away from Gandharv and throw her in the sea.

She held on to the strings of the hammock, its ropes cutting into her fingers. She looked at the moon, at the clouds drifting. She was pleased to see and recognise the constellations. The Orion, the hunter with the dagger. She searched the sky for a shooting star and slowly she calmed down.

Dipali could hear the revelry coming from the restaurant. She ached to go back, if only just to look at him. She saw a figure coming towards her. It was Gandharv. Once he'd spotted her, he strode purposefully towards her. She tried to sit up but the hammock wobbled and she hastily lay back to balance herself.

'Why did you leave?' he asked, standing above her. He held the can of beer tightly in his grasp.

She couldn't reply because her head was reeling. He looked so needy that she felt her resolve break. She wanted to tell him about her jealousy. About her desire for him. But nothing came out. He held his hand out and helped Dipali out of the hammock.

'My parents lived in a village by the sea.'

'Oh, where?' Dipali asked, aware of his fingers still on her arm.

'On the east coast. Chandipur-on-sea. My father was a marine biologist and for a long time he was stationed at Chandipur, researching the biodiversity of the place.'

'Were you born there?'

'No, I was born in Calcutta. My mother's home. I did my schooling in Calcutta. My father used to come down to visit us. My mother shuttled between the two places.'

Gandharv shook his head. 'If only we had known...'

'Known what?' But she didn't want to know. It sounded too familiar. If only we had known, he wouldn't have gone to the passport office that day. If only we had known, I wouldn't have argued with him that day...

Gandharv lit a cigarette. He was silent for a long time, just smoking and staring at the sea. He didn't let go of Dipali's arm, and she held on to him. They walked towards the surf. Then Gandharv spoke again.

'Strange isn't it? The thing that you love so much can repel you as well. I love the sea, but coming near, I always feel so sad. I feel my father's spirit there, and I want to be with him. Even today.'

'When did he pass away?' Dipali asked, pressing his hand tight.

'I was five. My sister was two. She doesn't even remember them. Both my parents gone at the same time.'

'Both?' Dipali flinched. 'Oh no! That is terrible, Gandharv. I'm sorry. You were so young.' How she wished she could have loved her father like that, even after all this time. 'How did it happen?' she asked gently, knowing he wanted to talk about it.

'Car accident. They were driving back to Calcutta, to see us. A speeding truck got in the way,' he said, not meeting her eyes.

Dipali pictured two innocent young children being told their parents were no more. What did they understand? His sister must have cried for her mother's arms in vain. He must have waited by the window every day, expecting his father's car to thunder into the line of his vision. 'Life isn't fair,' she said.

They walked along the beach, away from resort. A kite screeched from a palm tree, waking the other birds who cried out in protest. Dipali wished the night wouldn't end, that they could keep on walking, never stopping. She reached out and stroked his arm, feeling the texture of his skin, breathing in his smell.

Gandharv stopped abruptly and cupped Dipali's face in his hands. He bent down and kissed her hard. He broke away and looked at her. 'We need to move on,' he said. He laid her down on the sand and kissed her again. She embraced him, pulling him on top of her. Dipali's mind went blank as he touched her. Their hands explored each other's bodies until they heard a shout from the distance. The wind carried Gandharv's name to them. Her body trembled violently as she hugged him tight, not wanting to let go. She didn't care who saw. But he pulled away, pressing his fingers to her lips to quieten her.

205

15

The white clouds puffed along the horizon like a steam train. The sun had dipped, creating the perfect light for portrait photography and the team did not waste a single moment. Dipali watched from a distance, but a crowd had gathered around the photo shoot.

She waved to Moushumi, who was walking up towards her wearing a large straw hat, which she was trying hard to keep in place. They had been to the market earlier that morning, looking for souvenirs, but the market had been disappointing. Dipali wasn't interested in the colourful scarves and t-shirts and hats on display. She wanted to spend at much time as she could sitting on the beach, enjoying the breeze and the calmness of the sea.

Neha's little girl, Shreya, played on the sand. She was collecting shells in her small bucket, giggling as a crab tickled across her feet. Her ayah sat higher up the beach, sated after an evening snack of fried prawns and potato bondas.

In her imagination, Dipali saw her own little girl playing by the sea. It could have happened. Shreya could have been her child. The little girl was laughing, a sound so pure it shot through her heart.

The ayah called Shreya back. 'Don't go too far in,' she

shouted though her eyes fought to remain open. But Shreya shook her curls and ran into the sea. She jumped when a wave hit her feet and squealed in delight. Dipali smiled. To have such innocence was a gift. She tried to remember her own childhood. There was no running carefree in the water for her. Her parents didn't have time for such frivolities.

A scream ricocheted her back to the present. The ayah was waving her arms frantically and running towards the sea. Dipali jumped up. She couldn't see Shreya anywhere. The ayah was screaming hysterically – Shreya had been swept away. She could see her little head bobbing in the waves, but before she could act, Moushumi jumped into the water. She swam towards the child and quickly caught her in her grip. Then she brought her in and laid her on the sand.

Shreya was breathing heavily and staring at them with wild eyes. Moushumi pumped her chest in case she had swallowed water, but she hadn't. Instead, the little girl cried for her mother.

All the action had attracted the attention of the advertising team. Soon some of them were racing down the beach to see what was wrong. The ayah wailed and beat her breasts, swearing she hadn't once taken her eyes away from her charge. Neha swept the crying girl into her arms and held her tight. Tears coursed down her cheeks as she examined every inch of her daughter's body.

'She's alright,' Moushumi reassured her. 'It wasn't a very big wave. She's more frightened than hurt.'

Neha nodded, unable to take her eyes away from Shreya. 'Thank you, Moushumi. Thank you for saving her. It is my fault, I shouldn't have brought her. I owe you my life.' Neha wept. 'But I had no choice. I need to… get away sometimes. I hope you realise I love my daughter very much. I didn't mean to ignore her.'

'Don't worry, she needs you the most now. Calm down and be there for her.' Moushumi stroked Neha's hair and helped her to her feet.

Dipali clung to Moushumi's arm. She felt faint. She had been right there and hadn't been able to do anything. What if? She watched how Neha pressed her daughter to herself.

'Thank God you were here, Mou,' she whispered. 'Thank God you were here.'

❧

Moushumi punched the familiar numbers on the dial. Since Shreya's incident, she had wanted to hear her own mother's voice. To be comforted. To be told it would all work out right. Her hand trembled as she listened to the telephone ring on the other side. She counted each ring. On the tenth ring, it was answered.

'Hello?'

She heard the familiar voice and a lump formed in her throat.

'Hello? Hello?' The voice questioned again. Then became silent. But the phone didn't disconnect. Moushumi hung on, pressing the earpiece to her head, as if trying to ingest that voice into her mind. She knew.

'Mou,' The voice said.

'Ma,' she whispered.

'How are you, child?' Her voice was low as though she didn't want the others to know who had called. The others? Her father. Moushumi wanted to touch her mother, smell her. Nestle her head in her warm, turmeric-scented sari.

'I'm okay. And you? Baba?'

'Fine. We are okay. But it is not the same without you.'

Silence.

'Are you eating properly?'

Moushumi smiled. After all this time, that was her mother's first concern.

'Yes.'

'I wish I could have talked to you the last time you called. But you hung up. It's been ages since…'

'Yes.' Moushumi said. But had all this time changed their views? She couldn't get herself to ask, too afraid of the answer.

'You should come home,' her mother said tentatively. Moushumi felt the question hover above them.

'Would you accept me?' she said.

'You are my child, Mou,' her mother said. 'How can I not accept you? Whatever your faults. Even if you had killed somebody, I would not have disowned you.'

'I haven't killed anyone, Ma,' Moushumi said. 'I just loved another woman, that's all.'

There was a sharp intake of breath. 'Moushumi, do you still…?'

'What?'

'Are you still…?'

'What, Ma?'

'Your father is suffering because of it. Would you forget everything and return to us?'

'Forget what? Would you forget everything and accept me as I am?'

Silence.

'Mou, your Baba is home, I have to go. But please call me soon. Come back soon, we'll sort everything out.'

Sort everything out, Moushumi smiled at the irony. It meant getting a husband. That would be her family's way of sorting it out.

16

Neha took Shreya back to Mumbai. Everyone was very subdued after the accident. The shoot was wrapped up quickly and the team prepared to leave as well. Moushumi and Dipali returned to Mumbai, thankful of the little girl's recovery. As they entered Mumbai, the traffic slowed them down. But this was unusual for a Saturday afternoon. They hadn't moved for about twenty minutes when Moushumi started to get impatient.

'What's with this traffic? Bloody hell.'

A man sitting in front of them turned around. 'There's a morcha further up. I heard thugs have set fire to a cinema.' He spat out a stream of red spit expertly down the side of his window.

'What demonstration? What fire?' Dipali asked, panicking. 'What's happening?'

'Arrey, don't you know? That film released yesterday? Dirty picture. Two women having affair,' he said, lowering his eyes. 'People saw yesterday and now our political party is protesting. Not Indian culture, spoiling our sanskriti.'

'Bastard,' Moushumi muttered under her breath. 'He's talking about the lesbian film just released.'

Dipali nodded. Yes, of course. The local political party had threatened the cinemas not to release the film or else they'd have to pay. She'd forgotten about it in Alibaug. The police were resorting to baton charge. Chants and slogans echoed in the air. They waited in the bus, watching. There was a big bang and the cinema hall burst into flames. Glass shattered onto the road. People rushed out, shrieking. Some of them were on fire. They ran, flames leaping from their clothes, until some quick-thinking people tipped them to the ground and smothered the flames.

Dipali screamed. Memories of another time flooded her. It must have been like this. The violence, the confusion, the deaths. She covered her face and sobbed hysterically. 'Stop, Stop it,' she screamed again. Moushumi lunged towards her and shook her. 'We've got to get out of here,' she shouted. 'Calm down. Don't watch.'

Moushumi clung to Dipali, forcing her to sit still. There was nowhere to go. They were in the middle of a traffic jam. The cars tried to reverse into side lanes and alleys wherever possible. The police were trying to get the traffic to move back as well. 'All this for a bloody film,' Moushumi cursed. 'Imagine what they'll do to a real lesbian. She'll die a witch's death.'

ॐ

The next morning, it was all over the newspapers. *Lesbian film causes real-life tragedy. Cinema in Goregaon attacked. Innocent film-goers injured.* The Chief Minister (CM) was proclaiming that the party had done the right thing, lesbianism was not Indian culture. Saying that it was a product from the West; a disease and such films lured young girls into sin.

Moushumi couldn't believe it. She watched the news, anger rising up within. She wanted to slap that self-righteous CM.

Why didn't they just get it? Straight women would never become lesbians just because of some film. Lesbians were born that way, and there was no way for them to live respectfully in this society. What bloody disease? She thought. AIDS, TB, cholera, these were diseases. Not homosexuality. The director had called for a candlelight march in the capital in support of her film. A gay activist was shouting in another news snippet, asking all gays to come out in the open and fight for their rights. He was cut short rather quickly. But Moushumi had heard enough.

ॐ

The evening breeze played in her hair. Moushumi stood on the Marine Drive promenade, watching the people who had turned up to support the march. Gay people. Not a whole army of them, though. Moushumi thought maybe about two hundred. Some held banners, others wore slogans on their t-shirts, but the message was the same. Give us respect. She scanned the crowds, looking for similarities with herself. No one was different from her. There was man in stiff collar and tie, his arm around his boyfriend's waist. Young men in t-shirts and jeans chatted among themselves. There were a few women too. They were dressed mostly in trousers and t-shirts, a few in salwar kameez. They did not have fear in their eyes. For the first time, the women had come out as well. They looked at each other for support, at the same time their demeanour proud to have at least found a platform to present their true selves. There were hijras, complete in their make-up and gestures, but they too were here to fight for recognition and respect.

The police skirted round the edges, like vultures sizing up the prey. It was supposed to be a peaceful march, but still they carried lathis and wore helmets. Just in case. Moushumi edged towards the women, who flocked together in the middle of the crowd. She smiled tentatively at a young girl beside her. The girl acknowledged her warily.

There was a crackle on the loudspeaker and a voice came through the general buzz. It was the gay activist, Sudhakar Patil. 'Welcome,' he said. 'And congratulations for coming. It is a brave thing to do.'

There were claps and cheers and hoots. People gathered on the other side of the road, ogling at the spectacle. Some booed and threw stones in their direction. Patil turned on them. 'Listen, people of the public, I urge you not to create any problems. If you do not support us, please leave this place. Tonight, the world is ours.'

Moushumi found herself shouting and cheering as well. Her heart soared as her voice mingled with the rest. She found herself holding hands with the woman next to her, both their voices chanting, respect, respect along with the crowd. A slogan was thrust in her hand: I am gay and proud of it. She waved it in the air, shivering with excitement.

Patil addressed the police. 'Thank you for coming to protect us. We hope this march will remain peaceful and show the world, show Mumbai, that homosexuals are not crazy, diseased, aggressive creatures. WE ARE NORMAL HUMAN BEINGS.'

Shouts went up to the sky. Confetti was thrown and a drum began to beat. Patil led the parade towards the Mantralaya, the state secretariat. Cameramen followed the march, while journalists nudged to get in and interview the participants. The hijras danced and some men joined them, moving in circles, clapping and singing. In other circumstances, such a thing would never happen. No one wanted to have anything to do with the eunuchs, but today they were joined in the same cause.

A woman elbowed her way in and touched Moushumi on her shoulder. She turned and was face to face with a news channel cameraman. At first, Moushumi panicked. She didn't want to stand out in the crowd. The journalist thrust a mic in front of her.

'Since when have you been a lesbian?' She shouted above the noise. Moushumi stared at her, too nervous to think. The woman repeated her question, pushing the mic into her face.

'Er... ever since I can remember,' Moushumi stammered. She looked around for support, but everyone kept marching on, waving their slogans and shouting.

'Are you with someone now?' the woman persisted, looking around.

'No,' Moushumi said. And then, she was suddenly very mad. This was not about her and her sexual life. The journalist was trying to turn her into a circus act, for people to be entertained. 'No, I'm not,' she shouted. 'I'm here to support the gays and lesbians who've always been at the wrong end of the stick. I'm tired of hiding from society, my friends, my family, myself. I'm tired of hiding from you.'

The woman jerked back. But Moushumi clutched the microphone and pulled it to herself.

'We've suffered for centuries,' she shouted. 'But it was not always like this. Look at Khajuraho. Read the Kamasutra. Homosexuality existed then and it does now. I've done my homework, and so should the rest of the world before they pass any judgement. Why all the fuss? When did it become a dirty thing? When did it become a disease? It's normal to be gay.'

The journalist gave her a tight smile. 'So are you saying your family is okay with it?'

'No, they are not,' Moushumi said. 'Unfortunately not. They've lost a daughter through no fault of mine.'

'And you hope this march will make people accept homosexuality in India?'

The cameraman zoomed in to Moushumi, recording her facial expression.

'It is a beginning, but there is such a long way to go.' She returned the mic and left the journalist behind; sucked into the march again.

☙

Dipali watched with her mouth open. She saw Moushumi on screen, talking on the 7.30pm regional evening news. What was Moushumi thinking?

'That girl, isn't she your friend, Moushumi?' Her mother pushed her glasses up her nose and leaned forward.

On the TV, Moushumi thrust the mic back to the journalist and moved on, waving her banner for the world to see. For her parents to see. For Mother Superior to see. For her students to see. Oh Moushumi, what will become of you? Dipali couldn't bear to watch anymore. She switched off the television.

'She's, she's...?' Her mother couldn't even complete her question. 'Dipali, you knew?'

'Of course I knew,' Dipali snapped. 'She's my best friend.'

'Eesh,' Asha Devi shook her head. 'And you went with her on a holiday? Dipali, how could you? What's going on with the two of you?'

Dipali swung round to face her mother. Obviously she had jumped to conclusions. And how many others who knew them would? In school, especially. So Moushumi's sexual problems would involve Dipali as well. She sank back into the armchair.

215

'What do you think is going on between us, Ma?' she asked sharply.

'Chee, chee, don't even make me mention it,' her mother muttered and heaved herself up. 'Be careful, Dipali. Don't ruin your reputation and ours.' She shuffled towards her bedroom, to pray for Dipali's sins to her many gods and goddesses seated on the marble plinth in her room.

'Ma,' Dipali called. 'If I was a lesbian, in a relationship with Mou, I would be out there too, fighting for our future. Not hiding here in my house, ashamed of my lover. But no, thankfully for you, there's nothing like that. She's still my best friend, that's all.'

Her mother didn't turn around, but her shoulders relaxed. She walked into her room and shut the door.

Dipali reached for the telephone. She punched Gandharv's number and waited. 'Did you see?' she asked when he answered.

'Yes, of course. It's only a matter of minutes now,' Gandharv said.

'For what?' Dipali didn't like the tone of his voice. 'What's going to happen now?'

'Do you think they will even be allowed to reach the Mantralaya? After yesterday's rioting, tension is still running high. It's too soon to pull a stunt like this. They'll be attacked by the thugs.'

Dipali shuddered. More violence? More calamities? 'Why did she go?'

Gandharv was silent for a moment. 'I support her,' he said finally. 'It shows she has guts to stand up for herself. Be proud of her, Dipali, whatever the outcome.'

'Even at the cost of her life?' Dipali asked.

'Yes, even at that,' said Gandharv. 'This means a lot to her, so we need to be behind her every step of the way.'

'Yes,' Dipali said. 'Even if my mother is suspecting that Mou and me are in a relationship, since I have been quite vocal in my support.'

Gandharv laughed, and Dipali couldn't help but smile. She wished he was with her, in her sitting room having this conversation.

'Should I come and disprove her?' he teased.

'I wouldn't mind,' Dipali said, her mind easing. 'I honestly wouldn't mind.'

ॐ

They marched on into the sunset, gaining distance but not the full support of the public. Never before had such a morcha taken place. People weren't sure how to react. Some cheered while some booed and taunted. They were stared at as though they were aliens. And there, in front of Sudhakar Patil, stood the political activist, Chandrakant Hegde.

'Patil,' he boomed, twirling his long black moustache. 'You freak. Go home and hide in your lover's pyjamas. Why all this tamasha? Leave some decency in this city.'

There was silence. Each party was sizing the other up. There was no competition at all. Hegde and his men had come armed with lathis and chains. Patil's army had banners and a drum. Moushumi watched, her body tensing. It wasn't meant to end like this. The police were here to protect them. But the policemen were hovering around, unsure. Who would they support?

A man charged out of the group and escaped into a dark alley. Another followed him. A policeman, assuming an attack, brought his lathi down on the escaping man's head. The victim gave a guttural scream and fell to the ground. He dragged himself forward, trying to escape the policeman's reach and finally managed to run into the darkness. This was enough for hell to break loose. Hegde's goons fell on the protesters, beating whoever came in the way. They tried to fight, but this time for their lives, not for respect and homosexuality.

Moushumi watched in horror as this peaceful march turned into a bloodbath. The man in front of her was blinded by the blood running down his hairline into his eyes. He tottered and she grabbed him, pulling him to one side. She wiped the blood with her dupatta, and he kept whimpering and mewling. 'What was the use?' he moaned. 'What was the use of coming out? I have old parents to feed at home. This was not needed.'

Moushumi tried to comfort him, but she was feeling the same way. What was the use of this? Making a mockery of themselves. Did they believe the CM would listen to them? That India would suddenly start accepting them? Hell, no. This was not the way. She wanted to strangle the activist, Patil. But he was nowhere to be seen.

Patil escaped, but about fifty of them were rounded off by the police, Moushumi included, and taken to the police thana. Some went willingly, like martyrs for their cause, while others had to be pushed into the backs of the police vans, with a few doses of the lathis on them. Moushumi had never been inside a police station. It was nothing spectacular, it wasn't even frightening. It looked tired and lonely. The constable on duty was chewing tobacco and listening to the transistor. A couple of women in gaudy saris and make up leaned against the wall, bored. They kept looking at their watches, counting their losses as they wasted their time inside the thana. The constable perked up when the latest arrestees were brought in. He smirked to his colleagues who came running out to watch the procession.

'Gayyyys,' he taunted, poking the nearest man on his behind with his baton. 'Baaylya saala, you'll find plenty to fuck in the cell tonight. These men do it all the time inside, but they don't give themselves a fancy name and sway their hips in public.'

The policemen laughed. 'Chala, chala,' a policewoman appeared, looking efficient. She directed the crowd in, single file and started taking down their details. Moushumi tried to edge forward. She would explain to them it was only a demonstration. They were not breaking any laws. But of course they were and she knew that. Penal Code 377. The law against homosexuality in India. But they were not caught in the act, were they? Wasn't that what the law said: *whoever voluntarily has carnal intercourse against the order of nature with any man, woman or animal shall be punished with imprisonment for life, or with imprisonment of either description for term, which may extend to ten years, and shall also be liable to fine.*

She knew every word of that law. They were just protesting against the discrimination against gays, asking for respect. They weren't indulging in sex. So why were they brought here? She went up the police woman and demanded an explanation.

Inspector Divya Kulkarni's face was pockmarked and her hair slick with oil. She wore her uniform sari with pride. She narrowed her eyes at Moushumi. She seemed to be reconsidering. Then she spoke. 'Listen, you bitch. Weren't you just on the television, talking great things about this filth? Do you want a slap across your face? Ha? Do you?'

Moushumi was taken aback. She watched Inspector Kulkarni's mouth spew more abuses at her. Her mind went blank.

'You lot should be flogged and made to remain in jail forever,' the inspector shouted. 'People are fighting for food, for a place to live, to survive, and you fucking lot are fighting to have sex?'

The women were herded into one cell, and the men squeezed into another.

'We want a lawyer,' yelled one of the men. 'This is against the law.'

'What you do is also against the law. God's law,' the constable shouted. 'Now stew in there for some time.'

The air was becoming suffocating in the cell. Sweat, perfume, stale breath all came together to create a pungent atmosphere. The women sat listlessly, tired and emotionally drained. Moushumi smiled at the woman next to her. She's a lesbian, Moushumi thought. Yet, she looks so motherly, so housewifely. The woman was wearing a cheap chiffon sari and a big bindi on her forehead.

'I'm Moushumi. Can we talk?' One of their cell mates had begun snoring in the corner.

The woman nodded. 'I'm Charu.'

'How come? I mean, why are you protesting?' Moushumi didn't know what to ask. How to ask.

'Because I want freedom,' Charu whispered. She wiped her perspiring face with a large checked handkerchief.

'I'm sorry,' Moushumi said.

Charu tried to compose herself. She was pretty in a plump sort of way. Soft curves and tiny hands. Her eyes were red from tiredness and tears. 'My lover was taken away from me. I want her back,' she said softly. 'I want to win this fight.'

'How can we win?' Moushumi asked. 'I have lost too. My family. They don't want me anymore.'

'Of course not. Nobody wants us,' Charu said. 'Her husband found out, and he warned me off. She's my sister-in-law.'

Moushumi nodded. Like in the film. The two sisters-in-law

fell in love. Their husbands didn't fulfil their needs. What was Charu's story? It was this: she had always known she was not straight, but had to marry anyway. There was no choice. She now had two teenage sons. But for years she had a clandestine relationship with her sister-in-law. They lived in a joint family home, so it was easy in some ways, difficult in others. They were together in the afternoons, when the husbands were at work and the children at school. But they also had to put up with living a lie with their husbands. They cheated on their husbands and felt guilty about it. But there was no choice again. It went on for ten years, until one day, her brother-in-law came home early.

It was pure hell. The look on his face. Her husband's face. The two women begged, asked for forgiveness. Swore they'd never indulge in anything ever again. Just don't separate them. The two families split up. It was complicated, because they owned one flat. If they sold, they wouldn't have enough to buy two. But they sold, and rented a tiny flat in the suburbs. As far away as possible from each other. Charu's husband died earlier that year, due to a heart problem. And now she could claim Sukanya again. But Sukanya didn't respond to her. She was terrified of being separated from her children, stripped of her respect and thrown out on the streets. Sukanya wasn't interested anymore. And all Charu could do was shout at the top of her voice in a gay protest march and end up in jail.

17

Dipali paid the bail money. As Moushumi stepped out of the police station, Gandharv moved forward and shielded her and Dipali from the cameras. He tried to push the reporters back, but he was a known face in the profession, and the reporters pressed forward, thinking he wanted exclusive rights to Moushumi's story to himself. There was a scuffle, voices were raised, accusing him of meddling with their business. The two women threw themselves into the car and slammed the door shut. Faces appeared at the windows, cameras flashing and they had to cover their faces with their dupattas.

'Enough,' Gandharv shouted. 'Bus karo, yaar. Let us go.' The reporters shoved him away. They weren't going to be beaten to an afternoon scoop. Lesbians at large. Perfect headline news.

A woman shouted at Dipali. 'Are you two lovers? I'd like to interview you two. We pay for stories, you know.'

Gandharv jumped in and started the car. The reporters ran behind them for a bit and then gave up. There were other fish to bite the bait inside the police station.

'What a shithole I've got us into,' Moushumi whispered. 'I didn't expect this at all.'

Dipali reached out to hold her hand. 'I'm so sorry I stayed

away from you out there. I just don't know how to react. These people will just jump to conclusions.'

Moushumi shook her head and looked out of the window. The city was rambling on, people were breathing the dusty air and fighting to get ahead in the crowd. No one was bothered by who was travelling in this car. No one cared that she had spent a night in lock-up because she had spelled out her sexual orientation. She was just an ordinary woman in the backseat of a Fiat. But when they would recognise her as the woman who was attracted to other women, then they would come, talons out, to scratch at her eyes, pull out her tongue and shred her to pieces.

CR

Moushumi entered the Mother Superior's office. She was doomed, she knew that. The Mother was sitting at her desk, looking through newspapers. She gestured to Moushumi to be seated and continued to read. She knew what the principal was reading. There was a picture of her waving the slogan in the protest march. Another of her leaving the police station.

The Mother Superior looked up at her. 'What were you doing, my dear?' she asked softly. 'Getting into trouble like that?'

Moushumi looked up, shocked. So she wasn't angry? Disgusted? 'I was trying to acknowledge my true self,' she said finally.

The Mother Superior nodded and put the newspapers away. She rubbed her cheeks with her bony hands and leaned back in her chair. 'What do you propose to do now?'

'I don't know,' Moushumi said. 'I really don't know.'

'It was a very foolish thing to do. You should have thought of the repercussions.'

The Mother Superior placed the newspapers in front of Moushumi. 'Have you read these?'

'No, Ma'm, I haven't. I don't want to.' Moushumi averted her gaze from the desk full of newspapers. She looked out of the window. The students were playing in the field. The sports master blew his whistle relentlessly, trying to get their attention. How many of those girls were lesbians, Moushumi wondered. How many of them suffered secretly? Or would do so in the near future?

'I'm sorry, but you cannot escape from your actions, Miss Dutta.' The Mother Superior's voice took on a sharper edge. Moushumi turned to look at her. Her lips were set into a thin line. She was not going to stroke Moushumi's hair and murmur it's alright, my dear, now go back to work. 'I have a school to run,' she finally said, adjusting her sari. 'A convent school for girls. Your behaviour was unacceptable.'

'But, Mother, surely it is not my fault,' Moushumi tried to explain. 'Are you saying my being a lesbian is wrong, or that I was locked up in jail fighting for my rights is wrong?'

Mother Superior sniffed and looked down at the newspapers. She cleaned her glasses with a lace handkerchief and pushed them up her long, narrow nose. 'I cannot upset the management and our benefactors. They want respectability.'

Moushumi sat up straight. She was not going to go down so easily, she decided. 'But you haven't answered my question, Ma'm. What is troubling you?'

'You have committed a sin. What you do is not natural. It is against God,' Mother Superior said.

'No, I have not gone against God. He created me this way. He didn't have a problem with how he made me. It seems you do.'

'Calm down, Miss Dutta, I'm not going to argue with you. I would like your resignation letter on my table by the end of the day. At least I'm doing you a favour. I'm not sacking you. You can apply at any other school you like.'

CRASH

Dipali stared at Ashish, not believing what he had just said. She turned to look at her mother, but Asha Devi slumped in her arm chair, not willing to look at either of them.

'Say something, Ma,' Dipali hissed. 'Don't keep quiet.'

Asha Devi turned her face away. Tears coursed down her wrinkled cheeks. 'I have never fought, always given in,' she whispered. 'How can I now?'

Ashish looked smugly at his sister and then turned back to study the files and papers he had retrieved from his briefcase. He had appeared at their doorstep early in the morning, and Dipali had had to miss school. He had plans, big plans to sell this crumbling house to a property builder. He wanted the shares to be divided in such a way that Dipali got a share out of her mother's while he got the rest.

'That's not fair,' Dipali said. 'First of all, how can you alone make this decision? Ma is still alive, and we are happy to live here. And even if we divided the house, why should it be divided in half, when there are three people involved?'

Ashish looked at her as if she was a fly he wanted to squash and do away with. 'Why are you getting so involved?' he said. 'Too bad your in-laws donated all their money to charity. But they left you an income you've put away in the bank. Don't get your greedy mind on this property.'

Dipali had used her money for the upkeep of this house, and now he wanted to sell it and make a profit. After worrying most of the night about Moushumi, now she had her brother's selfish modus operandi to deal with. How she wished Gandharv was here. 'I'm not letting you get away with this so easily,' she said. 'I may have some money. But you never let me have my freedom. And I am entitled to this property as well. You cannot force Ma to sign. We're going to live here until the end.'

'Do you know what a gold mine you are sitting on?' he shouted. 'If we don't sell now, the underworld thugs will murder you, and capture the house. Then what?'

'Then what?' Dipali asked. 'We'll be dead, so it won't affect us. It will affect you though, left with nothing.'

'Shut up,' Ashish hissed. 'Don't argue with me, I know what is best for the whole family.' He slammed his briefcase shut and glared at her. The nerve on his temple was throbbing. Dipali knew it meant he was furious. When she was younger that also meant she would get a slap or two from him. Would he dare to now?

'What family?' Dipali said. 'I am not your family. Your wife and your son are your family. Ma and I are just burdens for you. You never treated us as family, did you?'

Ashish stood up, his eyeballs bulging. 'And since when have you grown a tongue? You shouldn't even be here. What inheritance are you talking about? You should be in your husband's home. You are a widow, remember that. We've taken pity on you and kept you here—'

'Enough,' Asha Devi said. 'I've heard enough. Money makes people evil. Ashish, you of all people, treating your little sister in this manner? She shuffled past them into her room. 'I'm tired now. I need to rest.'

'You haven't taken any pity on me,' Dipali said after her mother left. 'You've used me to look after Ma. You played me to your benefit...'

Ashish stared at her, his mouth moving but unable to speak. His face had turned dark. He rushed towards Dipali, his hand raised, but just as he reached her he stopped, as if deflated. He swore under his breath and charged out of the room as well.

Dipali sat down heavily on the sofa and looked around. Such a drab looking house, with peeling paint and leaking roof. Yet worth so much. It had finally happened. They were fighting for this house. If Ashish had been a bit more decent, she wouldn't have disagreed. If he had acknowledged her part in caring for their mother, that was all she wanted. But he behaved so badly, thinking he could decide for them, it was difficult to think well of him. She thought of Gandharv's words. No, she would fight her brother. She'd give him a hard time. She'd let him know she would not take things the way he wanted any more.

☙

Moushumi walked out of the school, her mind in a blur. She had just been kicked out of her job. She was shown on national TV as a lesbian. People were talking about her. Damning her, making fun of her. She shuddered when she thought what was going on in Calcutta. Would her parents be ostracised because of her? She remembered the newspaper article about the two lesbians who had killed themselves. She remembered the photograph of the mothers, devastated, broken women. She had done the same to hers. She screwed her eyes tight and felt panic rising up from her stomach. She couldn't take this anymore. She wanted Dipali's presence, but even she hadn't turned up at school.

She reached for a cigarette and sat under a bridge and smoked. The street children sniggered at her and shouted out derogatory comments. No decent woman sat on the street and smoked. Nothing could get worse than this. She should really kill herself, she thought. Jump in front of a train. Walk into the sea.

18

Dipali and Gandharv sat in his car, facing the sea at Bandra Bandstand. The moon shone brilliantly down on the faces of all the couples sitting on the low wall in front of the water. Cars and motorbikes lined the promenade, with more couples enjoying some private time before they headed their separate ways back to their homes. The kulfi-sellers were doing brisk business and so were the peanut sellers and coconut-water hawkers. Various types of music escaped from the cars creating a discordant blur of sound in the open air. Some lovers were quite adventurous, passionately engaged in view of everybody, while others preferred the sealed anonymity of their cars, the dark windows wound up and fogged while the cars rocked gently to a certain rhythm.

Dipali turned to look at Gandharv, who looked confused by the surroundings. 'Er, why are we here?' she asked.

'I didn't know,' he replied, scanning the scene. 'I told a colleague I was taking a girl on a date, and he suggested this place as the last stop before dropping her home.'

'Haven't you been to Bandstand before?' Dipali tried hard not to laugh. 'It's a place to make out. Gosh, I feel like a teenager again. My friends in college would come here with their boyfriends and then tell me what they got up to. There was fierce competition with how far one went. And I only ever listened.'

'Wow, I'm sorry. I didn't have such intentions.' Gandharv scratched his head and squirmed in his seat. They watched the car next to them get particularly bumpy and suddenly they both burst out laughing.

'Oh, I'm so glad to be here,' Dipali said and reached out to hold his hand. 'Finally made it to Bandstand. In my middle age. What should we do now?'

'Do in Rome as Romans do?' Gandharv grinned with a sideward glance towards her. 'But you said you wanted to talk.'

Dipali leaned back in her seat. She was too tired to banter with him. She wanted the exhaustion to seep out of her body. She wanted the diversion, the excitement she knew she could get from Gandharv. But even asking for that seemed like a huge task. 'It's been such a crazy week. First Mou, then my brother. I just want some normality in my life right now.'

'So what normal things do you want to do?' Gandharv asked. 'And I'm glad you regard me as the choice for your normality.'

'Oh, stop it, Gandharv.'

'We haven't really talked since we got back from Alibaug. So much has happened, we kind of left our lives in the backseat.' Gandharv opened his side of the door and leaned out to light a cigarette.

'I'm used to living in the backseat.' Dipali muttered. 'I'm pretty much used to it.' She sat up and rested her chin on her knees.

A peanut-seller approached her tentatively. 'Channa sheng?' he rasped. His lips parted in a grin, showing off his betel-stained cracked teeth.

Gandharv wound the car window up and turned to face her.

'What do you mean by that, Dipali? That's the problem with you. You always leave it to others to decide what to do with your life. You assume what people think about you, not bothering to find out what they really do. And you always play the loser. Why?'

Dipali was frightened by his words. She knew he spoke the truth, but she was too afraid to take action. Where would it leave her? Homeless? Humiliated? What good would facing up to the truth do? Look what it did to Moushumi. She spoke her mind, but in the end, it didn't help her, did it?

'For once, Dipali,' Gandharv raised his voice, claiming her wandering attention. 'Do what you want to do. If you want to live in your old house and not have it broken down, tell your brother so. If you want to rip my shirt and make love to me, then do, don't wait for me to make a move. No one will judge you. But if you just want to keep your distance and not have anything romantic between us, then please say so. Don't keep playing games with me. Don't think that just because you are a woman, and a widow at that, you are allowed to feel hurt. I'm human too, and just because you claim I have women falling at my feet, I'm incapable of feeling hurt. I don't want a relationship with just any woman. Let me know where I stand in your life. I'm willing to wait I'm not rushing you. But at the same time, leave me clues as to what you want to do with me.'

'I want this, Gandharv,' she whispered and pressed her lips to his. 'Like you said, do in Rome—'

They fumbled clumsily as they tried to embrace each other within the constricted space. They ignored the kulfi-wala asking if they'd like a kulfi to cool down.

'Oh, stop, stop,' she gasped, pulling away from him. They both faced each other, breathing hard. He put his head on the steering wheel and tried to calm down. She pulled down her kurta and began to ease out the creases. She had to hug herself tightly so that her hands didn't automatically reach out to claim him again. He sat up and straightened his clothes. He studied his own clothing and laughed.

'Hey, I wasn't serious when I said you could rip my kurta.' He pointed at the buttons hanging weakly to broken threads. 'You have to take me home now and mend it.'

She was grateful that he lightened the situation and she ruffled his hair. 'I could take you home and destroy your kurta altogether.'

'Wow,' Gandharv gave a low whistle. 'Now I am afraid to know what you fantasise about me. You will tell me, won't you?'

Dipali giggled and cuffed his arm. 'Maybe. If you kiss me just like before, I will.'

It was very late when they finally drove up to Dipali's house. The lights were on in every room.

'Shit,' Dipali looked at her watch and cursed. 'They're awake.'

'Good,' Gandharv smiled. 'Good time to introduce your toy-boy to the family.'

'Oh, shut up, Gandharv. I'm in deep trouble.'

'No, you're not. You are an adult, for god's sake, not a sixteen-year-old virgin. Go out and face them.'

She stepped out of the car. The door opened and Ashish stormed out. Gandharv got out of the car and walked round to Dipali. Ashish stared at his watch pointedly and then at her. He ignored Gandharv's presence altogether. 'Have you seen the time?' he muttered between his teeth. 'Ma's sick with worry. Is this what you normally do? Is this a decent time to come home?'

Dipali ignored him and waited till Gandharv reached her side. 'Meet Gandharv. Gandharv, my brother, Ashish.'

Ashish jolted back in surprise. He spluttered as Gandharv held out his hand. He took it half-heartedly and was rewarded a hard squeeze.

Dipali turned to Gandharv. 'Thank you for dropping me home. Really appreciate it.'

He smiled at her and then at Ashish. 'It was my pleasure. I hope to see you soon, Dipali. Nice to meet you, Ashish.'

Ashish said something incoherent. Gandharv winked at Dipali and the twinkle in his eye assured her that she had impressed him. She walked up the path towards the house, leaving Ashish to follow indignantly.

'What insolence,' Ashish muttered.

Dipali swung around. 'What did you say?'

'We are a respectable family,' he spat at her. 'So why are you whoring around?'

He sidestepped her and went into his bedroom and slammed the door shut.

Dipali stood there for a long time, staring out at the moon. Is that what he thought? Is that what the others thought? Was having a night out whoring? Was making love to Gandharv a sin? No, it didn't feel like whoring to her. She thought of his lips on hers. His hands caressing her body. His temper, his concern, his possessiveness of her. She wanted all of that for herself. She wanted to live again like she once had. But with a different man. And how easily Ashish made it sound so filthy.

19

'We'll have to call the police,' Dipali cried, tears streaming down her face. 'I should have called earlier. Damn it, why did all this have to happen?' She threw herself at the door, hoping it would give way. It didn't budge. This was a British built house with thick walls and a sturdy teak door. Built to last.

The landlady handed the telephone to Dipali and sank into her armchair. Dipali touched her shoulder gently as the old lady trembled and whimpered. She had been hysterical when Dipali had called by. Moushumi had locked herself in her room for hours and wasn't answering her knocks. Just as Dipali was about to dial, Moushumi's door creaked open.

'Mou,' Dipali cried, rushing in. 'Are you okay?'

Dipali touched her face, her arms, relieved she was still alive. Moushumi's face was immobile. Her hair was matted and her cheek creased with criss-cross lines.

On her bedside table were strips of paracetamol, and a bottle of Old Monk rum. Dipali felt a crushing pain in her chest.

'What have you done?' Dipali shouted, grabbing Moushumi's wrists to feel her pulse.

Moushumi shook her head. She gave out a high-pitched wail. That sound bounced back into Dipali's memory from the distant past. It was the same keening wail she had let out when she had identified Sunil's body.

She held Moushumi close and rocked her slowly. She tried to soothe her even though she was crying herself. She could hear the landlady moan outside. Khodai, oh khodai. Dipali took the old lady to her bed and laid her down.

'Moushumi's lost someone close to her,' she lied. 'Don't worry, Aunty. She's okay now. I'm here. You rest a bit.'

Dipali then rushed to the kitchen to look for some food. Some sort of sustenance, biscuits, bread, anything. She rummaged through the boxes in the cupboards. Through the window she could see people rushing about, going in and out of the cinema, standing outside the ganna-juice stall, drinking tall glasses of sugarcane juice. The sewage was belching out of the gutter, filthy water flowing past the juice stall, where the owner was washing the used glasses in a bucket of water.

There was so much wrong in this city. In this country. The politicians were eating up the money, not doing their jobs properly. There was scam after scam in the news every day. Sewers ran over, garbage spilled onto streets which were home to rabid dogs and rodents. Rich people's SUVs ran over homeless people sleeping on the streets and they got away with it too. And here was a woman, minding her own business, but one day spoke out for herself, and this was the result.

'Whatever you do, Mou,' Dipali said. 'Please don't ever think of killing yourself.'

Moushumi looked down at her hands. She didn't look convinced.

'You know Dipali, once I had read an article about two young women in Bengal, who killed themselves when their families separated them from each other. No one took their side except me. My father called them perverts. My mother said they were fools to destroy their families' names. Even Jasmine laughed and called them fools. No one does what they did. They deserved to die for being such idiots and coming out with it.'

Moushumi sighed and leaned back on her pillow. 'Only I supported them. I thought they were brave, they had principles. They wouldn't go down the path of cheating others and living a lie. I thought I could follow their principles. In a way, bring justice for their deaths, by proving I could do it. But I too have failed. I'm useless, a failure in every way, a freak.'

Dipali moved closer and stroked her arm. 'No, you haven't failed, Mou. If you want words to describe you, I'll tell you. You're beautiful. You're brave. Intelligent. Funny. And a lesbian. Which of them is supposed to be a freak? Be proud of who you are.'

'Proud of what?' Moushumi lashed out. 'Proud of losing my parents? My sister? My job?'

She buried her face in her hands and wept. 'Mother Superior said to me that I'm not normal. I have gone against God's ways.'

'Ignore her,' Dipali hissed. 'Who has the right to decide who's normal? I'm not normal either then. My brother called me a whore. Can anyone define what is normal?'

'I said to her, I haven't gone against God. He created me like this. I didn't choose to be a lesbian. He did. So punish him if you like, not me. I had nothing to do with it.'

'Good for you, Mou. Now don't talk about her. You need to rest. To recover. Will you come home with me? Stay a few days?' Dipali feared she might be driven to take her life if left alone. She longed to have Gandharv by her side. He would be full of solutions. He'd talk sense into Moushumi.'

'Dipali, lie down next to me, please. I don't want to be alone.'

It started to rain. The sudden shower caused some panic in the street below. People ran to take shelter under trees and shop awnings. The sun shone defiantly on the stray clouds, willing them to pass. Dipali went to the window, and like always, she looked out for the rainbow. It was there, a faint shimmer brightening up the polluted sky with its mellow colours. Dipali watched till the light faded away. The rain stopped as suddenly as it had come. Brushing the water from their clothes and hair, people reluctantly walked out of the shade. And again, they were back in motion, rushing about to resume what they had been doing.

Dipali slipped in next to Moushumi. She stroked her hair, like her mother used to when she had a headache.

'Don't blame yourself, Mou,' she said softly. 'Nobody has the right to pass judgement on anybody. Promise me you'll take care of yourself. Come home with me.'

'No,' Moushumi said. 'I can't go to your house. Your mother knows, right?'

'Doesn't matter,' Dipali said. But she stopped. Her brother was still there; how would he react? She hadn't thought of him. He'd go out of his way to insult Moushumi.

'It matters,' Moushumi said. 'I cannot have anyone look at me that way. I want to be alone. I promise, I won't kill myself.' She turned to face Dipali and smiled. 'I didn't do it, did I? I just stared and stared at the stuff I'd bought. But then I thought: I'm not going to give up.'

'The pharmacy just gave you so many strips of Crocin?' Dipali asked, astounded at the carelessness of the chemists.

Moushumi smiled. 'One gets very clever when planning things. I visited around ten pharmacies on my way home, and one stop at the liquor shop. No one batted an eyelid. It's easy to die of an overdose, you know.'

'Shush, don't say such things, Mou. It frightens me. I've been to that place before, and it is not a good place to be.' Dipali touched her finger to Mou's lips. Mou caught her hand and held it there, softly pressing her lips. There was stillness in the air. They didn't move. Dipali looked into Moushumi's eyes. She could see her need, her hunger. She felt Moushumi move closer to her until her breath touched her face. Moushumi buried her face in her hair, breathing deeply. She laced her fingers through Dipali's and they lay quietly together.

A knock on the door woke them up. Dipali jumped, pulling away from Moushumi. They had fallen asleep in each other's arms. Moushumi curled in, her back pressing into Dipali's bosom. It was dark, and the streetlamp was shining into the room. The landlady's voice came through the door. Dipali stood up, unsteady on her feet, eyes still adjusting to the dark. Moushumi reached out and switched on the bedside lamp. 'Coming,' she called.

Dipali straightened her clothes, feeling a hot flush run down her body. What would the landlady think, the two of them in the dark? She had no idea when they'd fallen asleep, so exhausted by their emotional states. She looked at the clock. It was nearly eight.

Moushumi opened the door and stuck her head out. She turned around to Dipali. 'Your mother's on the phone.'

ℜ

Dipali walked in, smoothing down her kameez. She knew her brother's eyes were on her. Her mother was complaining,

237

saying she nearly had a heart attack, not knowing where her daughter was.

She saw her brother smirk and look away. 'She was with her boyfriend, Ma. She's not bothered whether you were worried or not.'

Her mother's gaze wavered. She looked from him to her, mouth open. Her eyes questioned Dipali.

'Your daughter is a very modern woman,' Ashish continued to taunt. 'You've not met her boyfriend, Ma? She didn't bring him home?'

He leaned back in the armchair, one leg crossed over the other. His chappal slapped his raised foot as he shook his leg. He was wearing a white kurta and pyjamas, his hair glistening like he'd just had a shower. Dipali felt crumpled and sweaty; she ignored him and went towards her room.

'Bloody whore,' he said under his breath, but just enough for her to hear.

Dipali swung around, and raised her hand. He was going too far with this nonsense.

'You,' she said, shaking a finger at him. 'Don't you dare talk to me like that.'

Ashish stood up and towered over her, his eyes shining with hatred. 'Shut up, you bitch,' he said. 'I can break all your teeth if you talk back.'

Dipali looked up at him. 'I'm not afraid of you. You touch me, I'll go to the police. You better behave respectfully if you want me to sign those papers.'

Ashish stepped back. She heard his ragged breath. She knew he was doing all he could to stop himself from striking her. But Dipali knew she had the upper hand. Their mother gave out a low wail, but no one turned to look at her. Dipali and Ashish remained locked in each other's glare.

'What am I hearing?' Asha Devi cried. 'My son abusing his own sister? My daughter having a lover? Why so much hatred in this house?' She wept as she turned to go into her room. Dipali swung around.

'Ma,' she said softly. 'Why do you believe this man? He's insecure, greedy and jealous. Always has been. But this time, he won't get away with it.'

Ashish snorted and backed off. He gathered the newspapers on the coffee table and strode away. The door banged shut and a painting on the wall fell askew. Asha Devi did not reply. Her shoulders sagged and she slowly shuffled into her room. She closed the door quietly behind her. Dipali stood in the middle of the sitting room. She thought of Moushumi. She thought of Gandharv. She thought of Sunil. And from some crevice in her memory, she thought of that futile visit to the fertility clinic. Her head reeled. She had desired so many things. She hadn't got most of them. She realised now, it was really up to her to stand up for herself and achieve what she wanted. And, at this present moment, she wanted Gandharv.

20

Moushumi waited impatiently in reception. Gandharv had arranged an interview with his boss for her. A position for a copywriter was available. The receptionist eyed her from the top of her glossy magazine. Gandharv had not turned up at work yet. Did everyone in advertising have a late start? She shifted uncomfortably on the sofa that was shaped like red lips. Which idiot had designed this office, she wondered. The glass door swung open and Neha walked in. Moushumi's knuckles turned white as she gripped her file too tight.

'Oh hi, Moushumi,' Neha greeted her. 'Are you waiting for someone? Gandharv?'

'Oh, not really,' Moushumi didn't want to give much information. What if she wasn't offered the job? 'Mmm, yes, Gandharv. He's not in, though. Yet.' She looked at her watch and shrugged.

'Did you have an appointment with him? He doesn't come in some days. On location and stuff, you know.' She looked concerned and turned to the receptionist to ask about Gandharv's whereabouts.

'Oh, I didn't bother to check.' Moushumi got up. She felt silly sitting on that sofa. 'Is Gandharv in?' she asked the receptionist.

'I thought you were waiting for Chirag Mhatre,' the receptionist interrupted. 'Gandharv's not in today.' She jabbed some numbers on the phone and began speaking in a low, husky voice.

Moushumi bit her lip. 'Okay. Thanks.' She looked at Neha, embarrassed. 'He's not in, how silly. But I'll wait for Mr Mhatre.'

'I've got a meeting in a minute. But if you like, you could wait with me, have a coffee? Better than sitting on the smooching sofa,' Neha said.

Moushumi nodded gratefully. 'Yes, that would be good. Thank you.' Better than sitting under that snooty receptionist's nose. Moushumi followed Neha in.

'Arse-kisser sofa, we call it,' Neha whispered to Moushumi. 'Most people who sit there are usually waiting to do that.'

Moushumi stopped. Neha bit her tongue. 'Oops, I didn't mean you, of course. Sorry.'

They laughed nervously. Neha offered to get some coffee and disappeared into the pantry.

Moushumi looked around. It was a lovely office, minus that sofa. Bright artwork on the walls. Plants that looked watered and healthy. Big glass windows overlooking the city. It was situated in an old mill, which had been empty for years, ever since the textile industry in Mumbai closed down. But, one by one, the mills and their surrounding land were being converted into offices and apartment blocks.

There was a loud giggle and Moushumi saw Alisha Chopra sweep in, on the arm of the creative director. She dazzled in her white tank top and denim shorts. Her skin was like creamy cappuccino. They disappeared into his office.

Neha appeared with two coffees. 'Oh, I see Alisha is here. Do you want to go and say hi?'

'Um, no,' Moushumi looked away, embarrassed at being caught out. 'Not really. I'll have coffee with you, if you're not too busy.'

Neha laughed. 'Never too busy for you! You're my knight in shining armour.'

'How's Shreya?' She asked, fishing around for some conversation to make. Thank goodness she remembered the name of Neha's daughter.

'She's fine,' Neha said. She pushed a framed photo of Shreya towards Moushumi. It was a picture of her on a swing. Wind-swept hair. Toothy smile. Sparkling eyes. A beautiful, precocious child.

'She's lovely,' Moushumi said. 'She recovered well, didn't she?'

'Yes,' Neha said and hastily touched her wooden desk. 'Thank goodness. That was the worst day of my life. But thanks to you she's alive today.' Tears sprang in her eyes, and she looked away. The telephone on her desk rang and she answered it. 'Chirag's waiting for you,' she said.

Moushumi thanked her for the coffee and stood up to leave.

'And oh, by the way,' Neha whispered, leaning towards Moushumi. 'Alisha's not a lesbian. So you can give up on her.'

Moushumi's mouth fell open. Then shut. She tried to say something, but nothing came out.

'Moushumi, don't run after that bimbo. She's not what you want. I'll introduce you to someone. She may be interested.'

Moushumi stared at her, not believing what she had just heard.

Neha gently pushed Moushumi towards the door. 'But for now, good luck with the interview.'

The afternoon heat was making Dipali sluggish. She sat listening to the solicitor drone on about deeds and inheritance laws and other such jargon in between his profuse apologies for his air-conditioning not working. A man was perched on a high stool, fiddling with the air-conditioner, while another young boy, apprentice perhaps, stared at Dipali while passing him screwdrivers and whatever else was required.

Dipali wiped her brow and her shoulders drooped. Hopefully, by the end of the meeting, she'd have a bit more wisdom and knowledge about property and inheritance. She was now determined to make life. Later, she was meeting up with Gandharv. In his flat for the first time. The thought made her flush with excitement. She had dressed carefully for the occasion, and now this meeting was making her into a hot, smelly mess.

The solicitor talked on, his hands moving, trying to stress each word in between mopping his brow. His shirt had grown two dark patches under the arms. Perspiration trickled down the sides of his face. Dipali wished he would open the window, to diffuse the pungent air. The two repairmen reeked of stale sweat. She wiped her face with her dupatta and bit her lip in exasperation. She was paying for his time, but she wasn't absorbing much.

Finally, relieved of a good amount of cash, Dipali stepped out of the office. Outside was hot as well, but at least it was not suffocating. A fresh breeze blew intermittently. She ran across the road towards the sugarcane juice-wala and ordered a tall glass with extra ice. She knew she shouldn't be having that in her juice. God knows the source of the water. But she was desperate. If only she could have changed her clothes as well. Dipali sucked on the ice. Hopefully Gandharv wouldn't notice. She turned her nose surreptiously towards her armpit.

A faint odour of sweat. A trace of Ponds talcum powder. It would have to do.

Gandharv's flat was in a leafy corner of Andheri. Far from the airport traffic and rattle of autos. Dipali stepped into the building, arranging her hair as best as she could.

She rang the doorbell and he opened the door immediately, like as if he had been by the door the whole time, waiting for her.

'Hi,' Dipali said, suddenly shy. 'I'm here.'

Gandharv beamed as he showed her in. 'I saw you from the window. I was so scared you weren't going to turn up.'

They both looked at each other, not sure of their next move. Dipali noticed that Gandharv had showered and smelled very good. His hair was still damp, his face still red from shaving. She sat on the divan and looked around her. It was a neat flat, surprising for a man. It was sparsely furnished, a divan and a small table in front of it. An armchair by the balcony. A dining table with a pile of photography magazines and camera equipment. A rickety bookshelf, handmade probably, leaning dangerously to one side from the weight of the books. A few framed photographs stood on the bookshelf. Pictures from Gandharv's childhood, his parents, his sister, his grandparents.

'Your happy pictures,' Dipali said. 'And they do mean a lot to me,'

'Thank you,' Gandharv replied, flicking imaginary dust motes off the photo frames. He resembled his mother. She was a tall woman, standing nearly shoulder to shoulder with his father in one picture, her hands blurred as she was caught on camera in the middle of an action. Same curls framing her face, and that lopsided grin. It was difficult to believe that she no longer existed. She seemed so full of life, she could have jumped out of the picture into the room and completed the sentence that was frozen on her tongue. His father seemed more sedate, standing to attention, his lips smiling, but his eyes were far away.

'Baby Gandharv looks the same as the older version,' Dipali joked, pointing to a photograph of him squinting at the camera.

'Yeah. My dad had probably bribed me with a toffee, anything to keep me still for the shot. I'm still like that, you know. Show me a chocolate bar, and I'll follow you to eternity!'

'Not for a chocolate bar, you won't. A cigarette, perhaps,' Dipali said, looking pointedly at the overflowing ashtray on the table.

'You're right. I'm a shameless man. I need my fuel to burn.'

'That's just too bad, Gandharv. You are poisoning yourself, and that just makes me incredibly sad.'

Gandharv grabbed the ashtray and emptied the contents into the bin. He then reached into his jeans pocket and pulled out a pack of cigarettes. He stuffed that in the bin as well.

'For you, my lady, I have done the impossible. I have just given up smoking.'

Dipali looked at him incredulously. He bowed to her and then flung the lighter out of the window.

'I shall endeavour to do my best, to stay away from evil fags and protect my health and that of my loved ones for now and for ever, amen.'

'Shut up, silly,' Dipali giggled as she tried to dodge him and run towards the balcony. He did a mock curtsey and raced after her, cornering her, and they fell laughing on the divan.

'You may be rather silly at times, but you are very tidy for, you know, man standards. Bachelor standards,' Dipali said between fits of laughter and fighting him off her. 'I like your flat.'

'It's very small,' Gandharv said, 'but it does the job. There's a bedroom that way, but I've converted it into a darkroom. And a kitchen.'

'So where do you sleep?' Dipali asked.

Gandharv indicated the divan she was resting on and Dipali flushed. This was his bed and she was rolling in it with him.

'Oh,' she jumped up. 'I didn't mean to untidy your bed.'

'Don't worry,' Gandharv said. 'You'll get used to it.'

'Only if you pass the kitchen test,' she said and strode into the kitchen.

It was tiny and they had to stand close to each other. Everything was in its place. There were two pots on the gas, and Dipali wondered if Gandharv had cooked. She couldn't place him in this domestic situation. She was used to seeing him in his professional mode, and this gave him another dimension.

'You can cook?' she asked.

Gandharv looked towards the gas cooker and then back at her. He burst out laughing. 'Only for survival. I'm not going to offer you any food! Sri Krishna down the road does home delivery.'

'I can make tea,' he offered, but clearly the rows of glass tumblers on the window sill was proof enough that Sri Krishna delivered even his tea.

Dipali smiled, and before she knew it, she was stepping closer to him. She forgot being hot and smelly. She drew in his scent deeply, memorising it. They leaned far into the kitchen counter and paused only briefly when the steel cooking pots came crashing down to the floor.

21

Moushumi pushed past the door of the restaurant. She was so excited and nervous she hadn't slept very well the night before. She felt dizzy and the bright lights of the restaurant hurt her eyes. She was early so she picked a seat that allowed her the advantage of checking out her date first.

There was a table booked in her name, as Neha had said, in a quiet corner. It was a quaint Italian restaurant. The walls were terracotta with plaited garlic and onion bulbs hanging from the beams. The pizza oven was open for the diners to view. Waiters in chequered aprons and pencil-thin moustaches noted the orders on slate slabs. Moushumi looked at the drinks menu. She needed a bit of Dutch courage. She looked around for the waiter and waved to him. 'One vodka shot, please. And make it quick, thank you.'

She straightened her top and smoothed down her hair. What if she didn't come? What if she wasn't interested? What if it was the woman on the train? No, it wouldn't be. She certainly wasn't the only lesbian in town. She drummed her fingers on the table and sucked her lower lip.

The waiter brought her the shot. Moushumi downed it quickly and resisted ordering another one. Oh, that was good, burning all the way down to her stomach. And then it buzzed straight up to her head. I'm ready for her now, Moushumi pushed the glass away. She studied the menu, and waited.

'Hi,' said a familiar voice.

Moushumi looked up. 'Oh hi, Neha. You're alone? Where's your friend?'

Neha sat down opposite her. 'Oh, I don't know...' She flicked back her hair and leaned forward, rummaging into her handbag. 'I love this place, absolutely amazing,' she said absently. She pulled out a handkerchief and delicately patted her forehead with it.

Moushumi looked down, deflated. Of course it wouldn't be so easy, she told herself. 'So she didn't come?'

'Who?' Neha asked, still mopping her brow.

Moushumi looked at her, irritated. This Neha was being such a pain, wasting her time.

'Never mind. You should have called me or something to cancel.'

Neha looked at her and smiled nervously. 'And what if I say I'm your date?'

Moushumi didn't know how to react. She stared at Neha sitting opposite her, flaunting a mangalsutra and wedding ring.

'You're a married woman, Neha.' Moushumi's voice trembled as she gathered her handbag and stood up. 'I'm not sure what's going on here, but I don't want to get involved. I'm sorry.'

'Hey,' Neha said, standing up. 'I'm sorry if I was being all mysterious. I'm not sure about you either, but I'd like to get to know you better.'

Moushumi shook her head, thinking of Jasmine. 'I'm sorry. But I don't do bored married women. Not anymore.'

Moushumi began to walk out of the restaurant. Neha ran

after her, dodging waiters with heavy laden trays. People turned to stare at them, excited at the prospect of some drama.

'Hey, I'm sorry. I'm married but certainly not bored. Look, can't we talk like proper adults?' Neha called out.

Moushumi swung around and glared at Neha. 'Talk? About what? I don't know you. How dare you make assumptions? Just because I am a lesbian does not mean I would be interested in any woman who propositions me.'

There was silence as the diners registered what they had just heard. Even the waiters stopped in their tracks and turned to look at them. The manager hurried towards them, rubbing his hands together.

'Ladies, ladies,' he began. 'Please, what is the need for all this tamasha? Surely you can solve your problems outside?'

Neha took Moushumi's hand. 'Can we have a drink at least? We can talk as much as you want me to.'

The manager tried to lead them to the door, but Moushumi glared at him so hard he took a step back. People were whispering. They must have recognised her. Some were pointing to her and others had a look of distaste on their faces.

Neha led Moushumi back to their table. The in-house musician hurried towards them, guitar in hand, but Neha's glare made him scurry back to more amiable tables.

'You're married,' Moushumi said between clenched teeth. 'You have a child.'

'I have a child, yes,' Neha said. 'I'm married, but I had to do it to please my parents. I couldn't fight for my rights. I didn't even know I had rights. I thought I was abnormal, weird and that getting married would sort me out. Same old story, I'm afraid.'

'So, this husband of yours,' Moushumi asked. 'He couldn't sort you out? Does he know?'

'He knows,' Neha said. 'I couldn't keep him in the dark. He's such a nice guy. I had to tell him.'

Moushumi couldn't believe what she had just heard. For the first time, someone had owned up and not lied to her partner. She wanted to know more. Suddenly Neha was worth talking to.

'How come he didn't kick you out? And how did you two manage to have a baby?'

'Slow down, Moushumi,' Neha laughed. 'All in good time.'

They went back to their table and ordered some food. The waiter brought them their drinks and Neha settled down to tell Moushumi her story. At first she had hidden the truth from her husband, fearing that she would get hurt if she disclosed her secret. But trying to avoid him every night, or lying listlessly while he had sex with her was breaking her down. She didn't want to live that kind of lie any more. Besides, she felt bad for him. He didn't deserve such treatment from a wife he had married for love and companionship.

'So, one night, after another unsuccessful attempt, I told him why I couldn't respond to him.' Neha sipped her drink and played with her wedding ring. 'He was obviously shocked, then angry. But then, he was really upset. He said that technically he had raped me several times. I told him not to think like that, because obviously he hadn't known the truth, and I was the one at fault.'

'Wow,' Moushumi exhaled. 'I can't believe this. He blamed himself in spite of all this?'

Neha nodded. 'He's a real gentleman. I suggested we get a divorce and then he can marry a proper girl. He said it made sense to do that, but he also didn't want me to get into trouble. We talked about ways to get the divorce when I found out I was pregnant. And that was it. He didn't bring up the divorce subject again, and I left it too. With a baby and all, I had no option but stay with him. It wasn't even like I had a lover or someone to go to.'

'And you've lived together ever since?'

'Yes. He's become so busy with his career, he doesn't have time to spend with me. We just live in the same house and love our child.'

'Very strange,' Moushumi said. 'Why is he sacrificing his life into the bargain?'

'I suppose, one day he'll find someone he'll fall in love with. And then he will leave me. But until then, he's taking pity on me. Keeping me safe under his wings. That's what he said. It was his duty as a husband to look after me, whether or not I kept up my part of the bargain as a wife.'

The food arrived and they paused. Moushumi felt a lightness within herself. The woman opposite her had refused to live a lie. She had spoken out and told the truth about herself. Finally, Mou had met a woman like herself. A woman without double standards. It was such a relief to know that.

'Would you leave him if you did find that someone special?' Moushumi asked.

Neha tipped her head to one side and thought for a moment. 'It's difficult to say, Moushumi. I don't know what'll be at stake. Where Shreya will figure in all of this. What if the woman I love doesn't accept my daughter? What if society harms Shreya's upbringing? Will Ajay let Shreya go away from his life? These are questions I don't have answers to. So even if I am upfront about my sexuality, I'm not sure that is to my daughter's benefit.'

'Indeed,' Moushumi said. But she looked at Neha with new found admiration. There was a possibility here. They could share something special. Only time would tell.

251

22

The muezzin's call to prayer woke Dipali up. She opened her eyes, unsure where she was. Then she realised he was sleeping beside her. His arm was draped around her middle, his breath ruffling her hair. It was late and the sun had set. But today Dipali did not feel the need to rush home. She would not have to give excuses. She would tell her mother and brother where she had been. The thought excited her. Oh, to see the look on her brother's face.

As he slept on, she carefully removed herself from his embrace and reached for her clothes, then dressed. She went out on the balcony and took a deep breath. In the distance, the sodium streetlights glowed orange. Neon signs lit up adverts into the night and she listened to the film music streaming out of the security guard's booth. It was an old love song from the Sixties. It matched her mood.

Dipali wondered if she should turn the light on. She felt odd standing there in the dark. Gandharv stirred in his sleep. Dipali tiptoed to the bathroom and switched on the light. She caught her breath. Clothes lines criss-crossed the length of the passage to the bathroom. And hanging on the clothes lines, were photographs left to dry. Photographs Gandharv had clicked. She looked closer. They were nudes. The model looked like Alisha Chopra. On the beach at Alibaug. She pulled out a couple of photos. Yes, it was her, her lithe body draped over the rocks, morning sun in her eyes. Another one of her from behind by the palm trees. All this had happened when she had been present? After a night talking about love with her, had he gone and shot nudes of another woman the next morning?

She leaned on the tiled wall, staring at the rows of photographs. Why hadn't he told her? Why had he done this? Her body racked with sobs. She heard him leap from the bed. A light came on. But she didn't want to see him. Didn't want him to see her this way.

'Dipali? Dipali?' he cried. 'What's the matter?' He came running in and stopped. He saw the pictures in her hand and her distraught face. He didn't say anything.

'Why?' Dipali whispered. 'What does this mean?'

She watched his chest heave. He opened his mouth to say something and then closed it again. He looked confused. He looked at her and then at the photographs.

'What do you mean?' he said, finally. 'I'm a photographer, you know that. This is my job.' He grabbed the pictures from her hand and hung them back on the line. 'This is an assignment I got paid for.'

'But naked women?' Dipali said. 'Why do you have to shoot naked women for money? You're not so desperate for money, are you? This is Alisha in Alibaug, right? I was there, wasn't I? You didn't tell me.'

Gandharv ran his fingers through his hair. 'Dipali, can we talk about this in a more mature way? Please?'

Gandharv led her back to the room. Dipali winced when she saw the crumpled bed linen, his t-shirt lying on the floor on top of her dupatta. She sat on the armchair purposefully, turning herself away from the bed. She wondered if he had ever brought any other woman to his flat. She could believe anything now.

'Look, Dipali, this is a part of the profession, these are called nudes,' Gandharv started to explain, patiently. 'It is an artistic expression. A lot of models like to include it in their portfolios. It's nothing more than that.'

But Dipali was in no mood to be patronised. 'So how many other women have you clicked in the *nude*? Did it just stop at that? I want to know, Gandharv. Since I too have landed in bed with you, are you going to take my pictures as well?' Dipali wiped spittle from the corner of her mouth. She didn't want to hear the answers to her questions.

Gandharv held her gaze until she turned away.

'Do you think this is porn?' he asked. 'Have you seen what pornography is? Do you think I sleep with every Tom, Dick and Harry I meet? How can you accuse me of such shit, Dipali? You are behaving like a stranger, not like the person I love.'

'How can you say you love me, if you made out with me in Alibaug and then took pictures of a naked woman, and didn't even tell me about it?' Dipali shouted. 'In my world, my lover has to be truthful to me. Be open with me. As I will be with him. And you were the one lecturing me always – stand up for yourself. Don't play games with me.'

'Okay. And in my world, I don't have to prove my character or my virtue. In my world, I have to take photographs and nude women happen to be one of the many subjects. It is called art. These pictures are not for public consumption in sex magazines. She paid to have them taken. For her portfolio. For her career. You have no business to make assumptions about my character or business.'

'Of course not,' Dipali said. 'Even when you kissed Moushumi, you never told me. She came out with it. If I hadn't brought it up, would you have told me?'

Gandharv shut his eyes. 'It was stupid of me to do that, I agree. I honestly was very drunk and I thought I was helping her out. Anyway, we weren't even formally together. I didn't know what your feelings for me were.'

'Don't make excuses,' Dipali spat out. 'You were always flirting around. Even when we were together in Alibaug, you were all over Shilpa. And then you took those photographs.'

Gandharv paced up and down the room. He grabbed his t-shirt from the floor and put it on. He threw the dupatta in her direction. 'You'd better cover up,' he said. 'I don't want you accusing me of raping you next.'

Dipali stood up, flinging the dupatta over her shoulders. 'Fine,' she shouted. 'I asked you simple questions; you didn't bother to reply. Looks like our worlds are not destined to meet.'

'You make it so difficult for me,' Gandharv said. 'You always teased, and then withdrew. Always giving me a sob story of your helplessness. Everyone trying to get the better of you. How did that make me feel?'

'Don't change the bloody thing around,' Dipali said. 'I'm taking your advice now. I'm making a decision here.' She grabbed her handbag and walked out of the door.

23

It was a week since their fight. It felt like life had seeped out of Dipali. Her mind refused to function. School had become torture, especially when she felt tears coming to her eyes in the middle of a class. She spent most of her time avoiding others, resisting food and feeling miserable.

Moushumi wasn't in school anymore to talk to. She wasn't around much anyway, behaving very secretively. She did seem a bit more cheerful when they last spoke on the phone, and Dipali hadn't managed to tell her what had happened to her. She didn't want to burden Moushumi with her problems as well since she seemed to be only now recovering from her own.

Ashish produced papers for them to sign. He was leaving for Delhi that evening. Dipali felt weak. She couldn't fight anyone anymore. She would sign and give everything up. All these material goods were not worth it. No wonder widows were relegated to Kashi to live the rest of their lives in poverty and pain. The only thing they had to look forward to was death. It made sense now. They came in the way of inheritance; they were an extra mouth to feed; they were useless in society.

She looked at the papers on the dining table. Ashish had left them there and gone out. She could just take the pen and sign, but she found that it wasn't so easy to sign away one's respect and freedom.

'Are you hesitating as well?' Asha Devi said. 'I don't know what the best thing is for us. Dipali, what should we do?'

'What do you want to do, Ma?' Dipali asked. 'Why don't you make a decision for once?'

Asha Devi sat down at the table. She seemed to have aged quickly since Ashish's arrival. Her face was creased with fine lines and her mouth was turned down.

'I'm sorry, Dipu,' she said finally, her mouth trembling. 'Please forgive me, my daughter.' She buried her face in her hands and wept, shaking her head slowly from side to side.

'Sorry for what, Ma?' Dipali asked. If it had been a year ago, she would have gathered her mother in her arms and comforted her. Cried with her, felt helpless and sorry for herself. But she had changed too. She was no longer soft and vulnerable.

'I should have been stronger. The way your Baba treated you and Ashish, like animals. And I watched, too afraid to say anything. It turned you into a mouse and Ashish into a wolf. If only Sunil was here, he would do something.'

'But he's not here, Ma,' Dipali said. 'We are. We should do something.'

Asha Devi nodded and wiped her nose on the loose end of her sari. 'How? Ashish will never back out.'

'He can't hold your hand and force you to sign, can he?' Dipali raised her voice. 'He won't push a gun to your forehead, will he?'

'No,' Asha Devi replied. 'He can't. He won't. Tell me Dipu, tell me the truth. Is there someone else in your life now? Are you going to go away with him? Will you leave me here alone?'

There was desperation in her voice as she looked at her daughter. Dipali glared at her, unable to speak. Asha Devi rocked her body back and forth, crying noiselessly. But Dipali was not going to be sucked into being a martyr again. Without replying, she turned and left the room.

ॐ

Moushumi watched Shreya concentrate on the jigsaw puzzle she had presented her with. Neha sat cross-legged on the floor, helping her daughter along. Moushumi wanted to join in but felt too self-conscious. She did not belong to the set yet.

She thought of her nephew, Poltu. He had been so little when she had left. Such a little rascal. He would have grown a lot by now.

Neha was very good company. She was kind and sensitive. She was careful not to rush into a relationship. They were just friends, trying to figure out common interests and ideals. She had joked with Moushumi that this was like an arranged marriage system, where two strangers tried to see if they could spend the rest of their lives together.

Moushumi thought that made sense. Sex wasn't everything; it was nothing in fact, without caring for each other. She may have been in love with Jasmine, but that hadn't been love, actually. It had been a discovery of herself, the excitement of finding someone who understood her, but it had not been the right thing for her. The woman on the train had taught her that she wasn't going to jump into bed with anyone just because she was a lesbian as well. It had to be deeper, much deeper than that.

Neha had cooked lunch for them. As she brought out the

fish curry and rice, she told Shreya the story of how she had thrown her ice-cream cone into her curry and this aunty had bought her two ice-creams to make up for her lost one. Shreya wasn't too pleased that Ice-Cream Aunty had not produced any ice cream on this visit to her house. Neha's husband was away, like he was most of the time. His successful career made up for the unsuccessful marriage, Neha would say, and she was happy for him. He deserved that, at least.

Their home was simple. The walls were covered with photographs of Shreya in various poses. The rest of the space was taken up by books. The medical books were of Neha's husband. Neha's advertising annuals and creative books, novels, journals, Hindi classics, the entire bound volumes of *Amar Chitra Katha* comics.

'Wow,' Moushumi squealed. 'This is a treasure trove. The whole series?' She flicked through one volume, burying her face in to smell the inks and paper from her own childhood, when she and her sister saved every paisa to buy the latest copy of *Amar Chitra Katha*. They were the literary introduction to complex and entertaining legends, histories and mythologies of India for an entire generation of children.

Neha laughed and nodded. 'Every single one, to date and counting. I'm building the collection for Shreya. But it's also for me, in my old age, I will relive my childhood through them.'

'And in between Shreya reading them and you getting old, could I borrow a volume from time to time?'

'Hmmm, as a rule, I never lend out my books. But as I am about to break all the rules with you around, I might as well. But return them quickly, or else—'

'Or else what?'

Neha lunged on Moushumi and tickled her till she was

259

hysterical with laughter and Shreya jumped in, squealing and tickling and getting tickled by two pairs of hands.

CR

Dipali heard the click of the front door and knew Ashish had returned. She lay back on her bed and shut her eyes. He would create a scene and she did not want to be a part of it. Let her mother handle it for once. She was counting down to the minute he would leave the house to return to Delhi. But of course that would not solve any problems. He would not let go of the house so easily. So she slid under the covers and waited for the shouting to begin.

It was very quiet. She heard him shuffling around and she heard the ruffle of papers. So he was looking at the documents he had left on the table. Had her mother signed? Dipali tried to think of herself being far away from here. Images of Alibaug filled her mind. Those three complicated days. Her intimacy with Gandharv. The shock of someone known to her losing a child. That terror-stricken journey back home. And the discovery of Gandharv's other activities. Why wasn't there any good news anywhere?

'Why aren't these papers signed yet?'

Dipali heard him shout. He was striding across the room now, heading to her door. He banged on the door, but she didn't move. She was glad she had locked it. She held on to her pillow, hoping it was a real live person who would protect her from Ashish's wrath. But she realised there was no one to do that. She would have to protect herself. He moved away, and was now shouting outside their mother's room. Had she locked herself in as well? Dipali felt a laugh escape her lips. It was such a ludicrous situation. Both women locking themselves up to escape the inevitable future. Ashish was raging outside, threatening to take them to court. Suddenly he was quiet. Dipali lifted herself on her elbow and listened hard. Had he gone? She got out of bed and pressed her ear to the door. She heard a low voice. It was her mother's.

Dipali opened her door and walked out. She didn't want her mother to face Ashish alone. It wouldn't be fair. She looked at her brother, who had gone purple with rage. Any minute he'll collapse with a heart attack, Dipali thought. Her mother stood in front of him, straight and calm.

She looked at Dipali. 'I've told Ashish I'm not going to sign. We need to discuss options and ideas. I'm sure we'll work something out to everybody's benefit. I need to talk to a lawyer myself first.'

Dipali beamed at her mother. 'Of course, I think that's a very good idea. What do you think, Borda?'

Ashish was frothing at the mouth. He grabbed the papers from the table and stuffed them into his briefcase and then snarled. 'I will see you in court.'

The front door, slammed behind him. Asha Devi sank into the sofa. 'Dipu, I think I need a strong cup of tea.'

'You were good, Ma. He didn't expect that from you.' Dipali said. They looked at each and burst out laughing.

'I was shaking inside,' her mother said. 'But I realised I had to make a stand. Or I'd be letting you down. Letting *us* down.'

Dipali went into the kitchen to make tea. Things would work out for the better. Her mother had made her first brave step. Now all she had to do was support her mother every step of the way.

ભ

Shreya mumbled in her sleep. She was clutching her teddy bear and kicking her covers off. Neha went in and soothed her until she lay still and breathed deeply again.

'She often has nightmares,' Neha whispered. 'Especially after the Alibaug incident. I do too, you know.'

Moushumi nodded. 'Of course,' she said. 'Quite under-standable. That was a real nightmare.' She caught hold of Neha as she passed her by the door. Neha stepped closer, and Moushumi saw the fear in her eyes. She gently kneaded Neha's shoulders until she felt them relax.

They walked back to the living room and settled on the sofa. Neha had insisted Moushumi stay until the house was free as they were finally alone. The ayah had gone home and Shreya was put to bed early. Neha switched on the television to fill in the silence between them. They ate the afternoon's leftovers and watched the news. There was no more talk about homosexuality. The film had been banned and forgotten. Now the media was hounding a Bollywood scam with the underworld, far more interesting, showing famous faces brought more TV rating points. Moushumi was glad in a way. She had not expected what had happened. She imagined now every time any connection to homosexuality came up her parents would be reminded of her and be tortured mentally. It was better they forgot her.

She leaned forward and kissed Neha gently on the mouth. Neha held her breath and there was a pause between them. Then Neha put her plate aside and ran her fingers through Moushumi's hair. They kissed gently, thankful to be in each other's company.

'Thank goodness we're both eating fish curry. Sort of neutralises the aftertaste, huh?' Neha smiled.

'Yeah, sure does.' Moushumi leaned back and played with Neha's fingers. 'I'm beginning to get quite used to this, Neha. Be careful, or I'll soon be camping at your place.'

'I don't mind, Moushumi. I don't know what the future holds for us, though. I'll tell Ajay about us. I won't be able to keep it from him.'

'Tell me, Neha,' Moushumi said, refusing to get into the conversation as it frightened her. She didn't want Ajay to know, because he would then have the power to break them apart. Like Nandkumar did to Jasmine and her. Or at least, that was the excuse Jasmine had given her. 'What if Shreya turns out to be a lesbian? How will you react to that?'

Neha slumped on the sofa. 'I'll be sad, Mou.'

'But why?' Moushumi asked. 'Won't you be more understanding? Wouldn't you be able to relate to her better?'

'Of course I would. I would make sure she isn't forced to make decisions because of society pressures. But it won't be an easy life for her. She will have to struggle to live with herself, struggle to make others accept her identity. No one wants to see their child in pain.'

'But she will have you to cushion her. Parents are the biggest step towards pain and heartbreak, you know that. You chose to please them and you lost. I chose to please myself and I still lost.'

'What about her father? How will he ever reconcile with that?' Neha asked.

'He will blame you?'

'I don't know,' Neha said. 'He's been good to us, you know. We're still together, for Shreya's sake. He's a very decent person. I'm too scared to get out of this comfortable arrangement – financially, I can support the two of us. But socially, I don't want Shreya to be ostracised because of me.'

'Oh, I'm not sure what to do, Neha. Why is it so difficult? Why can't we live together, and bring her up together? Is it too much of a dream situation?'

263

'Yes, we are a minority. Or hey, maybe we are not. Maybe everyone is just hiding because they think of themselves as the minority. But for the moment, we are screwed.'

Moushumi reached out for Neha's hand. 'It has brought you to me. I'm not that romantic fool anymore, thinking I will lead an easy open life with my partner. This is not the right era for it perhaps. Maybe one day in our lifetime we will be able to do just that. And we'll be glad we waited and stuck through it.'

Neha nodded and rested on Moushumi's shoulder. 'I certainly hope we will see that day. For our sake. For Shreya's sake. Not just if she turns out to be like me. But also for her to recognise me for who I am, to respect me. To respect us.'

24

'It's been so long,' Moushumi said, hugging Dipali. 'I haven't seen you in ages.'

Dipali wriggled out of her arms and entered her room. Ever since Moushumi had started the new job, she hadn't had the time to meet up with Dipali much. For in her free time, she now spent it with Neha. Dipali was hurt by this sudden isolation. She was about to open her mouth and complain, but she stopped herself. She did not like confrontations. Not with her best friend. She had fought with the man she loved, but she was not going to lose Moushumi, despite all her faults.

Neha was fidgeting near the window. She flapped a napkin over the food laid out on a table. The flies buzzed incessantly in the October heat. She stood up and shook hands with Dipali. Then she leaned forward and hugged her as well. 'Hi Dipali,' she said. 'So good to see you again.'

Dipali nodded briskly, a tight smile on her lips. She felt like an outsider. She didn't know what to say. So she asked about Shreya and was told she was fine; she was with her dad, visiting grandparents.

Moushumi had organised a lunch at her landlady's flat. She had ordered Parsi food from Rippon Club, and the aromas of the dhansak and kebabs wafted out of the cardboard takeaway cartons, filling the room with a rich, cosy smell. There were drinks on the table – beers and orange juice.

Dipali had forgotten what Neha was like. It had been a while since they had met each other in Alibaug. She noticed her uneven teeth that made her smile even more endearing. She used her hands a lot when she talked, and she talked a lot. She was funny and clever. She was nothing like that cautious, nervous wreck of a person she had encountered in Alibaug. She felt happy for Moushumi. She hoped it would work for them.

Moushumi and Neha sat close together. They seemed comfortable leaning against each other, sharing a bowl of peanuts. Dipali remembered how she and Moushumi would sit close together, share a bhel and laugh about things. Now she was the odd one out again. It hurt her to think that she was always pushed out of a companionship just when she was getting comfortable with it.

It had been two weeks since 'the big fight'. She had stormed out but now she regretted it. Gandharv had not contacted her nor made any attempt to make up. Maybe in a way it was good. He had not been serious enough, hence the silence. Neha's chatter brought her back to the present. She was holding out a plastic plate full of food towards Dipali.

'So, you two, wooing each other and keeping me in the dark? Mou, you starting a new job and all,' she began, smiling through her nerves. 'Minus points to you, my best friend, for not keeping me up to date.'

Moushumi shook her head vigorously, mouth stuffed with rice. She leaned away from Neha. 'Dipali, I didn't mean to keep this from you,' she spoke with her mouth full. 'I did not do this on purpose. You've got to understand, we were so shaky and nervous about this, we didn't want to announce anything before we were sure ourselves.'

Neha nodded in agreement. Dipali noticed Moushumi was already speaking in terms of 'we' and not 'I' anymore. Good for her. Good for them. But it left her feeling very alone.

'As for the job,' Moushumi continued. 'I'm starting at the bottom, junior copywriter. But it's a start. I am so lucky to have got it so easily. I have Gandharv to thank of course, he pulled a few strings. '

'Congratulations,' Dipali conceded. 'You'll be working with him then.' She wanted to hear about Gandharv. She felt a prickle of envy at the fact that Moushumi would see him every day.

'I did invite him as well,' Moushumi was saying. 'But he declined.'

Dipali exhaled, and slumped in her chair. He really wasn't interested anymore then. He didn't want to see her again.

'Yes,' Neha said. 'Didn't you know, he's moving to Bangalore. He's going to lead the creative team in the new set-up there.'

'I didn't know that,' Moushumi gasped. 'He didn't mention it to me.'

Both Moushumi and Neha looked at Dipali. 'You knew, Dips?' Moushumi asked.

Dipali shook her head slowly, bright sparks appeared before her eyes. Her throat felt constricted. He was going? He was leaving? Moushumi moved to sit beside her. She took her trembling hand in hers and held it tight.

'What's the matter, Dips? Did something happen between the two of you?' she asked softly. She exchanged glances with Neha, who shoved her plate on the bed and jumped up. She ran her fingers through her hair and chewed on her lips, unsure of what to say.

'What did he say, Neha? Why is he going away?' Moushumi asked.

'We are working on an account together. He told me a few days ago to transfer the job to another creative. Moonworks had been after him for some time now to head the Bangalore team. He had been resisting, but then he accepted last week.'

'He didn't tell you, Dipali?' Moushumi asked her. 'I cannot believe that. He wasn't like this before, you know. I swear, he wasn't, otherwise I wouldn't have... you know...'

Dipali shook her head. 'No, no, it's not what you think.' She gulped down air and wiped her face. Be in control, be in control, she thought. 'We realised it wouldn't work for us. We decided—' A sob escaped her lips and she pressed her hands to her mouth. 'I can't talk about this now.' She went to the bathroom and washed her face. The cold water soothed her nerves. She felt bad, ruining their party, but she hadn't been prepared for what she had heard. He was leaving Mumbai. Technically, he was leaving her. It was the end then.

☙

Asha Devi watched Dipali as she flitted around the house. She had come home soaked in sweat with bleeding blisters on her feet. When she questioned her, Dipali burst into tears. She forced her daughter to sit down and she bathed her feet and applied Dettol. She asked her what happended, repeatedly, but Dipali refused to answer.

Dipali stood by the window, watching the world outside. It didn't matter to anyone what she was going through. The homeless man continued to sit contentedly under the streetlight, swatting flies and chewing tobacco. The Nepali security men from the opposite building laughed at jokes told in their mother tongue. The cyclists rushed passed, barely an inch away from pedestrians.

The telephone rang.

'Dipali, Dips,' Moushumi's voice came through. 'Are you okay? Did you get home alright?'

'Yes, Mou. I'm fine. I'm sorry. I didn't mean to ruin your party.'

'Oh, forget that,' Moushumi said. 'I don't know what has happened between the two of you, but please Dips, think hard. Don't let go of something so easily, unless he's been a jerk. Has he?'

'Mou. I'll think hard. I will. We've had some problems, but we'll see what happens.'

Dipali couldn't sleep. She tossed and turned, thinking, replaying all the moments she had spent with Gandharv. And all the moments she had not. All her thoughts stopped and stayed on him. His kisses. His warmth. His reassurances. What had she done?

CR

Dipali had slipped into a fitful sleep sometime as dawn arrived at her window. She woke with a start. The sun was high up and the parrots were bickering in the mango tree. It was Sunday. The day he was leaving. She leapt out of bed and ran into the living room.

Her mother was dusting the furniture. She raised her eyebrow and looked at the clock. 'It's ten o'clock. Do you want some tea, Dipu? Did you sleep well last night?'

Dipali nodded absently. She looked around for the

newspaper. Trains scheduled for the day would be listed in there. She searched for the Bangalore train. Udayan Express. There, it would be leaving at noon. Shit, she didn't have much time. She rushed to the bathroom, sat on the toilet and brushed her teeth. She wasn't sure what she was planning, she only knew she had to get there. On time. Throwing on some clothes, she checked herself in the mirror. Not perfect, but it would have to do.

CR

Dipali stepped off the local train at Dadar station and raced towards the long-distance train platform. It wasn't very crowded. The tannoy droned on incoherently, something about train timings and platforms. She could not understand what was being said. She needed to find out which platform the train would come to, as it stopped only for a minute. She had to find him before that.

She raced past the drinks stall, the shoe-polish boys, Wheeler bookstall, porters, travellers, beggars. She scanned every little space she possibly could. Where was he? She rushed down the stairs to platform six. There was still ten minutes for the train to arrive. Please, please let me find him. She walked the length of the platform, stumbling over suitcases and hold-alls. She searched, and prayed, and cried.

'Dipali?'

'Gandharv?'

They stood opposite each other, tongue-tied. She should say something, and quick, Dipali realised. The tannoy was announcing the arrival of the train.

'I'm sorry,' she had to shout over the din at the station. 'I'm sorry I doubted you. I wanted to say that.'

Gandharv's hair was damp, hanging limply around his face. Dipali wanted to reach up and smooth it down.

'—Well, now I'm going. I hope that will make it better for you.'

Dipali shook her head. 'No— It won't. It'll make it a lot worse. I realise I have made a mistake. I shouldn't have judged you without hearing your side of the story.'

'Yes,' Gandharv said. 'You did hear me out, but you didn't agree to my thought process.' He looked beyond her towards the railway tracks.

Dipali felt her heart thud louder. 'So is this the end, Gandharv?' If it was, it had to be done properly, with no bitterness between them.

His eyes flashed with an instance of tenderness, of longing, before it turned into a glare. 'The train will be here now,' he said. 'I'll have to go, you know.'

Dipali nodded. 'I know.' She took his hand in hers and pressed it. 'Don't become a stranger, Gandharv. Don't forget me.'

He held on to her hand. 'I won't forget you.'

The shrill whistle preceded the arrival of the train. Slowly it clanked and chugged into view. The people began to pull their luggage along, ready to board. Gandharv too started to walk ahead. But he held on to her hand. Dipali followed.

He stopped in front of his compartment and turned to her. Dipali was openly crying now.

'Dipali, look at me,' Gandharv said, wiping her eyes and lifting up her chin. 'We've always been struggling to express our feelings. We've had such a difference of opinions, of beliefs. I was okay with all of that. But you doubted me. I just couldn't take that.'

'I know. But you need to look at it through my point of view as well,' Dipali said. 'Your profession, your way of life is so new to me. You haven't given me the opportunity to learn, to adjust.'

People were rushing past them, jumping into the train with their luggage. Dipali held his arm tight to prevent him from entering as well.

'We need time,' Gandharv said. 'We can't rush into something to regret it later. Shall we use this separation to think about it?'

Dipali closed her eyes in disappointment. If she let him go, he would be gone forever. He was young with a career ahead of him. He'd forget her. He'd find someone in Bangalore.

'If that's what you wish,' she said. She let go of his hand and wiped away her tears. She wasn't going to beg. No, she was not going to beg anyone anymore. She stepped away from him. 'You better go in. The train will leave any minute.'

'Dipali, don't lose faith in me. I'll come and see you. We'll work it out.'

'Yes, we'll work it out,' Dipali nodded. 'This separation will help us realise our true feelings, won't it, Gandharv?'

The guard blew the whistle and the train rumbled into life. It began to move slowly, clanking and heaving its way out of the platform. He climbed into the train and waved to Dipali.

'I'll call you when I get there,' he smiled. 'Miss me, okay?'

Dipali smiled and walked along the platform, trying to keep pace with the train. 'And you me, okay?'

Gandharv saluted her. Dipali stood and watched until the train became a speck in the landscape. He was gone. But he had left her with hope. Whatever the outcome, it would be one for the best.

25

Moushumi's landlady called her to the phone. It's urgent, she
mouthed, waving her arms frantically. Moushumi ran across
the hallway towards the telephone. She could tell who it was.
She had written her phone number and posted it to her sister
ages ago. But she had never called.

'Mou, Mou,' Aparna's voice came through the line. 'Can
you hear me?'

'Yes, Didi, I can.' Moushumi didn't dare ask any more
questions. They wouldn't have called her if not for some bad
news. She leaned against the wall, her strength failing her.
She knew this was coming.

'Ma wants to speak to you,' Aparna said. There was the
sound of an exchange of hands. Moushumi heard bangles
clinking and voices. She couldn't understand what was being
said. And then,

'Mou, your Baba isn't well. He's in hospital.'

Moushumi nodded, unable to speak.

'Mou, Mou, can you hear me?'

'Yes, Ma. I can,' Moushumi said. 'What happened to Baba?'

There was a disturbance on the line and Aparna was
speaking again.

'Baba's had a heart attack,' she said. 'He's in hospital. It's under control, don't worry. The doctor says that he'll pull through.'

Relief. He hadn't gone. They were keeping him alive. Various thoughts jumped around in her mind. She should go. But would that cause him more stress? She wanted to see him. But would he want to see her? His words echoed in her mind. Neha's promise to stay by her nailed her to the ground. What was she going to do?

'Baba wants to see you,' Aparna was saying. 'He's forgiven you, Mou. He wants to see you. He said it didn't matter anymore.'

'Really?' Moushumi felt as if the cords that had been binding her, biting into her skin, had been snapped open. She felt free of all oppression. If it was alright with him, it was okay to be how *she* was. To live how she wanted. 'Should I come to see him?'

'Yes, do come quickly. Ma's desperate that you come too. It will give him strength to keep fighting.'

'I'll be there. I'll take the next flight home.' Moushumi smiled to herself. Home. She said that word after all these years. She was really going home.

In her room, she started to fling some clothes into an overnight bag. Neha. She needed to talk to her. But she was away for the weekend with her family. Moushumi stopped for breath. And once again, a feeling of despondence washed over her. Her two lives. Both so separate she'd have to cut herself into two to live them out. Her father had at last asked to see her. But she wasn't sure what he would say? What if he made her promise not to see Neha again? What if Neha said she couldn't see her again? That her family was more important to her?

Moushumi sank to the floor. She wanted to see her father and nurse him back to health. Yet, she didn't want him to hold her to ransom and make unreasonable demands of her. Focus, focus, Moushumi thought. Your father is dying, stop thinking about yourself.

She ran to the telephone again.

'Dipali, please come here. I need you.'

CR

'This is great news,' Dipali said when she arrived. 'Don't worry, family will always be family. They will accept you in the end, no matter what.'

'Will you tell Neha?' Moushumi ran around the room in circles, unsure what to pack and what to put away. 'She may feel offended I didn't tell her personally, but I don't want to—'

'Mou, just go. See your father. Your family. Don't worry about anything. I'm here. I'll take care of everything.'

Moushumi handed the keys to Dipali and hugged her. 'You are the best, Dips. Where would I be without you?'

'And me without you,' Dipali said, squeezing her friend tight. They rushed downstairs to the waiting taxi. And once more, Moushumi made her way across town, this time to the airport, to return home. To make amends. To make a new beginning. She opened her wallet and looked at the photos she had stuffed inside the tiny plastic covered display pocket. There was Neha and her, posing with Shreya in a park. Her own parents and sister's family, all posing in their fine clothes one Durga Puja. Dipali grinning in front of the goddess at the local pandal, squeezed on either side by frenzied worshippers. She made a mental note to remove that photo and replace it later. One of Gandharv and Dipali, she knew she had one somewhere, posing under a palm tree in Alibaug, his arm sneaking behind to hold her by the waist. She was positive things would work out for them. It had to, or she would have to interfere again.

She urged the taxi driver to hurry. Her father was waiting for her. She would taste her mother's food again. Lose herself in her sister's embrace. She prayed to Krishna, oh God of love, be kind. Be merciful. For once in my life, I ask you for my own interests. Let me have both, Lord. My family and my love.

The taxi driver leaned on the accelerator and sped towards the airport. Moushumi passed the sea, twinkling in afternoon sun. They got onto the highway, racing hundreds of cars, all beeping and honking their way forward. Every inch they progressed moved Moushumi closer to home. She clutched her bag close to her chest and smiled. Somehow she knew, things would turn out alright. They would have to accept her, because she was finally proud of who she was and now practically all of India knew her real identity, and life just moved on.

Acknowledgments

I'd like to thank Bella Kemble for those wonderful creative writing classes that inspired me to take writing seriously. Shelagh Weeks, John Freeman, Richard Gwyn and the students and staff on the Masters in Creative Writing course, Cardiff University 2006, for long hours of workshops, discussions, reading lists and friendship. The novel was conceived here. Literature Wales for awarding me a mentorship with Phil Carradice, whose advice was invaluable.

Thank you to Parthian, especially Richard Davies, for taking a chance with my book and thanks to the entire Parthian team. Susie Wild, editor and superstar, for believing in me and supporting me through to the very end. Bertel Martin (LiteratureWorks, Plymouth), cannot thank you enough. Shipra Bhattacharya for the use of the beautiful painting on the cover. Early readers John White, Bethany Rivers, Sandra Higdon, Andy Lavender and Hanna Silva, thank you for your patience with early drafts and excellent critiques. Romy Wood for being there for me through all drafts and for your precious friendship. Ronjita, my sister, for accompanying me on research trips across Mumbai and treating me to lots of cake! To Chirodeep Chaudhuri, Shobhna S. Kumar and the Humsafar Trust in India for answering my questions.

Thank you to all my family and friends who supported me and looked after me, the NHS, especially The Mustard Tree and Derriford Hospital, Plymouth.

Lastly, but most importantly, thanks to my two daughters, Rohini and Mihika for being my special girls. And to my husband, Syamantak, where would I be without you?

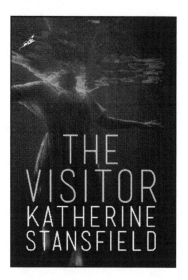

PARTHIAN

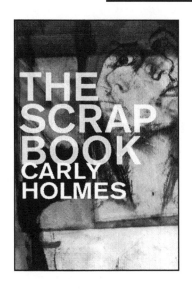

www.parthianbooks.com